DEC 06

Ralph Compton:
For the Brand

This Large Print Book carries the
Seal of Approval of N.A.V.H.

RALPH COMPTON: FOR THE BRAND

A RALPH COMPTON NOVEL

DAVID ROBBINS

THORNDIKE PRESS

An imprint of Thomson Gale, a part of The Thomson Corporation

THOMSON

GALE

Detroit • New York • San Francisco • New Haven, Conn. • Waterville, Maine • London

THOMSON
GALE
™

Thorndike Press® Large Print Western.

The text of this Large Print edition is unabridged.

Other aspects of the book may vary from the original edition.

Set in 16 pt. Plantin.

LIBRARY OF CONGRESS CATALOGING-IN-PUBLICATION DATA

Robbins, David, 1950–
    Ralph Compton : for the brand : a Ralph Compton novel
/ by David Robbins.
        p. cm. — (Thorndike Press large print Western)
    ISBN 0-7862-9130-3 (alk. paper)
        1. Large type books. I. Compton, Ralph. II. Title. III. Title: For the brand.
    PS3568.O22288R34 2006
    813'.54—dc22   2006027677

U.S. Hardcover:
ISBN 13: 978-0-7862-9130-4
ISBN 10: 0-7862-9130-3

Published in 2006 by arrangement with NAL Signet,
a division of Penguin Group (USA) Inc.

Printed in the United States of America on permanent paper
10 9 8 7 6 5 4 3 2 1

THE IMMORTAL COWBOY

This is respectfully dedicated to the "American Cowboy." His was the saga sparked by the turmoil that followed the Civil War, and the passing of more than a century has by no means diminished the flame.

True, the old days and the old ways are but treasured memories, and the old trails have grown dim with the ravages of time, but the spirit of the cowboy lives on.

In my travels — to Texas, Oklahoma, Kansas, Nebraska, Colorado, Wyoming, New Mexico, and Arizona — I always find something that reminds me of the Old West. While I am walking these plains and mountains for the first time, there is this feeling that a part of me is eternal, that I have known these old trails before. I believe it is the undying spirit of the frontier calling, allowing me, through the mind's eye, to step back into time. What is the appeal of the Old West of the American frontier?

It has been epitomized by some as the dark and bloody period in American history. Its heroes — Crockett, Bowie, Hickok, Earp — have been reviled and criticized. Yet the Old West lives on, larger than life.

It has become a symbol of freedom, when there was always another mountain to climb and another river to cross; when a dispute between two men was settled not with expensive lawyers, but with fists, knives, or guns. Barbaric? Maybe. But some things never change. When the cowboy rode into the pages of American history, he left behind a legacy that lives within the hearts of us all.

— Ralph Compton

CHAPTER 1

Willis woke up at the crack of dawn. He always woke up at the crack of dawn. It was as much a habit as breathing.

The sparrows helped. They started chirping and flitting about in the bushes beside the line shack at the first hint of light. Sometimes Willis would lie and listen and envy them their joy and their energy. His own vigor was not what it had been, and he had not known joy — pure, real joy — since his days with Mattie. Willis missed his sister more than anything.

Willis did not stir until the edges around the door brightened. Then he reluctantly cast off the blanket and sat up. The old bed creaked. So did a few of his joints. A hell of a thing, Willis thought, for a man who wouldn't turn fifty for pretty near ten years.

His bad knee twinged with pain as it was prone to do on brisk mornings, and he cursed himself as he was prone to do.

Willis flexed his left leg a few times, then glanced at the brace on the floor by the foot of the bed. To hell with it, he decided. He pushed to his feet and took three steps toward the stove before his leg reminded him that human bone and human sinew should never be taken for granted. Whoever did was liable to end his days a cripple. He pitched onto his hands and his good knee, and cursed himself anew.

His bouts of temper never lasted long. He had never been a hothead, not even as a boy. He had been mad at himself now for what seemed like forever but that was not the same. A man had a right to be mad when he did something stupid. The stupider it was, the madder he could be.

Willis curled his legs under himself and levered across the floor to where he had thrown the brace the night before. He had to be careful, he reminded himself, or he might break it, and then where would he be? Up the creek without a paddle. No, up the creek without a damn canoe.

It took a while to get the brace on. Willis had to place it just right or it would chafe something awful and, worse, his leg wouldn't hold him up. The thick leather straps had to be as tight as a woman's corset. Not that he had much experience with corsets. He had seen Mattie's, of course, but had never thought of touching it; you never thought like that about your sister. Then there had been that dove down to Kansas, at the end of a trail drive, with a corset it took what seemed like hours to undo. And that was it. Some of the punchers liked to boast of undoing more corsets than they had fingers and toes, and he could only boast of undoing one, and even then he had needed the dove's help.

Presently, the brace was secure. Propping himself against the wall, Willis slowly stood, and when he was satisfied he would not fall, he limped to the bed and pulled his pants and his shirt on over his long underwear. His pants were baggier than most but they had to be because of the brace. Next he forced his stockinged feet into his boots and donned his hat.

Willis studied his reflection in the square of glass above the washbasin. His eyebrows were too bushy and his nose was too long and too crooked from where a bronc had busted it one time, and his square chin gave his face the look of a box. The only good feature he had were his eyes. As green as the greenest pine, that dove had said. Or as his sister liked to say, as green as the prairie in the first bloom of spring. She always had a fine way with words, Mattie did. It made her fate all that more pitiable.

Willis shook himself and limped to the stove. He added wood from a pile under the window and kindled a new fire by puffing on glowing embers left over from the night before.

The shack always took a while to warm. Not that it was big, as line shacks went. In addition to his bunk there were some bunks he was required to keep ready for use at any hour of the day or night. The only other furniture was a small table with two chairs.

Willis held his hands to the flames, then rubbed them and walked to the door. He did not bother with his coat. It was not winter yet although that high up a body could be forgiven for thinking maybe it was.

A golden eyeball peeked at him over the rim of the world. Willis closed the door and limped around the side to the corral. The horses were there, his and the two extras, as they should have been. "No sign of that varmint?" Willis asked. Not one horse had the decency to look up. "Lazy no-accounts," he grumbled.

Willis looked off down the mountain. The woods were dark yet. A few low clouds hugged the treetops. It always tickled him being higher than the clouds. Some days in the winter, the valley was nothing but clouds from end to end, lending him the notion he was on top of the world. He wasn't, of course. The Tetons were high but they weren't as high as that mountain over in Asia somewhere, the one Charlie Weaver said was so high, a man could stand on his toes and about touch the moon. Charlie was known to stretch the truth, but other folks had said the mountain was as high as anything, so maybe it really was.

About to turn and go back in, Willis paused at a hint of movement far below. He figured it to be an elk or a deer or some other critter but the sky picked that moment to lighten a few degrees and he saw the unmistakable silhouette of a distant horse and rider.

"I'll be damned!" Willis blurted, too overcome with excitement to move. He had to remind himself that Indians rode horses, too. So did badmen, although badmen were rare in those parts ever since the Flour Sack Kid left that neck of the country and was giving folks down in Colorado fits.

Willis didn't really reckon it was an Indian. The Shoshones were all over to the Wind River region and the Blackfeet hadn't acted up in a coon's age. He rubbed his hands again and hurried back in. The shack was nicely warm and the stove was hot. He got down the Arbuckle's from a shelf and put a fresh pot of coffee on. Then he took down the flour and some of the precious butter and the Borden's condensed milk and the salt, and by the time hooves clomped outside he had a dozen hot flapjacks heaped and ready, plus the coffee and some potatoes, besides.

Willis limped to the door. The rider had drawn rein, and was framed by the rising sun. Willis had to squint to see who it was. "Well, this is a wonderment. Are you drunk? Or did you get lost and end up here by mistake?"

"Is that any way to greet someone who has come five hundred miles to bring you the news?" Charlie Weaver asked. He was half Willis' age and uncommonly plump for a cow hand but he could ride with the best of them and had the cheeriest disposition this side of a patent medicine salesman. Perhaps too cheery.

"It's only forty miles to the ranch house," Willis corrected him, "and more than likely the news you're bringin' is your new conquest over to the Lucky Dollar."

Charlie pressed a hand to his chest in one of his typical theatrics. "You wound me, pard. You truly do. How you can think so

12

little of me after all the great times we've had is a mystery."

"Climb down and I'll tend to your horse," Willis said. It was his job and he always did what was expected of him.

"No need," Charlie said. "This ain't official. It's a social call. I can do it my own self."

"Climb down," Willis insisted. "There's breakfast waitin'. Just be sure to leave some for me or I'll boot you out on your ear."

"Did someone mention food?" Charlie was off his sorrel so fast he practically sprouted wings. "Yes, indeed! I can smell it from here! Pard, you are a gem of a gent and I'll punch any uncouth clod who says different."

"Shut up and go eat, you jackass," Willis said gruffly. His friend's fondness for flowery words was often an embarrassment. Willis led the sorrel to the corral and stripped off the saddle and the saddle blanket and the bridle, then carried the saddle and the bedroll and saddlebags inside.

Charlie was at the table, forking a large piece of flapjack into his mouth with a smile of contentment. "You know, Willis, if you ever give up bein' a cowboy, you could always hire out as a cook. You're not half bad."

"I'm passable." Willis would not accept the false praise. "You must have ridden all night to get here this early."

"That I did," Charlie allowed, chomping lustily, talking with his mouth full. "I have to be back day after tomorrow and didn't want to spend two nights on the trail comin' out."

"Day after tomorrow?" Willis repeated. "I figured you were ridin' the line."

"Told you," Charlie said between chomps, "this is a social visit."

Willis digested that while forking a couple of flapjacks onto a plate and reaching for the molasses. He told himself he should wait until Charlie was done before he brought it up but he was burning with interest. "So what's this big news?"

"There's a new girl at the Lucky Dollar."

"I knew it," Willis said.

"Her name is Gertrude but everybody calls her Gerty. She's from Ohio. A little too wide at the hips for my tastes and she has the biggest damn feet you ever saw on a female, but she hums real pretty."

"Hums?"

"When she's not talkin' and you're not talkin', she just sort of sits there and hums," Charlie related. "About puts me to sleep."

"So you've had her?" Willis took it for granted.

"No, sir. Not her. She's a mite finnicky. Hasn't invited any of the punchers under the sheets, nor any of the townsmen, besides. Jim Palmer tried, and Lord knows he hasn't failed yet, but he met his match in Gerty. She told him flat out no man could take liberties with her unless she cottoned to him and he cottoned to her more than any other."

"Sounds like she's throwin' a loop for a husband," Willis said. Jim Palmer was the handsomest ranny in the outfit, maybe the most handsome man in all of Wyoming. Any female who could turn Jim down had to be up to no good.

"My thinkin' exactly," Charlie said. "But Gerty ain't the big news. Neither is the Flour Sack Kid."

Willis gave a mild start. He could not help himself. "How does the Kid fit into your news?"

"I figured you hadn't heard," Charlie said smugly. "Word is he made it so hot for himself down in Colorado, vigilantes came within a whisker of treatin' him to a strangulation jig. They say he's driftin' up our way again."

"Who says this?" Willis asked, alarmed.

"Oh, you know, the boys at the Lucky Dollar. Slim says he heard it from a drummer, who heard it from a friend of a lawdog down to Denver or some such place."

Slim, the bartender at the Lucky Dollar, was as reliable a source of information as Cottonwood had except for the parson, who never, ever lied, and reminded everyone of that regularly. But Willis hoped it wasn't true. God, how he hoped it wasn't true. "Well, if Gerty ain't the news and the Kid ain't the news, what in blazes is so important you rode all night to see me?"

Charlie looked him in the eyes. "Abe is thinkin' of sellin' the Bar T."

This time it was more than a start. It was shock. Pure and total shock. Willis was so numb, he couldn't say anything.

Charlie chuckled. "Set you off your feed, did I? Word reached the bunkhouse two days ago. One of Elfie's friends got it straight from Elfie at a quiltin' bee and the friend told Jim when he went courtin'."

Willis' spirits sank. "I bet it was Elfie who put Abe up to it. Abe would never sell on his own." Abe Tyler had built the Bar T from nothing into a prosperous ranch and was as proud of it as a man could be proud of anything on God's green earth.

"It would be a rigged bet," Charlie said.

16

"Of course she prodded him. She never liked it here. She's a city gal at heart and country livin' doesn't agree with her refined disposition." Charlie snorted. "Abe should never have brought her back from Saint Louis. What he sees in her is hard to untangle."

Not for Willis. Elfie had a bosom that resembled twin watermelons, and Abe always had been exceptionally fond of watermelons. "How soon before you reckon Abe finds a buyer?"

"Is your brain sluggish today?" Charlie rejoined. "He already has one. We don't know much about her other than she's from Texas, of all places."

"She?" Willis said. He couldn't take many more of these shocks. As it was, he had a hankering to crawl under his blankets and sleep a while and hope when he woke up he would find out it had all been a bad dream.

Charlie was nodding. "You heard rightly. Laurella Hendershot. I guess her pa has a spread in Texas and she wanted one of her own, so she made an offer for the Bar T."

"Why doesn't she buy a ranch in Texas?"

"You're askin' me? How in hell would I know. I can't explain Wyomin' women, and Texas women are twice as female."

"That makes no kind of sense," Willis said.

"All I can tell you is that she made a more than fair offer and Elfie is interested even if Abe ain't, and Elfie always gets her way." Charlie speared a piece of potato with his fork.

"What will I do?"

"What will we all do? That's the question." Charlie rested his elbows on the table and grew uncharacteristically glum. "Some of the boys are for pullin' up stakes. Sam says he won't work for a woman. Hank says he won't work for a Texan because Texans are naturally bossy."

"What does Reuben say?"

"He's for waitin' and seein' how the wind blows. It could be things will go on just as they are. Then again, this Laurella *is* female, *and* a Texan, so it could be she'll shake the whole tree from top to bottom and maybe bring in her own outfit."

"There's that," Willis said. He almost wished Charlie had not come. His day had been ruined. Hell, his life had been ruined, and he had no idea what to do. "Abe's been awful kind to me."

"Abe's kind to everyone," Charlie said. "It's part of why we've all been so loyal to the brand. The Bar T won't be the same without him." He speared another piece of potato almost savagely. "Damn that Elfie, anyhow. She'll drag him back to Saint Louis, I reckon, and turn him into a citified dandy who will wait on her hand and foot."

"He does that already."

Charlie chuckled, shoving the potato in his mouth. "Ain't that the truth! That's what he gets for pickin' such a poor runnin' mate."

"Abe loves her," Willis said.

"He probably thinks he does. But when it comes to women, a man can't ever be sure how much is his heart and how much is below his belt."

"There you go again."

"What?" Charlie washed down the potato with coffee and sat back and patted his belly. "I'm halfway to full. The way you cook, if you were female, I'd marry you."

"Say that again and I'll hit you."

Unflustered, Charlie said, "I figure to stay on long enough to see how the new owner stacks up. If Hendershot lets things go on as they are, maybe I'll stick. If she puts curtains in the bunkhouse and makes us sweep the floor and make our beds, then I'll light a shuck for other parts."

"Is she married?" Willis really didn't care. He was making small talk while pondering the weightier issue of what he was going to do if the ranch indeed was sold.

"Somethin' strange there," Charlie said. "Word is, she's over thirty, but she doesn't have a husband nor any kids. What do you suppose is wrong with her?"

"Maybe she had a husband and he died before she could have any," Willis guessed, "or maybe she's a spinster."

"Lord, no," Charlie said. "A man hater *and* female *and* from Texas. How could it get any worse?"

"I didn't say she hates men."

"She might as well. Half the boys hate her and they haven't even set eyes on her yet."

Willis had lost his appetite but he forced himself to eat the rest of his flapjacks. He listened with half an ear as his friend prattled on about how each and every hand at the Bar T felt about the impending change.

"When?" Willis interrupted.

Breaking off in midsentence, Charlie glanced at him. "When what? When will the first snow fall? When will Armageddon come? When will horses speak English?"

"You say the damnedest things," Willis said. "When will Abe sell the Bar T?"

"No one knows for sure. There's talk that this Hendershot woman is comin' to give the ranch a look-see sometime in the next couple of weeks and if she likes what she

20

sees, the deal will go through."

"How did she find out it was for sale, anyhow?"

"That blamed Elfie," Charlie said. "She went to Denver on another of her shoppin' sprees and met the Hendershot woman somewhere or other and they got to jawin', and the next thing, Elfie came back and told Abe she had a buyer lined up."

"Women!" Willis said.

"Can't live with the critters without goin' loco and can't shoot them dead without bein' thrown in jail," Charlie lamented. "It's a cruel world."

Willis got up and stepped to the stove to refill his tin cup. "Now you're talkin' plumb nonsense."

"How do you feel about Arizona?" Charlie asked.

"I've never given it enough thought to have feelin's about," Willis said. He liked Wyoming. He had been born and lived his whole life there, and he would die there, if he had his druthers.

"Well, start thinkin'. You and me could make a heap of money. Or haven't you heard about all the silver strikes and how folks are takin' ore out of the ground like it was as common as dirt?"

"I've heard there are Apaches in Arizona

and that's all I need to hear," Willis said.

"Apaches have you spooked? They ain't any more fierce than the tribes we have hereabouts."

"You can say that with a straight face?" Willis marveled. "You should give up nursemaidin' cows and be a gambler. You're a natural." He took a sip of the piping hot coffee. "For one thing, the Shoshones ain't never been fierce. They're the friendliest tribe this side of creation. For another, the Blackfeet and the Sioux can be right fierce when they want to but they can't hold a candle to Apaches."

"Says the jasper who's never set foot in Arizona."

"I don't need to jump off a cliff to know it will hurt when I hit the bottom," Willis observed.

"All I ask is that you think about it, pard," Charlie coaxed. "It's no use worryin' about how high a bronc will buck until you climb —" He suddenly stopped and frowned. "Sorry. I shouldn't have."

The coffee turned bitter in Willis' mouth. "That's all right," he said. But it was not really all right. He did not like it when anyone made more of it than they should. Setting the tin cup on the table, he announced, "I need some fresh air." He was angry even though it was stupid to be angry.

"I really am sorry."

Willis almost slammed the door. He hated it when he got like this. Most times he could control himself but there were others when the bitterness rose in him like a river in flood, and it was all he could do not to throw back his head and curse the heavens. It was so unfair.

Breathing deep of the brisk morning air, Willis limped a few yards from the shack and put his hands on his hips and hung his head. "I'm actin' childish," he said aloud. Talking to himself was a habit he could do without, but when he was alone for days and sometimes weeks on end, it helped to hear a human voice, even if the voice was his own.

Shaking his head, Willis was about to turn and go back in when he saw the track. It was clear as clear could be in the soft earth near the stump where he split wood for the stove. Whistling softly, he bent down, stretched out his right hand, and held his fingers over the print. The track was larger. "He came back."

"Who did?"

Willis had not heard his friend come out. "What did, you mean. Take a gander." He stepped back.

Charlie whistled softly. "That there has to be the biggest mountain lion since Hector was a pup. And you say he's been payin' you regular visits?"

"I think he's interested in the horses. Last week one night they were actin' up, and I came out with my rifle and the lantern and stayed with them until they quieted down. The next mornin' I found a partial print at the far end of the corral."

"Drecker would pay good money for a cougar skin," Charlie mentioned. "It's the only animal whose hide he doesn't have on his walls."

"All I care about are the horses," Willis said. He was responsible for them and he would not let them come to harm.

"Let's hunt it," Charlie proposed. "You and me, like in the old days when we did things together."

"I don't know," Willis hesitated. It would take a lot of riding and he could not ride like he used to.

"Come on," Charlie urged. "What can it hurt? You must be tired of bein' cooped up in that old shack all damn day. Why not get out a little?"

"What if the line rider shows up and I'm not here?" Willis argued. "I'd let Abe down, and he's been powerful kind to me."

"You're in luck, pard. I happen to know that Hank drew the short straw this month and he's busy down near Dutch Creek roundin' up strays. He won't make it up this way for a week or more."

"You're sure?"

"As God is my witness. May a rhino run up and poke me in the backside if I'm fibbin'."

"A what?"

"A critter from Africa. Lou the barber told me about them. He read about it in one of those periodicals he gets. A rhino is as big as a horse with a horn growin' out of the middle of its head."

To Willis it sounded suspiciously like the unicorn in a story his grandmother used to read to him when he was knee-high to a calf, and he said so.

"Could be. They also have antelopes with necks as tall as trees and snakes that can swallow a man whole and lions as big as buffalo." Charlie nodded at the track. "What do you say? Are you up for some big-game huntin', as they call it in Africa?"

"Why not?" Willis said.

Charlie laughed and said, "It will be just like old times. All we have to do is make it back alive."

CHAPTER 2

Willis hated to climb on a horse anymore. He hated it because more than anything else it reminded him of his stupidity. It threw his affliction, as Elfie once called it, smack in his face. Worst of all, it reminded him that he was no longer the man he once was, and would never again be.

But with Charlie Weaver looking on and waiting to head out, Willis had to swallow his shame. He gripped the saddle horn with both hands, tensed his good leg, and swung up and over the saddle in one smooth motion so that his right boot slid into the stirrup as he straightened. As for his left leg, he had to help it a little. He had to bend and slide his hand under the brace and lift the leg enough to insert his boot into the left stirrup.

"Ready, pard?"

Willis nodded. He did not like it that Charlie was watching him like a mother hen. He patted the Winchester in its saddle scabbard and replied, "Ready and rarin' to kill me that cat." He touched his right spur to the zebra dun.

"He won't have gone far," Charlie predicted. "He'll be holed up somewhere above."

"Let's hope," Willis said. They only had until sunset. Charlie was heading back in the morning and would need his sleep.

They followed the tracks to the top of the ridge, and drew rein. Below, wisps of smoke curled from the line shack. It would be a while before the stove went out. The two horses in the corral were staring up as if they yearned to go along.

"I envy you," Charlie unexpectedly said.

"What on earth for?" Willis didn't see where being a cripple was anything worth envying.

Encompassing the Tetons with a sweep of an arm, Charlie said, "It's beautiful up here. The forest, the snow on the peaks, the wildlife. And you don't have anyone lookin' over your shoulder sayin' as how you should do this, that, or the other."

"There's never anyone to talk to, though."

"Peace and quiet," Charlie said. "Go to bed when you want, get up when you want, do what you want. Yes, sir. This is the life."

"If it's so damn wonderful, why don't you ask to take my place?" Willis asked, more harshly than he had intended.

"Whoa there, pard. Did you get up on the wrong side of the bunk this mornin'?" Charlie grinned his most amiable grin. "I didn't mean to rile you. I honestly and truly think you have it great here."

"What's so great about being banished?" Willis asked, and gigged the zebra dun on up the mountain.

"How do you reckon?" Charlie asked.

"Do you think I don't know? Abe gave me this job because there's nothin' else I can do. I can't break the wild ones anymore. I'm useless at the thing I loved most in this world. Hell, I can't even cowboy."

"You're too hard on yourself."

"Am I? How can I handle a brandin' iron when I can't hardly bend? What good would it do me to rope a cow when it would take me a month of Sundays to climb down and undo the rope?" Willis shook his head. "I'm useless except for mindin' a line shack that doesn't need mindin' and cookin' meals for line riders who don't need anyone to cook for them."

"Still, it was nice of Abe."

"It was nice of Abe," Willis echoed, but his bitterness worsened.

After that, they did not talk for a while. Willis concentrated on finding tracks. It was a challenge. Cougars were almost as crafty as foxes when it came to leaving no sign.

Then Charlie asked another unexpected question. "Ever had a hankerin' to have your own cow bunny?"

"No," Willis lied, and when his friend did not go on, he asked, "Why? What brought that up?"

"I don't know," Charlie said. They were ascending a steep slope but Charlie rode as if he and his bay were one, with the natural ease of a master horseman. "I'm not gettin' any younger, and it occurs to me that maybe I ought to find me one before I'm too old for a woman to take any interest."

"What are you talkin' about? You're younger than me."

"It's that Gerty," Charlie said. "She sure is easy on the eyes. And I like how she hums. At night I'll lie in bed and hum to myself like she does. That shows me some-thin'."

"It shows what can happen when a person thinks too much," Willis said.

"Thinkin' ain't got nothin' to do with it," Charlie disagreed. "A man can go on bein' a boy only so long before he has to hitch up his belt and be a man whether he wants to be a man or not."

"If that made any kind of sense, it did so without me noticin' " was Willis' assessment. "You could go ten years yet without gettin' hitched."

"You're missin' the point," Charlie said. "You're not the only one who gets lonely. I like the notion of comin' home to a woman every night. Of havin' warm meals waitin' and someone to hold close under the covers."

"That's enough," Willis said sternly.

"You should think about it," Charlie suggested.

"When I say that's enough, I mean it." Willis refused to think about women. There was no point to it.

"You know, you're gettin' to be a grump. Time was, you would joke and laugh with the best of us."

"Time was, I had the use of both my legs," Willis stated flat-out, and regretted the words the instant they were out of his mouth.

"I never took you for the kind to wallow in pity," Charlie said. "The Willis Lander of old had more fire."

"I'm not the man I used to be." Willis would have said more but a lump formed in his throat and his eyes moistened, and he mentally cursed himself for being so weak. Sometimes it felt like there was no bottom to the well.

"Who of us is?" Charlie's plump frame was stooped forward to better distribute his weight. "There are days when I suspect the Almighty made us the way we are just so He can laugh at our antics."

"You come up with the most preposterous notions."

"Think about it. Why are we born just to die? Why have us be young just so we grow old?"

"Hellfire, where do you get this stuff?"

Charlie wasn't done. "Why give us teeth if all they're goin' to do one day is fall out? Why give us hair just so we can grow bald? What's the purpose in all this, if there even is one?"

Willis shook his head. "You're askin' the wrong person. If you really want to know, see the parson."

"All he'd do is quote Scripture. Which is fine for a sermon but doesn't always apply to real life."

"That's blasphemy."

"Since when did you go and get religion?" Charlie countered. "As I recollect, until your accident, you were the wildest and wooliest of the bunch."

"That was then and this is now," Willis said, skirting a deadfall. "I don't make a habit of livin' in the past."

"That's good," Charlie said as insincerely as was humanly possible.

Now Willis was mad. Fortunately, he spied another clear track and reined over to examine it from the saddle. The cat had headed almost due west from the line shack and was steadily climbing toward the peaks that gave the rugged range its name. In the distance reared the Grand Teton, flanked to the north by Mount Owen and Teewinot. To the south was the snowcapped knob of Middle Teton. At that time of year the snow was sparse but in a couple of months it would be deeper than the line shack was tall. South of Middle Teton reared Nez Percé and South Teton. Five peaks, five towering ramparts of stone and earth thrusting skyward as if to tear at the fabric of heaven.

"He wasn't in much of a hurry," Charlie commented.

Willis grunted. The length of the mountain lion's strides showed as much. It must have fed before it visited the shack, he reasoned, and now was looking for a spot to lay up during the day. Or more than likely, it had a den it used whenever it was in the area. An old hunter once told him that a male mountain lion's range could cover as much as seventy-five miles, a female's as much as fifty.

On they rode, the hooves of their mounts ringing on rock and now and then sending pebbles and loose dirt rattling down the slope. A raven flew overhead, the rhythmic beat of its wings unnaturally loud in the quiet of the high country.

Fifty yards higher, Charlie pointed and blurted, "Look there!"

Several elk were off in the shadows under tall firs. Willis peered hard but could not tell if any were bulls. Probably not. It would be another month yet before rut set in and the bulls set the slopes to ringing with their trumpeting cries and clash of antlers as they fought for their harems.

"Say, did I tell you about the gunfight?" Charlie asked out of nowhere.

Willis looked at him. "There are days when I want to beat you with a branch," he said in mild disgust.

"Sorry. It plumb slipped my mind. I missed it myself, but I heard all about it the last time I was in Cottonwood."

"Anyone I know?"

"Sure. Johnny Vance. He tangled with three drifters who accused him of cheatin' and now one of them is six feet under and the other two are on the mend."

Willis knew Johnny Vance well. He had played cards many a time at the gambler's table in the Lucky Dollar, and on several occasions Vance had bought him a drink after cleaning him out. As gambler's went, the Reb was damned decent. Vance was also as deadly as a rattler when riled. "That's it? Hell, if you were a newspaper, no one would read you."

"Oh. It's *details* you want?" Charlie said with a smirk. "Why didn't you say so?"

Willis made a show of gazing all around. "Where's a handy tree limb when you need one?"

"All right." Charlie grinned. "It was two Fridays ago. Three drifters came into Cottonwood from the East. Scruffy bunch. One wore a Union cap and another wore a Union coat."

"Uh-oh," Willis said. Johnny Vance was from the Deep South. Vance had served on the Confederate side during the war and was known to be touchy about the subject of Rebels and slaves and such.

"Exactly," Charlie said. "Anyway, they tied up outside the Lucky Dollar and went in and paid for a bottle and hunkered at a table for a while, drinkin'. Then one of 'em got the bright idea to go over and sit in on Johnny's card game."

Willis was watching for tracks. He had not seen any in a while and was beginning to worry they had lost the trail.

"Slim the bartender saw the whole thing," Charlie related. "Those three boys went on drinkin' and playin' and losin' their money, and along about midnight they were plumb broke and didn't take it well."

"A man who can't afford to lose shouldn't gamble."

"I hear that," Charlie said, "but these three peckerwoods didn't have the sense of a lump of coal between 'em. They started makin' remarks. They could tell by Johnny's accent that he was a Southerner, so one of them said as how the South got what it deserved for darin' to fight the North and another one said as how all Southerners were lower than pond scum and the third one said as how the only thing worse than a Southerner was a gambler and the only thing worse than that was a Southern gambler."

"Hell in a basket," Willis said.

"Slim says Johnny Vance took it pretty well until that last comment. Then he stood up and pulled his frock coat back from that fancy pearl-handled Remington of his and told those three gents they were Yankee trash with no more manners than a billy goat, and their mothers were whores, besides."

"How did that go over?"

"About as you'd expect. The three Yankees took to cussin' and blusterin' and then one of them went for his hardware and the other two took that as a sign they should be as dumb as he was."

"Damn. Wish I'd been there," Willis said. He had only ever witnessed one shooting in his whole life, and he witnessed that only because he was involved in it.

"You and me both, pard. Slim says it was a wonder to behold. Johnny Vance drew and put a slug into the chest of the first Yankee before the jackass cleared leather. Shot him smack through the heart, it turns out. The second one took a slug in the shoulder. The third one was hit in the neck and blood was sprayin' everywhere and he dropped his revolver and screamed like a little girl. Slim's own words."

"Only the one died?"

"The one who was shot in the neck lost a lot of blood but the wound wasn't that deep. Babies come in all sizes, I reckon."

Willis drew rein. He had spotted another partial print but this one was to his left and not ahead or to his right as the others had been. He reined over and announced, "The cat has changed direction."

"Goin' south now," Charlie observed.

The ground was harder. Willis had to go slowly or risk losing the sign. After a while he asked, "Vance get into any trouble with the law?"

"Are you kiddin'? Marshal Keever says the three idiots had it comin'. The two who lived were lucky he didn't throw them in jail and throw away the key."

"How is Johnny doin'?"

"How do you mean? It ain't like that's the first time he's pulled on a man. Slim says after he shot 'em, he sat back down as calmly as you please and shuffled the cards and asked if anyone else wanted to sit in the game."

Willis chuckled. "That sounds like him." He sobered. "But killin' always leaves its mark on a man."

"How would you know?" Charlie teased. "You've never shot anyone your whole life."

Willis did not reply.

"You would think most folks had put the war behind them," Charlie rambled on. "It's been, what, pretty near fifteen years? I guess some hatreds run so deep there's no ever gettin' over them."

"I reckon." Willis finally asked about the thing that was uppermost on his mind. "The Flour Sack Kid. How do folks know he's headin' our way?"

"He robbed a drummer near Fort Collins and a sawbones up toward Cheyenne," Charlie revealed. "Popped out of the dark with that flour sack on his head and hollered for them to fork over their valuables or go straight to hell."

"He robbed a doctor?" In Willis' estimation, that was almost as vile as robbing a schoolmarm.

"The sawbones was in his buggy, returnin' from a call. He didn't have any money on him so the Flour Sack Kid took his watch and a ring and a couple of cigars." Charlie chortled. "What sort of outlaw steals cigars? If the Flour Sack Kid ain't careful, he'll become a laughingstock."

"He hasn't amounted to much as an outlaw," Willis agreed. "Him and his short-cuts to the top."

"How's that?"

"Nothin'," Willis said, and abruptly drew rein. The mountain lion had changed direction again.

"Now that contrary cat is headin' east," Charlie noted. "Maybe it's lost."

The idea of a mountain lion not knowing

where it was going was so silly, Willis laughed.

"You don't think animals can get lost?" Charlie asked. "Critters do it all the time. Horses, dogs, cats, turtles."

"Turtles?"

"My brother had one when we were small. He'd set it out in the yard on sunny days for it to warm itself. One day he set it out, and the next we looked, it was gone. It strayed off and never found its way back."

Willis looked at him. "Remind me again why I put up with you?"

"Because I'm about the only cuss who can put up with *you*," Charlie rejoined. "It might come as a shock, but you don't have the sunniest disposition around."

"Go to hell."

"See?" Charlie grinned at his triumph. He glanced at another partial print in the dust and then down the mountain, and stiffened. "I just had me a thought, pard."

"There's a first."

"I'm serious," Charlie said. "Is it me, or is this cat of yours headin' back the way we came?"

Willis blinked, and recoiled as if he had been slapped. "Son of a bitch." He resorted to his right spur and descended as fast as he dared, which was not fast at all because the slope was too sleep.

"Don't get all agitated," Charlie hollered. "It could be I'm wrong. Since when do they hunt in broad daylight?"

Not often, Willis thought, but it did happen. He recalled a sheepherder who lost twenty or thirty sheep to a cat that got into the pen in the middle of the day and went on a slaughtering spree. "Oh God," he said softly. He was responsible for the other two horses. If anything should happen to them —

"Didn't you hear me? I could be wrong. Or is it you want to break your fool neck?"

"You could be right, too," Willis yelled. Lord help him, but he had a feeling deep in his gut that the cougar had drawn them off and was circling back for a purpose.

Willis buckled down to riding. Once, he had been as good a rider as Charlie. But now whole days and weeks went by and he refused to step into the stirrups and be reminded of the man he had once been.

The thud of hooves, the clatter of dirt and stones, the breathing of the zebra dun and the feel and the creak of saddle leather conspired to make Willis feel the loss that much more. God, how he had loved to ride! His father had thrown him on a pony when he was six and he had been on a horse every

40

day thereafter. Truth was, he had *lived* on horseback. Twelve, fourteen hours a day in the saddle had been nothing to him. What did he care if he was saddle sore so long as he could *ride.*

Willis gave an angry toss of his head. He had not thought about how much he loved riding in a long time. It always made him sad and mad. Sometimes more of the one and sometimes more of the other, depending on whether he was feeling sorry for himself or mad at the world and everyone and everything in it.

The line shack came into view. It was still a long way off and partly hidden by the trees. So was the corral. Willis started to rise in the stirrups and caught himself in time. His left knee had a habit of giving out when he did that, brace or no brace. He reined to the right in the hope the corral would be visible but there was too much vegetation in the way. His gut was balled into a knot and his mouth had gone as dry as a desert.

"Over yonder, pard!" Charlie bawled.

Willis glanced at his friend and then in the direction Charlie was pointing. There was the cat. The mountain lion was streaking to the south in long bounds that would put an antelope to shame. The cat had seen them and was running away from the corral, not toward it.

The tightness in Willis' belly lessened. They were in time! Shifting, he snatched his Winchester from the saddle scabbard and levered a round into the chamber. He wedged the stock to his shoulder to fire one-handed but the cat was too far off. They came to level ground and he spurred the zebra dun into a gallop, holding himself and his right arm as steady as he could.

The mountain lion looked back and ran faster. A tawny streak, it flowed across the ground like feline quicksilver.

"Shoot, damn it!" Charlie urged.

Willis had always been the better shot. He was not much good with a pistol but with a rifle he was more than passable. When he was younger, much younger, he had won the Thanksgiving turkey shoot two years in a row. But it was one feat to hit clay targets and another to hit a running animal, especially one as swift as a cougar. He fixed the best bead he could, led the cat by a yard or so, and squeezed the trigger.

A dirt geyser erupted next to the mountain lion's forepaw. Willis had missed but not by much. Levering in another round, he centered the sights but the Winchester would not steady no matter how hard he tried to hold it level. He banged off a shot anyway. Predictably, he missed.

"Don't let it get away!"

Willis would like to see Charlie try. Again he worked the lever one-handed. Again he jammed the stock to his shoulder. Again he tried to sight down the barrel. He might as well have done it from the back of a bucking bronc. His frustration mounting, he slowed so he could use his left arm as well as his right.

"There!" Charlie cried.

The mountain lion was almost to the pines. Another thirty seconds and it would be lost amid the boles.

Willis slowed even more, took a deep breath and held it, and stroked the Winchester's trigger. At the same instant as the sharp *crack*, the mountain lion veered to the right and moments later was swallowed by shadows.

"You missed."

Bringing the zebra dun to a stop, Willis slowly lowered the Winchester. "Tell me somethin' I don't know."

"Do we go after it?" Charlie asked.

Willis would have liked to but he had seen flecks of red on the mountain lion's jaw and neck when it glanced back. Reining around, he galloped toward the line shack. He told himself he was mistaken, that it had not been blood, that the horses were fine and he shouldn't fret.

Then the zebra dun rounded a small pine and another part of Willis deep inside shriveled. He reined in shy of the rails and sadly stared at the twin scarlet pools. In all his days he had never felt so useless. "I should do the world a favor and die."

CHAPTER 3

Burying the horses took hours but it had to be done. Left to rot, they would stink and draw every scavenger for miles. Willis refused to let Charlie Weaver help. "It's mine to do."

"But I can spell you diggin'," Charlie offered for the third time. "Why wear yourself out if you don't need to?"

"No," Willis said, and that was that. It was noon before he finished. He had to dig the holes a good distance from the shack, then use the zebra dun to haul the bodies over. He let Charlie lend a hand dragging but only because with the bay to help it was easier on the zebra dun.

"Want me to say a few words over them?" Charlie asked after the last shovelful of dirt had been tamped down.

Willis glanced sharply at him but his friend was serious. "I never took you for religious."

"I'm not," Charlie admitted, "except when it comes to dyin'. When my time comes, I want you to have the parson do me proper."

"You'll outlive me," Willis predicted. He had long thought — it could be said he had long hoped — that he would die before he was fifty.

"You never know." Charlie took off his hat, bowed his head, and intoned, "Ashes to ashes, dust to dust." Then he put his hat back on and adjusted his bandanna.

"That's it?"

"No need to make that much of a fuss," Charlie said. "They were only horses." He stretched, then yawned. "I reckon I'll catch up on my sleep before I head out."

"I'll be in shortly," Willis said. He wanted to be alone a while.

A log a stone's throw from the line shack was his favorite spot to sit and ponder. His right elbow on his right knee, his chin in his hand, he gazed off down the mountain and forlornly contemplated his future. "What future?" he asked himself, and regarded his left leg with loathing. He couldn't bend it more than an inch or two, so when he sat down, he always had to stick it out in front of him like the useless appendage it was.

Willis was lower than he had ever been, and he had been low a lot since his knee was shattered. He closed his eyes and thought of the old days and a dreamy smile creased his face, despite his mood. It was a shame people could not go back into the past and fix their mistakes. He would go back to that fateful morning when he tried to break the man killer and do what he should have done in the first place: shoot it.

Horses that killed were always shot. It was an unwritten law. But Willis thought he could tame that stallion. He would do what no one had ever done and turn a man killer into a usable horse.

That had been his first mistake: thinking he was God Almighty. His second mistake had been to go into the corral alone. His third had been to let himself be distracted for a few seconds. That was all it took. The stallion had him down and nearly stomped him to death. As it was, he had lost the knee, and his other broken bones took months to mend. He would have died that day if not for Abe, who saw what was happening and ran into the ranch house for his shotgun and rushed back out and did what should have been done in the first place.

Willis suspected Abe felt partly to blame. After the stallion killed Joe Sennet, the smart thing to do, the only thing to do, was kill the stallion. But Abe had let him try to break it, and now he would spend the rest of his days half the man he used to be.

"I wish the damn critter had killed me."

Clouds were scuttling in from the west, darkening the sky to match his mood. It was early in the year for rain but rain it did, forcing him indoors. He sat at the table a while listening to the patter of drops on the roof, what he could hear above Charlie's snoring.

The hours crawled by, as they always did. When Charlie woke, Willis fed him, and soon his friend was saddled and ready to leave.

"You should come down with me and tell Abe about the horses."

"You tell him," Willis said. "My job is to be here for the line rider when he comes."

"I told you Hank won't be here for weeks yet, but you do what you want." In a rare show of emotion, Charlie placed a hand on Willis' shoulder. "Are you all right, pard?"

"What kind of fool question is that? Of course I'm all right."

"Then why do you always look as if your ma just died and you're waitin' for the funeral to commence?"

"My mother died years ago."

Charlie sighed and slung his saddlebags over a shoulder. "You know what I mean." His spurs jangled as he went out.

Willis leaned in the doorway. The rain had stopped but the sky was overcast. "Give my regards to the boys in the bunkhouse."

"Will do." Charlie tied his saddlebags on and swung onto the saddle with a fluid ease his plump form belied. "Try not to be so hard on yourself — you hear?"

"I'll try." Willis watched until his friend melted into the timber lower down. The ache deep inside him grew worse and he went to the cupboard for his flask. He had half left, the best sipping whiskey money could buy. He sat at the table, his right leg propped on the edge, his useless left leg jutting under it, and sipped and thought and sipped and thought.

Thinking was bad for him but Willis had nothing else to do. The shack was tidy and clean, the beds all made, the floor swept. There was enough venison to last a week so he did not need to go hunting.

Night came and went and the day after that and then the next until a week had gone by, and then two weeks. Willis did his daily chores in a sort of daze. They were something to do but he had done them so often he could do them with his eyes closed. He was going through the motions of life, not really living, but he did not have the courage to do what he should.

Then came a sunny morning, and Willis was out brushing the zebra dun even though it did not need brushing when the animal raised its head, looked down the mountain, and whinnied.

A rider was coming. Willis figured it was Hank but then why was the riding coming from the east when Charlie had told him Hank was riding line to the south? He limped into the shack and put a fresh pot of coffee on and was outside waiting when the rider was near enough for him to identify.

To say Willis was shocked did not do his reaction justice. He was more than shocked. He was stupefied. He would not believe it if he was not seeing it with his own eyes, and as it was, he wondered if his eyes were really seeing it.

His visitor smiled and wearily reined up. "Hello, Willis. It's been a while, hasn't it?"

"Hello, Abe."

The Bar T's owner surveyed the line shack. "Aren't you getting tired yet of being way up here alone?" He did not wait for an answer but dismounted and started to lead his sorrel to the corral.

"I'll do that," Willis said, reaching.

"No, you won't." Abe was not a tall man or powerfully built, but when he spoke, other men listened. His head, framed by bushy sideburns that lent his face a bearish aspect, was almost too big for his body. "I don't need coddling." He stripped his buttermilk and hung the saddle and saddle blanket over the top rail. "I suppose you have coffee on?"

"It should be ready," Willis said, and respectfully waited for his employer to precede him.

Abe paused in the doorway to admire the mountains. "I had almost forgotten how beautiful they are." He shifted his gaze to Willis. "But hiding is still hiding, and it's time you gave some thought to rejoining the human race."

"I'm happy here," Willis said.

"Lie to yourself if you want but not to me." Abe went over to the stove. "Do you want a cup, too?"

"It's not right you should wait on me."

"Listen to yourself," Abe said, "as if I'm someone special. I pull my pants on one leg at a time, just like you." He filled two tin cups and set them down. "We should have done this long ago."

Willis ignored the coffee. "What brought it on?"

"Charlie told me about the cat and the horses," Abe said, "and how you insisted you had to stay — that it's your job and nothing else matters."

"It is and nothin' else does."

"That's where you're wrong." Abe swallowed, sat back, and studied Willis intently. "You can't go on beating yourself up over it. Time to get on with your life whether you want to or not."

"It's my life to do with as I want," Willis sullenly reminded him.

"I thought so, too. That's the only reason I let you come up here. But I was wrong and you are wrong and we need to own up to our mistake while we still can."

"You've changed, Abe," Willis said softly.

"Elfie changed me. She made me see things don't always need to stay the same. Life is a river, not quicksand, and we should flow with the current."

That was too much for Willis. "As much as I respect you, and I respect no one more, that's plain silly. I'm here because I want to be. Because it's best for me. Because you were kind enough to keep me on when I was worthless."

"Ah," Abe said, and was quiet a bit. "A man's worth isn't measured by whether he has the use of both his legs."

"Now you're gettin' personal."

Abe regarded each of the four walls. "This whole setup is personal. The line riders did just fine before you became the Teton Hermit."

"Is that what folks are callin' me?" Willis was joking and was taken aback when his employer nodded.

"Some, down to Cottonwood. Hell, you never go there anymore. You hide up here in your burrow and hope the rest of the world will leave you alone."

"There's nothin' wrong with a man bein' by himself," Willis grumbled.

"You're not worthless," Abe said bluntly.

Willis was so angry he stalled by drinking coffee. At last he said slowly, "You've been kind to me. You've treated me more decent than anyone ever has. But you're strayin' outside your pasture and I won't have you or anyone tellin' me how I should or shouldn't live."

"Fair enough," Abe said. "I respect your honesty. But the truth is, you don't have a choice anymore. Charlie told you I'm selling the Bar T, didn't he?"

"He said there's a rumor you are."

"The woman who is buying the ranch will be here in a week for another look and to sign the papers," Abe disclosed. "Then the Bar T will be hers, lock, stock and line shack."

Willis said, "I never thought I'd see the day."

"What can I say?" Abe responded. "She offered me a good price. More than I ever thought I could get. Enough for Elfie and me to spend the rest of our days comfortably. I'll miss the spread, sure. Impossible not to, seeing as how I built it up from free graze land into the third largest ranch in the territory. But it takes a lot of hard work and sweat to keep it running as it should, and I'd like to take it easy from now on. I'd like to enjoy what life I have left, not work myself into an early grave."

That's Elfie talkin', Willis was tempted to say, but did not.

"I admit it took a while for me to warm to the idea," Abe confessed. "Men are like mules. We get set in our ways and don't want to change even when the change is good for us." He glanced meaningfully across the table.

"So what you're sayin' is that this Texas filly won't want me stayin' up here," Willis said.

"She won't see the sense to it, no. And I wouldn't refer to her as a filly. Her name is Laurella Hendershot and she is every inch a lady. She knows all there is to know about ranching and cows. Don't underestimate

54

her because she's female."

"Where will I fit into her scheme of things?"

"That's up to her," Abe said. "She wants to meet all the hands personally. Including you."

"One week, you say?" The niche Willis had carved for himself was no longer his to carve, and his bleak existence had just become that much bleaker. "What if I don't come?"

"I'll send four or five of the boys to carry you. I'm sorry. It has to be. Your only other choice is to quit and that would disappoint me no end."

Willis stood, limped to the cupboard, and brought over his flask. "There's not much left but we can share."

"I'll go you one better." Abe reached inside his coat and pulled out a silver flask of his own. "I took a few nips on the way up but there's plenty left." He poured some into Willis' cup and poured some into his and replaced the flask. Raising his cup, he held it out. "How about a toast?"

The last time Willis had toasted anything was before his life was ruined, but he raised his cup and clinked it against Abe's. "What are we toastin'?"

"The future. May yours be as happy as

mine will be."

The whiskey and the hot coffee made for a fine mix. It burned a path clear down Willis' throat to the pit of his stomach. "If you don't mind my askin', are you honestly and truly happy, Abe?"

"Never more so. Yes, I know what people are whispering behind my back. That she holds the reins. That I'm acting like a lovestruck kid. That I don't really want to sell and I'm only giving up the Bar T because she's making me. It's all hogwash," Abe spat. "But then people will think what they want to think, and the truth be damned."

"There's an awful lot of folks out there who don't have enough brains to grease a skillet," Willis agreed. "I'll miss havin' you as the big sugar."

"I thought we were more than that. You've been with me from the beginning. The one man I could count on through thick and thin. We've shared many a drink, many a game of cards, and many a night around a roundup campfire."

"That we have," Willis said quietly.

"You've been as loyal to the brand as any man could ever be, and a whole lot more. I could no more cut you loose than I could cut off one of my fingers or toes."

"I appreciate that," Willis said. To disguise

how deeply it affected him, he tilted his tin cup to his lips.

Abe wasn't done. "I relied on you a lot in those early days. There I was, green as grass, an upstart from Ohio who thought he could make his fortune at cattle ranching when I hardly knew the first thing about cattle. Oh, I thought I did, from my farm days, but farm cows and ranch cows aren't the same."

"You did fine though."

"With a lot of luck and a lot of help from men like you," Abe said. "You're a big part of the reason I am where I am today, and that's why I've taken the liberty of coming up here and meddling in your personal life. This has gone on long enough. You need to pull yourself up by your bootstraps and get on with your life."

Again Willis grew angry but not quite as angry as before. "It's hard for me to think of livin' when I already have one foot — or make that one leg — in the grave."

"In all the years I've known you," Abe said, "that's the first damn stupid thing I've ever heard you say."

"Insults as well as meddlin'? If you're tryin' to cheer me up, you'd do a better job just shootin' me."

"Oh, Will," Abe said, "what will it take to get through that hard skull of yours? You're not washed up. A lot of good years are ahead of you. All you need to do is ask God to guide you."

"I've never been much for prayin'," Willis said. "It makes no sense to ask for help from someone who ain't listenin'."

"You better hope the parson never hears you say that. He would blister your ears." Abe sighed and stared into his cup. "I've overstepped my boundary, I know. But I'm done. I'll say no more. It's up to you what you do. But you might as well pack your things and ride down with me and meet the new owner. I doubt very much she will let you stay on up here when there is no reason for you to."

Now it was Willis who sighed. "I reckon I don't have any choice. Maybe it's just as well. When she lets me go, maybe I'll drift down Denver way. Maybe I can get a job sweepin' stores or shovelin' horse droppin's."

"Don't talk like that."

"Abe, you're as decent as they come, but you just don't savvy. All I ever wanted to be in life, I was. All I ever wanted to do, I was doin'. I was as happy as a man could be. Maybe too happy, and that's why the Almighty struck me down."

"You're saying stupid things again," Abe

said. "God doesn't hurt people to make them suffer."

"Sounds to me like you're the one who doesn't listen to the parson. Or have you forgotten about all those plagues and such? Or that she-bear God sent to kill those boys who were pokin' fun at that prophet? Seems to me the Almighty did an awful lot of hurtin' in the old days and liked it so much He's still doin' it today."

"I should have brought the parson," Abe said.

And that was where they left it. They drank more whiskey and made small talk about the ranch and mutual acquaintances and how much Cottonwood had grown, and by nightfall when they turned in, Willis was feeling a little better. He genuinely liked Abe, and it was nice Abe genuinely liked him.

The next morning, however, Willis balked. "I'd as soon not," he said when shortly after breakfast Abe Tyler suggested they get ready to head out.

"I knew you would try this. So as your boss and not your friend, I'm telling you to pack and be ready to go in half an hour."

"Whatever you say."

It was like leaving a part of himself. The line shack had been his home for so long that Willis stared over his shoulder until they were too far down to see it anymore. He thought of all the cold winter nights when he slept by the stove and the hot summer nights when he spread his blankets outside and slept under the stars. He thought of rain pattering on the roof and the many, many mornings he had gazed out over the mountains and felt, if not at peace, content with having the shack, and the world, to himself.

"Nervous?" Abe asked.

"Why should I be?" Willis said, but he was as nervous as he could ever recall being. He had not been down from the high country in so long, he had the impression he was entering a world he did not fit into. He much preferred the line shack. There, he was not a freak.

"Elfie will be glad to see you," Abe said. "Believe it or not, she's always liked you. Says you're the only hand who never looked at her as if she were an insult to the ranch."

Willis had always been good at poker.

"It's a shame the men never gave her a chance. She's not the shrew they make her out to be. Deep down, she's as kind and caring as any woman who ever lived, and I'm honored she took me for her husband."

Suddenly Abe stiffened. "Say, who are they?"

Absorbed in his fretting, Willis hadn't noticed riders to the southeast. He counted eight, in all, white men, not Indians, traveling westward. They were only a half mile away. "They're not any of the outfit?"

"The only one up this way is you," Abe said, and reined toward them. "Let's go see. I don't like trespassers on my range."

One of the riders saw them, stood in his stirrups, and pointed. Soon the whole group was trotting to meet them. A bright flash of light on the vest of the rider in the lead compelled Willis to say, "Why, it's the marshal."

"What on earth is he doing way up here?" Abe wondered.

Before coming to Cottonwood, Marshal Walt Keever had been a deputy in several cowtowns in Kansas. He never shot anyone or had his name written up in the newspapers like shadier lawmen always did. Keever was a rarity. An honest lawdog who applied the law fairly to one and all. When it came to drunks and troublemakers, he usually let his big fists do his talking. He wore a pistol but no one had ever seen him draw it. When firearms were called for, he was partial to a scattergun. As he once mentioned to Willis,

"Buckshot means buryin', and most hot-heads would as soon wrestle a grizzly as go up against a shotgun."

Keever smiled as he approached. With him was his deputy, Ivers. The rest were townsmen. "Abe! Lander! This is a surprise. What are you two up to?"

"I could ask you the same thing," Abe said as he came to a stop, and grinned. "On an early elk hunt?"

"A manhunt is more like it," Marshal Keever said in that great rumbling voice of his. "Care to join the posse? Seein' as how it's your land, you're more than welcome."

"Who are you hunting?" Abe inquired.

"The Flour Sack Kid."

Willis was so jolted that he thought for sure all the blood had drained from his face.

"I heard the Kid was heading this way," Abe mentioned, "but he must have sprouted wings to get here so fast."

"It's that damn Appaloosa of his," Jared Ivers declared. "It can whip any horse in the country."

"It's outrun ours," Marshal Keever said.

Willis had to clear his throat to ask, "What has the Kid done now? Killed someone again?"

"What do you know that I don't? He's never killed a soul, accordin' to the circulars," Marshal Keever said. "No, he went and robbed the general store. Fred Baxter had just opened when the Kid waltzed in with that flour sack over his head and shoved a revolver in Fred's face. Got away with close to fifty dollars." Keever paused. "Strange thing, though. When he walked in, he called Fred by name, as if the Kid knew him."

"How far behind him are you?" Abe Tyler asked.

"About an hour," Marshal Keever said. "Care to tag along?"

"Why not?" Abe said excitedly. Twisting, he gestured at Willis. "What do you say? Up for a manhunt?"

With all eyes on him, Willis could hardly refuse. "Why not?" he echoed, and then did something he had told Abe he rarely ever did. He prayed — prayed with all his might that they would not catch the Flour Sack Kid.

CHAPTER 4

Marshal Keever in the lead, the posse climbed toward a timbered slope. The tracks were plain enough. Abe Tyler rode beside Keever but Willis rode at the rear, lost in his thoughts, worry gnawing at him like termites on wood. He had pulled his hat brim and did not take part in the general gab of the others.

Jared Ivers was saying, "— can't savvy why the Kid came back. He's been gone, what, four years? You would think he'd have learned. He barely got away with his hide last time."

"Who can think like outlaws?" Floyd Treach said. "Hell, if they had brains, they wouldn't be outlaws to begin with."

"It has to be somebody from around these parts," Deputy Ivers said. "But for the life of me, I can't figure out who."

"I don't care one way or the other," remarked Ted Yost, a clerk at the Bank of

Cottonwood. "Just so we catch him and hang him."

Marshal Keever overheard and turned in his saddle. "This isn't a lynch posse. We catch him and we take him back for trial, just as we would do with anyone else."

"I didn't mean we should hang him ourselves," Yost replied. "Everyone knows you're a stickler for the law, Walt."

"It's not so much that," Marshal Keever said, "as doin' what's right." He tapped his badge. "When I pinned this tin star on, I took an oath."

"Who is under that sack, is what I would like to know," Deputy Ivers would not let it go.

"My word!" Abe Tyler suddenly exclaimed, pointing. "Look there!"

A horse and rider were silhouetted against the sky on a sawtooth ridge to the northwest. They were too far off to tell much other than the horse appeared to be an Appaloosa and the rider had something white over his head.

"Son of a bitch!" George Crowder blurted. "It's him!"

"Doesn't he ever take that damn flour sack off?" Floyd Treach asked.

The rider raised an arm and waved.

"Did you see that?" Crowder sputtered.

"Did you see what he did?"

"The gall!" Bill Krebs said. "The unmitigated gall!"

It looked to Willis as if the rider reached into a saddlebag. Something metal glinted in the sun.

"He's fixing to shoot us!" Harvey Stuckman cried. "Find cover boys!" He raised his reins to dash off.

"Calm yourself," Marshal Keever said. "That's not a gun. Unless I miss my guess, it's a spyglass. He's watchin' us through a telescope."

"He is?" Deputy Ivers said, and made a gesture.

Someone laughed. Then young Timmy Easton rose in his stirrups and smiled and waved. The Flour Sack Kid waved back.

"Son of a bitch!" George Crowder said. "Son of a bitch!"

"The gall," Bill Krebs said.

Willis bowed his head and closed his eyes and thought of his mother. He had not thought about her in a long time. He pictured her in the rocking chair by the fire, whistling softly to herself as she knitted.

"Well, he knows we're after him," Marshal Keever said, and sighed. "The circulars never said anything about a spyglass."

"He sure is a crafty devil," Floyd Treach

said. "Robbed my cousin once. I'd sure like to get my hands on him." The town blacksmith, he had more muscles than all of them combined. At the annual Cottonwood Days, he would entertain by bending iron bars with his bare hands.

Deputy Ivers rested a palm on his Smith & Wesson. "I'd like to put a slug into his head."

"That's no way for a lawman to talk, Jared," Marshal Keever scolded. "We're not executioners. We apply the law to him the same as we would to anyone else."

"Sure, sure," Deputy Ivers said. "But he's worse than most. At least his luck can't hold forever. Sooner or later he'll make a mistake. Maybe kill someone and have the bounty doubled." Ivers looked back at Willis. "If he hasn't killed someone already."

"Enough jawin'," Marshal Keever said. "Let's try to catch the coyote while he's bein' so obligin'."

The others started off. Willis raised his head to follow. He saw the Kid, and for a few seconds he had the unmistakable impression the spyglass was fixed on him and solely on him. He froze, and the Kid raised an arm and waved again. Willis was willing to bet that under that flour sack the Kid wore a mocking smile. Damn him, he thought. Damn him to hell.

The posse rode hard but when they reached the ridge the Flour Sack Kid was gone. The Appaloosa's tracks led on into the tall timber.

"We'll never catch him," Harvey Stuckman said.

"You just want to get back to your butcher shop," Deputy Ivers responded.

"Of course I do," Stuckman snapped. "I don't make money traipsing all over creation after a will-o'-the-wisp. The Kid won't ever be caught so long as he has that horse of his."

"I'd like to have me a fine animal like his," Timmy Easton said enviously. "It sure would impress the ladies."

"So does takin' a bath once a week," Harvey Stuckman said, "but as I told my wife, I'll be hanged if I'll risk my health just to wash off a little blood."

The timber closed around them — firs so high, the sunlight could not reach the forest floor, and firs so close together, there was barely space for their horses to thread through. Silence prevailed, an unnatural silence, where there should be birds and squirrels and other wildlife.

"I don't like this," George Crowder said. "He could be anywhere."

Harvey Stuckman was nervously glancing from side to side. "Grizzlies live up here. The last thing I want is to run into a grizzly."

"You worry too much," Deputy Ivers said.

"Hush, all of you!" Marshal Keever commanded. "This is a manhunt, not a church social."

Willis was grateful. Their jabber annoyed him. He had a lot on his mind and he could not work it out with all the distractions. Unlike the rest, he was not worried about the Flour Sack Kid shooting them, especially now that the Kid knew he was along.

The timber went on and on. Most of the others were on edge but not Willis. He was actually beginning to enjoy being on horseback when they came to a clearing and Marshal Keever reined up and declared, "What in the world?"

In the center of the clearing a length of fairly straight tree limb had been stuck into the ground. The top had been split, probably with a knife, and a piece of paper wedged into the split. Arranged around the base of the stick were ten pieces of jerky.

Keever rode over and climbed down. He plucked the paper from the stick, read what had been written, and chuckled. "He has sand. I'll give him that."

"What does it say?" Abe Tyler asked.

"See for yourself."

The paper was passed from man to man. Some laughed. Some swore. Willis was the last to read it.

Figured you boys might be hungry,
                              The Flour Sack Kid

"The gall," Bill Krebs said.

"Too bad he didn't leave us some whiskey to wash it down," Timmy Easton said, helping himself to a piece.

"How do you know it's not poisoned?" Harvey Stuckman asked.

Bill grinned and took a bite. "Harve, you're a caution."

Everyone else dismounted. Abe Tyler picked up two pieces and brought one over to Willis. "Here's yours."

"No," Willis said. "You eat it." He would not touch anything the Kid left for them even if he were starving.

"Are you sure?" Abe asked, and when Willis nodded, he shrugged and stuck one of the pieces in a pocket. "Quite the character, this Flour Sack Kid. Ever wonder why he decided to wear a flour sack instead of a bandanna like most badmen?"

"Maybe his ma did a lot of bakin' and sold

pies and cakes to folks," Willis said. "Maybe she used a lot of flour and made him tote it home when he was little and it got so he hated flour and flour sacks. Maybe he figures it's his notion of a joke." Willis stopped, fearing he had said too much.

"Could be," Abe said slowly, regarding him quizzically. "Takes an imagination to come up with that."

Ted Yost was making for the trees. "Don't leave without me," he said. "I need to answer the call of nature."

As soon as the bank clerk was out of earshot, Harvey Stuckman said, "I'm glad my bladder isn't as weak as his. He can hardly ride five miles without having to moisten the landscape."

"You shouldn't poke fun at a condition a man has no control over," Abe Tyler chided. "That's as bad as poking fun at a cripple."

Willis was aware of the glances he received but he pretended he did not notice and turned away. His bad knee was paining him but he refused to adjust the brace. He would wait until later when he was alone.

"What if we don't catch up to the Kid today?" Floyd Treach asked Keever. "I can't afford to be away from my shop for much longer."

"My wife won't take kindly to me being

gone, either," Harvey Stuckman complained. "She can't handle a cleaver like I can."

"As a posse we'd have made a good sewin' bee," Timmy Easton said.

"What is that supposed to mean?" Stuckman demanded.

"It means some of you gents act like biddy hens," Timmy Easton replied. "When you're not gripin', you fret about takin' a bullet."

Stuckman bristled and shook his fist at the cowboy. "Bite your tongue! You're barely old enough to shave, yet you insult your betters. I have half a mind to pound some respect into you."

Abe Tyler had been talking to Marshal Keever but now he advanced on the butcher. "That's enough of that kind of talk, Harve. Tim rides for me and I won't have him manhandled by you or anyone else."

"Thank you, Mr. Tyler," Timmy said, "but I can fight my own fights." Spurs jangling, he hooked his thumbs in his gun belt and brazenly sauntered past Stuckman and over to Willis. "The nerve of some folks, huh?"

"The nerve," Willis agreed.

"Ain't seen you in ages, Lander," the young cowboy said. "How is it Abe pried you out of your hidey hole?"

"He came up to tell me about the sale."

Willis had only ever talked to the young puncher two or three times. Easton joined the Bar T a year ago after a stint with an outfit in Oklahoma.

"How do you feel about workin' for a female? I can't make up my mind whether I should stick or find me a ranch where a petticoat's not in charge."

"What do the others say?"

Easton nonchalantly pushed his wide-brimmed hat back on his curly mop of hair. "The other night at the bunkhouse we took a vote. Half are for stayin'. Half are for ridin' the grub line and maybe rustlin' up work elsewhere."

Willis thought of something. "You like to spend a lot of time in town, as I recollect. Were you there when the Kid robbed the general store?"

"Sure was. I had some time off, so I went in to bend my elbow and cogitate on the sale. I had more than I should, and somehow or other Mabel ended up invitin' me to her place after she got off."

Willis suppressed a grin. Mabel Kline had been at the Cottonwood Saloon longer than any of the other girls. Sweet and friendly, she had a nice smile and weighed almost as much as his horse.

"I woke up to her snorin' so loud, she

shook the walls," Timmy Easton continued. "I picked up my boots and snuck on out, and wouldn't you know it? I wasn't hardly down the stairs when the marshal corralled me to join his posse. Five minutes more and he'd have missed me and I'd be enjoyin' some coffin varnish along about now."

"Mabel will be mad you left without sayin' goodbye," Willis said. "She likes a little fun in the mornin'."

"How would you know that?" Timmy Easton asked with a smirk.

"So I've heard tell." Willis was going to say more but just then the undergrowth rustled and out stepped Yost, the bank clerk, with his hands in the air and a dumbfounded look on his face. Yost was as pale as the flour sack worn by the man behind him, who held a cocked revolver to Yost's head.

"Howdy, gents," the Flour Sack Kid greeted them, his words muffled by the sack. "Let's not do anythin' hasty, hear, or your friend will have a new ear hole."

Everyone turned to marble. Then Deputy Ivers swore and stabbed for his pistol but Marshal Keever was next to him and gripped his wrist before Ivers could clear leather.

"What in hell do you think you're doin'?

Do you want Yost dead?"

"But it's the Kid!" Ivers protested.

"That's the spirit," the Flour Sack Kid said. He had cut large holes for his eyes, which were as green as the surrounding pines, and holes for his ears, as well, through which tufts of black hair poked. "Now I'd take it kindly if all of you would shed your hardware. Nice and slow, if you don't mind."

"Like hell I will," Deputy Ivers growled.

"Do it," Marshal Keevers said, already unbuckling his gun belt. To the Kid he said, "I've got to hand it to you. The jerky was a nice touch. Made us let down our guard."

"It was supposed to," the Kid said glibly, then wagged his black-handled Colts at Harvey Stuckman and Floyd Treach. "What's the delay? Are you hard of hearin'? Or is it you don't mind if I blow windows in this greenhorn's skull?"

Glares and muttered oaths accompanied the relinquishing of revolvers. Willis was last to unbuckle his belt and lower it to the grass. He could tell the Kid was staring at him and he burned with resentment.

"There? That wasn't so bad, was it?" The Kid moved to the left so he had a clear shot at all of them. "Now I want you gents to turn around and take ten paces and stop with your arms over your heads."

"What the hell for?" Deputy Ivers demanded. "So you can shoot us in the back?"

A chuckle fluttered from the flour sack. "When the Good Lord made peckerwoods, you must have been first in line. If I'd wanted to bed all of you down, I could have bushwhacked you. Picked off a few at a time until none were left."

"I don't trust you," Ivers said.

The eyes in the flour sack shifted to Marshal Keever. "Can't you talk some sense into your pup? I'm tryin' to be reasonable but he's makin' it mighty hard." His left hand dropped to his side and he drew his other black-handled Colt. "Need I add I'm not the most patient cuss alive?"

"Sooner or later you'll be caught or be bucked out in blood," Marshal Keever told him. "You know that, don't you?"

"We all of us die," the Kid said. "Now do as I say, or so help me I'll shoot each of you in the knee and you'll have to limp everywhere like Lander, there."

Willis was in motion before he could stop himself. He limped two steps, then halted when the twin muzzles of the Colts swung toward him. "You had no call to say that."

The shoulders under the flour sack rose and fell. "And you're awful touchy. Comes from bein' too proud, I reckon."

A nigh-overpowering urge came over Willis to wrap his fingers around the Kid's throat and squeeze until the skin under the sack turned purple. "You're a fine one to talk about pride, mister."

"Maybe so," the Kid allowed, "but I'm the one holdin' two pistols and you're unarmed. So I wouldn't prod, were I you."

"Killin' innocents now?" Willis asked.

"I haven't killed anyone since the war, and you —" The Kid caught himself and an amused gleam came into his green eyes. "Nicely done. But I don't have time for your high-and-mighty judgments. Do as I've told you and no one will be hurt."

"Your luck can't hold forever," Willis echoed the sentiments expressed by Deputy Ivers earlier.

"That's where we think different," the Kid said. "The way I see it, a man makes his own luck. If he's careful, he can go as long as he pleases."

"Name me an outlaw yet who hasn't been hung or shot?" Willis countered, the old heat coursing through his veins. "Name me one who stole enough money to live carefree as a bluebird the rest of their days?"

The Kid did no such thing. Instead he thumbed back the hammers to his Colts and announced, "I've got twelve pills in these wheels and there's only ten of you. So what will it be?"

Marshal Keever was the first to turn and raise his arm and take the required ten strides. As he did he said, "You've got the upper hand for now, Kid, but if you hang around long enough, it will be me who gets the drop on you and your robbin' days will be over."

"Just remember," the Kid said, "when you corner a wolf, it fights back."

"A wolf?" Deputy Ivers scoffed. "You're too generous. You're nothin' but a mangy coyote who likes to hear himself flap his gums."

The Flour Sack Kid was still for all of ten seconds. Then he chuckled again, and said with an edge to his tone, "If I was half as vicious as some folks say I am, I'd bed you down where you stand. But you're in luck today. Because I'm goin' to let you live. That is, if you don't insult me again."

Ivers opened his mouth to respond but Marshal Keever was quicker. "Jared isn't goin' to insult anyone, are you, Jared? You're to do exactly as the Kid tells you or I'll have your badge when we get back."

Ivers turned his spite from the Kid to the marshal. "I can't believe you would side with the likes of him against your own deputy."

"There's more to this world than you," Marshal Keever informed him. "If the Kid were to throw lead, it could be Treach or Yost or Abe or Stuckman or somebody else takes a bullet." He placed a hand on Ivers' shoulder. "A good lawman always thinks of others before he thinks of himself."

Since most of the rest had turned and raised their arms, Willis began to do the same and was surprised when the Flour Sack Kid said, "Not you, limpy. Stay right where you are."

Like a line of condemned men walking to the gallows, the other nine posse members took the required ten paces. Several looked over their shoulders but most gazed straight ahead to avoid tempting fate.

The Flour Sack Kid walked up to Willis and said so softly that no one else could possibly overhear, "It's been a while."

"Not long enough."

"Aren't you even a tiny bit happy to see me? I'm happy to see you. Happier than I've been since I took to the owlhoot trail."

"You made the choice," Willis refused to show sympathy.

"You're still upset, by God," the Kid whispered. "But you've always been a marvel at holdin' a grudge. You can never forgive and forget, can you? Between the two of us, when it comes to flaws, you have me beat."

"Leave before they suspect," Willis said, and was spiked by dread when Deputy Ivers called out.

"What in God's name are you two jawin' about? If we didn't know better, we'd think you were in cahoots."

"Thanks," Willis whispered.

The Flour Sack Kid sidled to the right and said to Ivers, "In cahoots with a cripple? I couldn't spend more than five minutes with someone who goes around feelin' sorry for himelf all the time without blowin' his brains out."

Abe Tyler came to Willis' defense. "I'll thank you not to call Mr. Lander a cripple. He's been in my employ for years, and he lost the use of his knee breaking a horse for me. He has my highest respect. I won't see him humbled."

"Well now," the Kid said, "it's nice some- one thinks so highly of him since he doesn't think highly of himself. But you can sheath your horns, mister. I'd as soon stomp a puppy to death as pick on a cripple."

"Quit sayin' that," Willis warned.

But the Kid wasn't listening. He was backing toward their horses. "Any requests, gents? Anythin' besides your canteens I can leave you so the walk back is easier?"

"You are stranding us afoot?" Harvey Stuckman blurted.

"Give me one good reason why I shouldn't and I won't," the Flour Sack Kid said.

"We might die!"

"I said a good reason." The Kid came to their horses and angled to the left so he was behind them. He pointed a Colt at the ground, then seemed to reconsider and went up to Willis' zebra dun and took hold of the reins and brought the zebra dun over to Willis.

"Better hold tight," the Kid said. He returned to where he had been and suddenly let out with a whoop worthy of a Sioux warrior on the war path while simultaneously firing three shots into the dirt. It had the desired effect. Nickering in fright, half the horses bolted and the rest took that as a hint they should do the same. The Kid added two more shots as further incentive.

"No!" Harvey Stuckman wailed, and made as if to run after them but he stopped dead when the Kid fixed the other black-handled Colt on him.

"Back in line. If you've trained your horse right, all you have to do is whistle and it will come back."

"No one trains a horse to do that," Stuckman said.

The Flour Sack Kid tilted his head back and trilled like a meadowlark. The brush crashed and crackled and into the clearing trotted the Appaloosa, truly as fine a specimen of horseflesh as Willis had ever set eyes on. Backing toward it, the Kid hooked a boot in the stirrup without taking his eyes off the posse members and, with a graceful swing of his other leg, forked leather and holstered his left Colt so he could unwind the reins from the saddle horn. "Be seein' you around," he baited them. Then he looked at Willis and one of the green eyes under the flour sack winked. "I left you your horse because I'm feelin' charitable today." He laughed and rode into the trees.

Willis had never hated anyone so much. Except maybe himself.

CHAPTER 5

A strange thing happened when Willis set eyes on the Bar T. It was the first time in months and he expected to feel as he always did. At the sight of the corral, his insides would churn and his blood would boil and he would curse the fate that made him a mockery of a man. That was how he always felt since the day that forever changed his life. But this time was different.

It was late morning when Abe Tyler and Willis came to a broad valley nestled in the heart of the range. The home valley, as the hands called it. Lush with grass, as always, watered by a tributary of the Snake River. Cattle dotted the valley floor. More cattle, Willis knew, grazed in adjoining valleys.

Abe drew rein and smiled. "A beautiful sight, isn't it? To think. Twenty years ago this was nothing but wilderness."

"You've done yourself proud," Willis said. He could not resist adding, "Yet you're

83

sellin' it off."

"Don't start. We've been all through that. Yes, I'm selling the Bar T, and yes, I'll have regrets, and yes, I'll miss it. I'll miss it terribly."

"I don't see how you can," Willis said.

"Some of the boys blame Elfie," Abe said, and held up a hand when Willis went to speak. "I know they do and I don't resent it. But the truth is, Will, I'm not getting any younger. I have more gray hairs every year. It's harder to do some of the things I used to take for granted. Fetching you, for instance. I'm so sore, I won't be able to sit down for a week."

"You've still got plenty of years left."

"Maybe I do," Abe said. "If so, I'd like to spend them enjoying more of life than I get to enjoy working twelve hours a day every single day of the year. I'd like to sit back and relax and not have to worry about the thousand and one things a rancher has to worry about."

"I hope Saint Louis turns out to be all you want."

"Thank you. Coming from you, that means a lot." Abe clucked to his mount. "Some of the others aren't as forgiving. Gus told me that he thought I was a traitor for turning my back on him and the others."

Willis was amazed. Gus, the cook, had been with Abe almost as long as he had. "That old goat said that? He called you a traitor?"

"His exact word," Abe confirmed. "It stung. It really did. I tried to reason with him but he said if I cared about the Bar T, I wouldn't sell it for all the gold in the Rockies."

"I'll talk to him."

"You're welcome to try. But Gus has announced he's packing up and leaving as soon as the sale is final. I understand five or six others have said they intend to do the same, and more might join them." Abe paused. "What will you do?"

"I haven't made up my mind yet."

"That's honest, at least." Abe looked at him. "All I ask is that you give Laurella Hendershot a chance. Who knows? You might even like her. It's not as if she's an amateur. She knows ranching and she knows cattle and she'll run the Bar T as it should be run."

"She's a woman."

"So? Don't tell me you're one of those who thinks females are born inferior? You do recall, don't you, that Wyoming Territory was the first to give women the right to vote and run for political office if they want?"

"I recollect it just fine," Willis said. It had been a contentious issue. He had voted on the side of the women, mainly because he remembered how sad his mother was that she could not cast votes in elections. "All I'm sayin' is that I never heard tell of a woman rancher before."

"Women can do practically anything men can do," Abe declared, then laughed lightly. "I would have loved to see the faces of all those snobby Easterners who look down their noses at cowboys and cows when we gave women the same rights as men. We're supposed to be so ignorant, so backward. Yet it was cowboys who did what all those snobby Easterners couldn't or wouldn't."

Willis wondered how much of that was Abe and how much of that was Elfie but he did not say anything.

By then they were near enough to see the ranch buildings: the two-story house with a wide front porch; the long, low bunkhouse; the cook shack, where Gus ruled the roost; the sheds and other outbuildings; the stable and the corral.

It was the corral that always made Willis' gut churn. But not this time. All he felt was a peculiar emptiness, as if he were a water-skin that had been drained dry. Images flashed through his mind: of the stallion caught in the north valley; no one knew where it came from or how it got there but it had run wild and free for so long that it fought the ropes every foot of the way, and when it was placed in the corral, it tried again and again to break out. Another image: of Joe Sennet, his helper, going into the corral to snub the stallion to the post, a task Joe had performed countless times, and performed well. But the stallion reared and Joe tried to turn, and slipped. A flailing hoof caught him on the crown of his head and crushed it.

Man killers were routinely put down. Once a horse killed, it was liable to do so again. But something about the black stallion, about the way it stood straight and defiant and proud, stirred Willis deep down, and he had gone to Abe and asked that the stallion be given another chance.

Abe was against it. He pointed out the risk. He offered to shoot the stallion himself. But Willis said that it would be a waste of a good animal, that just because man killers were usually killed didn't mean they always had to be killed. Abe, reluctantly, gave in.

Looking back, Willis often wondered what in hell he had been thinking. The next day he had taken his rope and gone into the corral, speaking softly and soothingly to show the stallion he meant it no harm. He wasn't one of those punchers who believed in breaking a bronco by brute force. Gentle but firm was how he tamed a horse.

A lot of the other punchers were on hand to watch. Some shouted encouragement. Charlie Weaver hollered for him to watch himself.

Willis had glanced at Charlie and smiled. He heard the thud of hooves and whirled. The stallion was almost on top of him. He swung his rope to shoo it off and the stallion turned aside. Quick as a darting snake, Willis had flicked his wrist and the loop sailed out and over the stallion's head and settled around its neck. He dug in his bootheels as the stallion reared and strained.

The next step was for him to snub the stallion to the post and hobble it. Willis had started to take up slack as he maneuvered the stallion to the post. All had gone well and Willis had the stallion where he wanted it when the stallion snorted and plunged. He sidestepped but the stallion's shoulder caught him and he was spun like a top and lost his hold.

Charlie and some of the others had yelled a warning. Willis looked up, and there was the stallion, rearing over him, a mountain of muscle and fury determined to do to him as it had done to poor Joe Sennet. He had thrown himself to the right as the heavy hooves crashed down. Somehow his legs became entangled in the rope, and he sprawled on his stomach.

Punchers sprang to help but they could not get close. Willis had rolled to escape the flailing hooves as they thudded down again and again. Then he rose to dart behind the post. Only he never made it. A blow to his left leg crumpled him. Pain exploded like a keg of powder, and there were other blows — terrible, brutal blows — and the next he knew, it was a week later and he was in his bunk, bandaged from head to ankle, and Abe and the doctor were next to the bunk and he heard the words that seared into his being like a red-hot branding iron.

"I'm sorry, Abe, but he'll never be able to walk again. Oh, he can get around, but he'll never have full use of his left leg."

"Dear God," Abe had said. "How about riding?"

"I'd have to say his days of living in the saddle are over."

Now, staring at the corral where his life had been destroyed, Willis swallowed and blinked and wished, for the umpteenth time, that the stallion had killed him. He became aware Abe was talking to him.

"— up to the house and have supper with Elfie and me? She would be delighted to have you."

Willis wasn't sure his ears were working. Sure, he had worked for Abe for decades and they were friends, but he had not been invited to the main house since Abe married. "Today?"

"No, you infant, next year." Abe chortled. "Of course today. This evening. Say, about six."

"All right," Willis said, but he was anything but sure about why the invite had been extended. Elfie had never been all that fond of the cowhands. It showed in how she looked at them and how she talked down to them. "But I can't make it into town and back in time."

"What do you need in town?"

"New clothes. I've worn these so long they're a mite ragged," Willis said. "And I can do with a haircut and a bath."

"Your clothes are fine as they are," Abe assured him. "As for the haircut, have Charlie clip it if you feel you need to. And the tub is right where it's always been. Not that many of you use it all that much except Timmy Easton and he only uses it because he's so young and so fond of petticoats."

They were almost to the stable when who

should come strolling out but Elfie, herself. She had on a pretty blue dress and a pretty blue bonnet. She had nice sandy hair and a nice smile but the smile seldom touched her brown eyes. "Abe! You're back!" She came to meet him and they embraced. "I was expecting you back yesterday morning."

"The Flour Sack Kid ran off our horses and Will had to round them up," Abe explained. "They were scattered to hell and back."

"The Flour Sack Kid?" Elfie said in concern. "Please refrain from using that kind of language. Remember, you're married to a lady."

"Sorry," Abe apologized, chastised. "I'm tired and hungry and not myself."

Elfie bestowed her cold smile on Willis. "And how are you, Mr. Lander? Has my husband invited you to supper tonight?"

"Yes, ma'am," Willis said, his puzzlement growing.

"Good. Very good," Elfie said, linking her arm in Abe's. "We have something very important to discuss with you."

"You do?"

"Now, now," Abe said. "The proper time and place is this evening. Remember, promptly at six. My wife is cooking the meal herself and she doesn't like it when her soup grows cold."

"I'll be there on time," Willis promised. As Elfie and Abe walked happily off toward the ranch house, he stiffly dismounted, and stretched. His left leg was paining him but what else was new? He led the zebra dun into the stable. Familiar smells rekindled more memories: the odor of the hay, of the horses, of droppings and urine. He breathed deep as he brought the zebra dun to a vacant stall.

"My eyes must be playin' tricks on me! It can't be I'm booze blind because I haven't had a drink since last Saturday."

Willis smiled and turned. "Reub, you son of a bitch, how the hell are you?"

Reuben Marsh was the ranch foreman. He was tall and rugged and no one in Wyoming Territory was better with cows or could run a ranch more smoothly. He had the respect of every hand on the Bar T, and he had it because he had earned it a thousand times over. Thrusting out a callused hand, his spurs jangling, he advanced down the straw-strewn aisle. "I wasn't sure Abe could talk you into comin' down from your roost."

"He didn't leave me much choice." Willis shook warmly, and Reuben clapped him on the arm.

"Damn, it's good to see you. We had us some great times in the old days, didn't we? You and Charlie and Hank and me."

"That we did," Willis agreed. "Where are they, anyhow?"

"Hank is due back from ridin' line sometime tomorrow or the next day, and Charlie is down in the south valley countin' head but should be back anytime now." Reuben paused. "I reckon you've heard about the new owner?"

"Have you met her?"

Reuben nodded. "I talked to her for about ten minutes. She wanted to know all there was to know about the Bar T, and let me tell you, that gal knew which questions to ask. She didn't miss a thing."

Willis began removing his saddlebags and bedroll. "Have you decided whether you'll stay?"

"I'm leanin' toward stayin' if she'll have me," Reuben said. "The thing is, she's a bit hard to get along with."

"How so, exactly?"

"Crusty, you might say," Reuben said. "I'd better let Abe and Elfie explain. They know what's best."

Now Willis was certain the Tylers were up to something and it involved him. "It's not like you to keep secrets."

"Nice try." Reuben folded his long arms and leaned against the stall. "Mind if I ask you a question?"

"Is it personal?"

"It's personal."

"Then no."

"What do you plan to do with your life?"

Willis looked at him. "Whatever happened to manners? First Abe, now you. Abe I can savvy because he's always been a nosy cuss but you've always had the sense not to pry where you shouldn't."

"It's our future at stake," Reuben said.

"And my future is my own, thank you very much," Willis testily remarked. "I'd as soon everyone would stop bringin' it up."

"You are havin' supper with Abe and his wife tonight, aren't you?" Reuben asked.

"What does that . . . ?" Willis began, and frowned. "Hell in a basket. What in blazes is that woman up to now?"

"I have work to do," Reuben declared, and made for the open double doors. "We'll jaw some tomorrow, after."

"After what?" Willis called out but the foreman merely waved and left the stable as if his britches were aflame. "Damn." He reached down to undo the cinch. "If I had any sense, I'd run."

Shortly, with his saddlebags over his right

shoulder and his rifle in his left hand, Willis limped toward the bunkhouse. He avoided gazing at the corral. More familiar odors, and a familiar sight, greeted him when he pushed open the bunkhouse door. The hands were off working. All the bunks were neatly made, and the floor had been swept clean. Some outfits had bunkhouses that looked as if a tornado had ripped through them but not the Bar T. Abe was a stickler for tidiness, and Reuben saw to it that whatever Abe wanted done *was* done.

Since he had been staying at the line shack, Willis no longer had a bunk of his own but several spares were always available toward the back for grub-line riders and the like, and he chose one at random.

The washbasin was out back. Willis examined his reflection in the mirror and was shocked at how drawn and haggard he appeared. "I'd give that Texas gal nightmares," he told the mirror.

A bucket of water was always kept handy, and soon Willis had shaved and snipped the hair around his ears. He considered filling the metal tub and taking a long overdue bath but after sniffing under his arms decided he did not really need one. He did spruce himself up, though, even going so far as to slick his cowlick down so when he took off his hat later it would not stick straight up like it usually did.

"That should do it," Willis said, and vowed then and there to stop talking to himself. It was all right to do up at the line shack, where he only had himself for company, but if he continued to talk to himself at the ranch, the other punchers would brand him as peculiar.

Willis donned his hat and went back into the bunkhouse. He was pleasantly surprised to find two hands had shown up while he was out back. "Well, look at this!" he declared. "They'll let anyone cowboy at this outfit, I reckon."

Charlie Weaver and Sam Tinsdale greeted him as if he were long-lost kin.

"You ornery varmint!" Charlie happily exclaimed. "When did you get in? I'd heard the boss went to fetch you and figured you would hide in the woods until he tired of waitin' and came back down."

"Now why didn't I think of that?" Willis grinned.

Sam Tinsdale was another of the older hands who had been with the Bar T almost from the start. "You're a sight for sore eyes, hoss. You've been gone too damn long, and that's a fact."

More memories flooded through Willis: of

days spent tending cattle when there were no horses to break; of nights spent in Cottonwood drinking and playing cards; of living instead of dying; of being a man instead of half a man. "So you missed me, did you?"

"Why wouldn't we?" Sam rejoined. "You were a great friend until you took to feelin' sorry for yourself."

Willis' memories dissolved in a burst of anger. "There's a little more to it than that, don't you think?"

"It's not my place to pass judgment," Sam said, "but you've been up in the mountains too long. You're overdue to socialize."

Charlie glanced from one to the other, and laughed. "Listen to him, will you? Sam's on the mossy side of thirty and he's never been hitched, yet he talks like he's an authority on socializain'."

"Go wrestle a grizzly."

"Now, now. Let's be nice," Charlie said. "We should be celebratin', not squabblin'. If it wasn't so early, I'd break out my flask."

"Early, hell." Sam smacked his lips. "Abe is up to the house and we passed Reuben on the way in, ridin' west. A few sips won't get us in much trouble."

"Not so long as we're not caught," Charlie agreed.

"The sips can wait," Willis said. Alcohol

was another thing Abe was a stickler about. No drinking was allowed in the bunkhouse, ever. Anyone who broke the rule was fired so fast, they were dizzy.

"Shucks," Sam said. "When you were younger, you took more chances."

Willis stared at his left knee. "I know."

Charlie went to his bunk and pulled a deck of cards from under his pillow. "How about a few hands, then? So long as we play for toothpicks, Abe doesn't mind."

Barely had the cards been dealt than more punchers showed up and Willis had to again go through the ritual of being greeted and teased about his long stay up in the mountains. He didn't mind, though. He was genuinely glad to be among his own kind again, to be with friends and acquaintances who did not judge his worth by whether or not one of his legs worked.

Willis was having such a good time, it stunned him when Charlie Weaver commented, "Didn't you say you have to be at the Big Augur's by six? It's a quarter till now."

Willis had never been much of a clock watcher. He yielded his chair to another cowhand and limped out back to redo his hair and recheck his shirt and pants. He was as ready as he was going to be.

His mouth went dry as he climbed the knoll to the house. Abe Tyler opened the door at his second knock. Elfie relieved him of his hat and hung it on a hat tree. As they ushered him to the dining room, Willis passed a full-length mirror and checked that his cowlick was behaving.

"I do so hope you are hungry, Mr. Lander," Elfie was saying. She never called the hands by their first names. "We're having chicken with all the trimmings, and for dessert apple pie fresh out of the oven."

Willis' stomach chose that moment to rumble. He had not realized how hungry he was.

"You're in for a treat," Abe said, rubbing his hands together. "My wife is about the best cook west of the Mississippi."

That was not how Willis heard it. Elfie was passable in the kitchen, if by passable it was understood she cooked chicken for every special occasion.

"Oh, Abe, please," their modest hostess gushed, "don't be flattering me or Mr. Lander is bound to be disappointed."

Willis was about to sit at the big oak table when he saw she was waiting for Abe to seat her, so he politely waited, giving thanks to his ma for her insistence on learning proper manners. He wondered who was going to wait on them if she wasn't, and soon found out. The Shoshone girl Abe had hired to clean the house five days a week did the honors. Little Sparrow, Willis believed her name to be.

Whoever taught her had done the job well. Wearing what Willis took to be a uniform of some sort, with her hair done up white-woman style, Little Sparrow was a whirl-wind of efficiency. She brought dish after dish from the kitchen, and between trips hovered at Elfie's elbow.

The soup was occasion for Elfie to say how happy she was that Willis accepted their invitation, and how glad she was he had come down from the line shack, where he never should have gone in the first place.

The main course was occasion for Elfie to extol the many and sundry virtues of Saint Louis, and how much she looked forward to moving back and enjoying the delights of "polite society," as she phrased it.

During dessert she did not say much. She was too fond of the apple pie.

Then they were done, and Little Sparrow was filling their coffee cups, and Abe cleared his throat and finally got down to business.

"You must be curious about why we invited you tonight."

"To put it mildly." Willis was drowsy from

all the fine food and had to struggle to concentrate.

"It has to do with Laurella Hendershot," Abe said.

For the life of him, Willis could not think of how, and commented as much.

Abe and Elfie swapped adoring glances, and Elfie grinned and said, "It's simple, Mr. Lander. We would like for you to be her escort."

CHAPTER 6

Willis was always annoyed with himself when his brain did not work as he wanted. He was not the fastest of thinkers, and when he had too much to drink or eat, he was slower yet. So much so, his thoughts tended to plod along like turtles. "Escort?" he repeated uncertainly. "You want me to fetch her here from Texas?"

Elfie squealed in mirth. "No, goodness, nothing like that. When I say escort, I'm thinking of someone who escorts a woman to a cotillion or a quadrille."

"You want me to dance with her?" Willis was even more confused.

Elfie laughed again.

Abe leaned forward on his elbows and said, "Permit me to explain to him, my dear. You see, Will, before the papers are signed and the sale is finalized, Miss Hendershot wants to spend four or five days looking over the Bar T. She'll need someone to show her around. We would like for it to be you."

Astonishment replaced Willis' confusion. "But that's rightly Reuben's job," he objected.

"Mr. Marsh is a top-notch foreman," Elfie said, "but a special touch is called for, and I happen to think you can provide that special touch."

"Ma'am?"

"My wife believes you can do a better job than Reuben," Abe elaborated. "I've already talked it over with him and he agrees."

"You have?" Willis was desperately trying to make sense of this startling development but it was beyond him.

Elfie folded her hands and smiled benignly. "Miss Hendershot and you have a lot in common, Mr. Lander. The two of you will hit it off quite well, I should imagine. Trust me. I'm a woman and I know about these things."

Willis was at a loss. "I don't see how that's possible, ma'am." He looked at Abe. "Not to show any disrespect, but can't you get somebody else? Charlie Weaver is a friendly cuss. And Hank is as polite as can be."

"I'd rather it was you," Abe insisted.

To cover his bewilderment, Willis swallowed some coffee and aligned his cup on the saucer, then said, since he saw no way out of the predicament short of quitting, "All right, I'll do it."

Elfie beamed. "Marvelous."

"But I want one thing understood," Willis said. "Don't blame me if it doesn't work out. I don't have much experience with females. I'd as soon be in the company of a rabid wolf as most women I've met."

Elfie's smile faded. "That's hardly flattering, Mr. Lander."

"It's not got anything to do with you personally, ma'am," Willis assured her. "It's just that females scare me."

"Scare you?" Elfie was amused, and winked at Abe.

"Yes, ma'am. Females are peculiar, if you don't mind my sayin' so. The only one I ever halfway understood was my ma, and then only because she wasn't out to throw a loop over me."

"Is that your opinion of womanhood?" Elfie asked, taking the subject more seriously. "That all we care about is marriage?"

"No, ma'am. There's been a few doves I've met who were more partial to havin' fun than they were to cookin' or mendin' or raisin' sprouts. Although the older they get, I've noticed the proposition has more appeal."

"Why, Mr. Lander, I had no idea you were

such the philosopher," Elfie said gaily.

"I only know what I've seen, ma'am," Willis said.

"Well, rest assured Laurella Hendershot is not out to throw a loop over you, as you cowboys so quaintly describe wedlock," Elfie said. "She's never been married, and from the few comments she's dropped, I would say she evidently never wants to be."

"She's a man hater?" The last one of those Willis ran into was in Laramie. He'd been drunk and taken a shine to a mousey dove named Marabelle but the dove's friend, a woman twice his size had come over and pushed and poked him, saying as how she would be damned if she would let him take liberties with *her* Marabelle, and the next thing, she had pushed him so hard he nearly fell over a chair. That got him so mad, he broke a whiskey bottle over her head. Then he and Charlie and Hank hightailed it out of there before the law showed up.

Elfie was speaking. "Not at all. She just has no interest that I could see."

"Yet you want me, a man, to be her escort?" Willis said. "Wouldn't it be better if maybe you did the honors?"

"We have already decided you should do it," Elfie responded a trifle stiffly. "And it *is* an honor, I hope you realize. My husband is taking an awful chance. Miss Hendershot was here once and liked what she saw, but she wants to go over the entire ranch from end to end before committing herself. If anything goes wrong, anything at all, it could jeopardize the sale."

"I wouldn't want to spoil it for you," Willis said. The extra weight did not sit well on his shoulders.

"We're counting on you, Mr. Lander," Elfie said earnestly. "Our future is in your hands."

"He'll do fine," Abe said.

"I can't stress enough how important this is to me," Elfie said. "I miss Saint Louis. I miss it more than I have ever missed anything in my whole life, Mr. Lander. Does that give you some idea?"

"Yes, ma'am," Willis said, recalling Charlie's comment that it was a mistake for Abe to marry a city girl because you could take the girl out of the city but never take the city out of the girl. Sometimes Charlie was downright smart.

"If something should go wrong, no matter how small a trifle, I will be most displeased."

"Yes, ma'am."

Elfie rose and placed her napkin on the table. "Stress the importance to him, Abe. I'll be back in a few minutes." She went down the hall with Little Sparrow trailing in her wake.

"I apologize for my wife," Abe said. "I'm sure I don't need to stress anything."

Willis wanted to say that Abe had changed. The old Abe would never have dragged him down from the line shack so his wife could ramrod him. Instead, Willis said, "If I had my druthers, I'd rather not do it."

"I'm sorry. You'll understand, I hope, in time." Abe paused. "Let's talk about something else." He glanced down the hall. "Reuben tells me the tally from the south valley came in six head short."

"Maybe the cows strayed into the high timber," Willis said.

"Maybe. But two weeks ago I had a tally of the north valley cattle taken so I would have an accurate count for Miss Hendershot. It came in a dozen cattle short."

"A whole dozen?" The implication hit Willis like a physical blow. "Has there been any talk of brand artists hereabouts?"

"None that I'm aware of," Abe said, "but eighteen cows in a month is a lot of cows to go missing."

"Hell in a basket. What are you fixin' to do about it?"

"I told Reuben to add extra men to the

herds and to have them be on the alert for sign. But these things take a while to work themselves out, and Miss Hendershot will be here in a few days." Abe stopped and stared hard at Willis, then said, "She'll want you to show her the whole ranch."

Willis was not quite sure what his boss was getting at. "I said I'd do it and I will."

"The thing is," Abe said, and abruptly averted his gaze, "do we tell her about the missing cows or do we keep quiet?"

Like the sun rising to light the new day, comprehension lit Willis. "You're afraid if she finds out the Bar T is havin' rustler problems she might not go through with the sale?"

"There is that possibility," Abe conceded.

Willis felt a funk coming on. It was bad enough he had been forced to serve as an escort, now Abe wanted him, in effect, to deceive the woman. Abe wasn't asking him to lie — probably because Abe knew lying went against his grain. "Spell it out for me."

"I would take it as a personal favor if you would not tell her about the rustling. Unless, of course, the subject comes up."

"Of course."

"It could be nothing. Like you said, maybe the cattle drifted into the high timber. It happens."

"Sure it does," Willis said.

"For what it is worth, I dislike imposing on you. If it were up to me, I would show Hendershot around myself."

"We go back a long ways," Willis said, letting Abe know that was the only reason he was going along with the proposition. "I owe you for keepin' me on when I became useless."

"Will you stop that?" Abe asked with a touch of exasperation. "You are as good a hand as any on the spread."

Willis refused to ignite another argument. "It will be, what, three or four days before the Hendershot woman gets here? What do you want me to do in the meantime?"

"Elfie has a lot to do to get ready. She'll need to make several trips into town, and I have too much to do around here to go along. I was hoping you would drive the buckboard."

So it's come to this, Willis thought. "That's one thing I can still do, I reckon." But his bitterness deepened. He had been able to hold it at bay at the line shack. Up there, he could convince himself he was doing something worthwhile. He could pretend he was still a valued hand. But down here all he was good for was minding a buckboard.

Later, after Willis had thanked the Tylers

and gone to the bunkhouse, he lay staring morosely at the ceiling, oblivious to the snores that threatened to shake the rafters, and pondered his lot in life.

In his estimation he had fallen as low as he could fall short of moving to town and spending his days with his mouth glued to a bottle. It was an insult to a top hand to be asked to watch after womenfolk, but then, he wasn't a top hand anymore, was he?

Reaching down, Willis touched the brace. At moments like this, he wanted to take a hammer and beat his leg to a mashed wreck. Why not, when it was already next to worthless?

Sometimes Willis thought about ending it, about taking his pistol and putting the end of the barrel to his head and leaving the world to those who could enjoy it. He sure couldn't. Any zest for life he had once had was long since dried up.

Willis slid his right arm off the bunk to the pile of his clothes beside it, and the holster lying on top of the pile. He slipped his Colt free and held it close to his face so he could see it clearly. All he had to do was cock the hammer and squeeze the trigger. Cock and squeeze, and the shame would end. He put the muzzle to his temple.

The metal was cool against his skin. Willis

curled his thumb around the hammer and took a deep breath. The seconds became a minute and the minute became two minutes, and he replaced the Colt and said in a whisper, "I'm worse than useless. I'm a coward to boot."

Cottonwood had not changed much since Willis was there last. There was the same lone dusty street flanked by buildings that looked fit to blow away with the next chinook, some with false fronts and some with boardwalks. But mostly Cottonwood had the air of a tired old woman who had been out in the elements too long.

The Bank of Cottonwood was an exception. Built from mortar and stone brought from the Tetons, it could withstand any tempest. Directly across from it was the Lucky Dollar, the most popular establishment in town. To the east of the saloon was the Cottonwood General Store, recently made the talk of the territory thanks to the Flour Sack Kid. Further east, at the end of the street, stood the church, painted as white as snow, with a belfry and a bell that could be heard for miles when the parson rang the call to services.

Willis brought the buckboard to a stop near the general store. His backside was ferociously sore from the trip, so sore he could barely stand to sit. He was scanning the street to see if there were any faces he recognized when there was a low cough besides him.

"You *are* a gentleman, I trust?" Elfie Tyler asked.

Willis flushed red. "My apologies, ma'am." He shifted in the seat and lowered his right leg to the ground, then carefully slid his left leg down. He held on to the side while he made sure the left leg would bear his weight; then, as quickly as he could, he limped around to the other side and held out an arm. "Here you go."

Elfie daintily draped a hand on his wrist and swung down. "Thank you. I'll be a couple of hours, so feel free to indulge yourself as you desire. Only no whiskey, you hear? I need you sober for the ride back."

"Sober it will be, ma'am," Willis said, thinking thoughts that would make her madder than a wet hen were she to read his mind.

With a sweep of her dress, Elfie whisked into the general store.

"Consarn it!" Willis muttered, and limped across the street to the Lucky Dollar. Pushing through the batwing doors, he limped to the bar, where Slim was rolling dice with a man Willis had never seen before. At a table along the south wall Timmy Easton and Jim Palmer were sharing a bottle. At a corner table, playing solitaire, was Johnny Vance, the gambler. The doves were not in evidence but it was much too early for them yet.

Slim's lower jaw dropped. "As I live and breathe! Is it a ghost or have my eyes stopped working?" He pumped Willis' hand. "It's great to see you again, you ornery cow nurse."

"Howdy, Slim," Willis said, pleased by the reception. "I didn't think anyone would miss me."

"Not miss one of my best customers? Are you loco?" Slim gestured. "What will it be, a brandy sour or a bimbo? You never could make up your mind which one you liked more?"

Willis' mouth watered. He was enormously fond of brandy sours, which consisted of brandy mixed with lemon or lime juice, but he would love to have a bimbo just then, which was brandy mixed with sugar and a dash of lemon. He could down five or six without them having an effect. But he had to settle for saying, "A beer will do."

"That's all? Are you feeling all right?" Slim

teased. He was a human bean pole with a rare trait for a saloon owner — he never indulged in the liquor he sold.

"I'm nursin' Abe's wife today, not cows," Willis explained, "and she thinks poorly of buckboard drivers who reek of hard spirits."

"Beer it is, then."

It had been so long, Willis' mouth puckered at the first sip. Swishing the beer in his mouth, he savored the taste, then plunked down a coin and limped over to his fellow Bar T punchers. "It must be nice to be takin' the year off."

Timmy Easton, who found more excuses to spend time in town than anyone at the ranch, chuckled. "Believe it or not, we're workin'."

"I don't believe it," Willis said.

Jim Palmer's handsome features creased in a grin. "He's right. Reuben sent us in to keep an eye out for strangers."

"Strangers?" Willis said, and remembered the tallies. "Oh. Did he twist your arms or were you saddled up before he asked?"

"That's a good one," Jim Palmer said, and pushed an empty chair out from the table with his boot. "Join us, why don't you? We'll tell you about the new girls Slim has workin' here, and you can tell us all about the pretty does and owls you saw up in the high country."

At that, Timmy Easton roared. "Pretty does and owls! Jim, you're a hoot."

"The ladies think so." Palmer wasn't bragging. He was stating fact. Females flocked to him like she bears to honey. "Have a seat, Will."

"In a minute."

Johnny Vance did not look up from the cards when Willis sank into a chair opposite him. "I heard yuh were minglin' with people again," he said in his thick Southern drawl.

"I heard you were involved in a corpse-and-cartridge occasion," Willis mentioned.

About to place a black nine on a red ten, Vance swore. "Some longhairs just don't know when to sheathe their horns."

"I'm surprised you came back to Cottonwood," Willis said. "There can't be much for you to win except when the Bar T boys blow in. How do you stand the peace and quiet?"

"There's a lot to be said for tranquillity," the gambler remarked, "for not havin' to worry that the next gent who ambles through the door isn't out to shoot you in the back."

There was a rumor — Willis tended to believe it — that Johnny Vance came to Cottonwood so often because it was the one place Vance felt safe. Apparently the Reb had made a few enemies in his travels, both poor losers and Yankees who resented any hint of Southern pride. "How long are you here for this time?"

Johnny Vance shrugged. "Another week or two at the most. I've had a hankerin' for Creole food, so I might pay New Orleans a visit."

"I envy you," Willis said.

"That's fittin' since I envy you."

"Did a bullet crease your noggin? What is there about to envy me, a crippled, used-up buster?"

"A man envies what he doesn't have," Johnny Vance said. "You spend almost all your time up in the mountains without a care in the world."

"There's no shortage of cares. Believe me." Willis was thinking of the mountain lion and the two dead horses.

Just then hooves drummed out in the street. Riders came to a stop at the hitch rail. Saddles creaked and spurs jangled. The batwing doors were thrust wide and into the Lucky Dollar strode four dusty men in wide-brimmed hats and slickers. Two were burly and middle-aged and looked enough alike to be brothers. The third had wispy corn silk hair and a wispy mustache and was dressed all in gray. The last was the runt of the bunch. Scrawny and bucktoothed, he glared at everyone and everything as if daring the world to make fun of his size.

All four, Willis observed, wore revolvers. Nothing unusual in that. But the way their hands hovered near their hardware was not ordinary, as was the constant darting of their eyes to the right and the left.

Jim Palmer and Timmy Easton had sat up and were scrutinizing the newcomers with keen interest.

"What will it be, fellas?" Slim asked.

"Monongahela," the runt said, thumping the bar, "and don't water it down or there will be hell to pay."

"I never water my drinks," Slim said, insulted. "Ask anyone."

The man in gray turned so he faced the door and rested his elbows on the edge of the counter. "Any chance of gettin' a mint julep, suh?"

Johnny Vance turned his chair half around. The scrape drew the attention of the man in gray, and they locked eyes. "Perhaps you will indulge me in a card game later, suh."

"Well, I'll be," the man in gray said. "Whereabouts did you get that accent? Macon, Georgia, for me."

"Atlanta," Johnny Vance said.

The runt with the buck teeth grunted and smacked the man in gray on the arm. "Share your whole life, why don't you, Mason?"

"Don't touch me, Varner."

"Or what?" Varner demanded. "Me and my cousins are gettin' mighty tired of your airs. You ain't no better than we are. It's time someone knocked you off your high horse."

The man called Mason stepped away from the bar and swept back his gray slicker, revealing a matched pair of Griswald and Gurnison revolvers with ivory grips, worn with the grips forward. "Start knockin'."

Varner glanced at the burly twosome for support but his cousins were not interested. "Let's not make a spectacle of ourselves."

"You started it," Mason said. "Always on the prod. Always lookin' for trouble. One of these days you'll get more than you bargained for." He moved to the bar and stood facing his companions. "Let's get our drinks and get back to work."

Jim Palmer called across the intervening space, "Just what is it you boys do for a livin'?"

Varner glared suspiciously at the Bar T's handsomest cowpoke. "Who wants to know

— and why?"

"The outfit I ride for, the Bar T, is lookin' for new hands," Palmer answered, which was a bald-faced untruth. "If you gents are any kind of cowhands, you could hire on."

"I've worked cows," Varner said, "but it'll be a long day in January before I do it again."

"Somethin' wrong with bein' a puncher?" Timmy Easton threw in.

"Nothin' that a konk on the head won't cure," Varner responded. "It's damn hard work. In the saddle from sunup to sunset. Havin' to put up with dust and flies and critters that try to run off. No, thanks."

"So what do you do for a livin'?" Jim Palmer inquired as politely as could be.

"Right now we're between jobs," Varner said, which was no real answer, "on our way to Utah."

"You're Mormons?" Timmy Easton blurted.

"Hell, do you see eight wives waitin' on me hand and foot?" was Varner's reply. "We just heard there's work there, is all." He turned to the bar, signifying their exchange was over.

Johnny Vance was playing solitaire again. Speaking so softly Willis barely heard, he said, "Palmer told me about the missin' cattle. I'd say those four are prime candidates."

"Could be," Willis said, "but there's nothin' we can do unless we catch them in the act."

"Go heeled," the gambler said. "They're a gun outfit, as sure as shootin'. And the cure for that isn't a konk on the head. It's a necktie social."

"Whoever it is will be hung, for sure," Willis said. Wyoming ranchers as a rule did not bother lawmen and judges with minor nuisances like rustlers.

"Yes, suh," Johnny Vance said, and he was grinning, "rustlin' is as low as a man can go. The only thing lower is a Yankee rustler." He glanced pointedly at Varner.

CHAPTER 7

Willis had been raised to treat women with respect. Most of the time, he did. The incident with Marabelle and the whiskey bottle had been when he was a lot younger, and booze blind; it was the only stain on his record with regard to females. So he was as surprised as anyone when he looked Elfie Tyler in the eye and bluntly said, "It's a bad idea, ma'am. I'm against it."

Elfie was out front of the general store. She had made more than a dozen purchases and Willis had dutifully deposited them in the bed of the buckboard and tied them down. While doing so, he made the mistake of mentioning the four men at the Lucky Dollar.

Now, her eyebrows arched in indignation, Elfie said, "*You're* against it, Mr. Lander? And since when do *you* make decisions about the Bar T?"

"It's not my place, true," Willis sheepishly

admitted, "but we should check with Abe first."

"I'm positive he would say the exact same thing." Elfie stared across the street at the Lucky Dollar. "Go bring them right this instant."

"Yes, ma'am," Willis said, blaming himself and his big mouth. He limped back over. Varner and his two burly cousins were still at the bar. They hardly gave him a glance as he hobbled past and over to the table where Jim Palmer and Timmy Easton were working on their bottle.

"Back so soon?" Jim Palmer said. "I'll pour you a tall one."

"Can't," Willis said. "I'm on official business. Abe's cow bunny wants to see you, and I'm sorry as hell, boys."

"Mrs. Tyler wants to see us?" Timmy Easton repeated, brightening and adjusting his bandanna.

"Kids," Willis said.

Elfie was waiting by the buckboard, impatiently tapping a foot. She got right down to it. "Mr. Palmer, Mr. Easton, Mr. Lander has told me about the four newcomers, and voiced his suspicion they might be the rustlers responsible for our missing cattle."

"They could be, ma'am," Jim Palmer said, "but all we have to go on is a hunch and you can't hang a man for that. Well, not usually, anyway."

"Your hunch is good enough for me," Elfie said. "Good enough, at any rate, that I would like for the two of you to trail them when they leave and see where they go."

Willis brought up his main objection. "That could be dangerous, ma'am. They're not friendly sorts, and they don't wear their hardware for bluff or ballast."

"Are you afraid?" Elfie asked Palmer and Easton.

If she had been Willis' wife, he would have kicked her. There was no surer way to get a man to do something he shouldn't do than by questioning his courage. He quickly said, "I'm sure they're not, ma'am." But the harm had been done.

"Why, yellow ain't hardly my favorite color," Timmy Easton bragged. "If you want those coyotes trailed, then by God, we'll trail them. Won't we, Jim?"

"If that's what Mrs. Tyler wants," Jim Palmer said reservedly. He was older and had more sense.

"Be careful," Elfie cautioned. "Don't get too close. Follow from a distance, and if they lead you to their camp and our cattle, head for the ranch and don't spare your horses."

"We can do that," Timmy Easton said.

Elfie bestowed a smile. "With a little luck, we can dispose of these rustlers before Laurella Hendershot arrives. The sale would go that much more smoothly."

Inwardly, Willis cursed the sale and cursed his boss for marrying a woman who always thought she was right and cursed the four newcomers for showing their faces in Cottonwood. But most of all he cursed his leaky mouth.

"I'm counting on you," Eflie said, then amended, "*We're* counting on you, my husband and I. It would mean a great deal to us, and I would be eternally grateful."

Timmy Easton had yet to learn that a woman's eternal gratitude usually lasted a day, if that. "You can count on us, ma'am."

"Good." Elfie bobbed her chin and smiled sweetly. "Off you go then."

Jim Palmer glanced at Willis with a pained expression but he did as she had told them.

"You're makin' a mistake, ma'am." Willis would not let the matter drop.

"It's mine to make. We'll see what Abe says when we reach the ranch. In the meantime, find something to occupy yourself for another hour or so. I have a few people to see and a few more items to buy."

"Yes, ma'am," Willis said, and if it was

possible to make those two words convey his belief that she was an idiot, he did it.

"I can't say as I like your tone, Mr. Lander. Abe told me you can be crotchety, what with your leg and all, but I should think you would know which lines you can cross and which you cannot." She walked off in a huff.

Willis let out a sigh and placed his hands on the buckboard and bowed his head. He toyed with the notion of going over to the Lucky Dollar and telling Jim and Timmy not to do as Elfie had instructed them but that might make Abe mad and he owed Abe too much. Damn, he thought, what a pickle.

"Are you holdin' up that buckboard or is the buckboard holdin' you up?"

Willis had rarely been so glad to see anyone. An idea occurred to him, and he grinned at his genius. "Marshal Keever!"

"Either you have a female problem or you need some prunes," the big lawman said with a smile. "Nothin' else could make a man look so miserable."

"How are you at keepin' secrets?" Willis asked.

"It depends on the secret. If you're in love and don't want me to tell anyone, fine and dandy. If it's the prunes, and I've had enough coffin varnish, I might joke about it in public."

"It's not prunes," Willis said in mild exasperation, and proceeded to relate the details of the missing cattle and the four men at the Lucky Dollar and Elfie's interference. The lawman listened with interest, and when Willis was done, he thoughtfully rubbed his square jaw.

"Well, now, maybe I should have a look at these gents. Could be they're wanted, and if I have circulars on them, it would solve your problem, wouldn't it?"

"That it would," Willis heartily agreed.

Marshal Keever scoured the street. "Now where did that deputy of mine get to?" He shrugged his big shoulders. "Oh, well. I doubt I'll need him. Tag along if you're inclined."

Willis wouldn't have missed it for all the whiskey in the saloon. He limped in the lawman's shadow, tingling with glee at his brainstorm.

The lawman went through the batwing doors as if they were not there. Keever paused just long enough to let his eyes adjust, then made a beeline for the bar, the badge on his vest shining with authority.

Willis hung back. The four might get the notion he had gone to fetch the lawdog, and that might not sit well. He saw Varner tilt a glass and glance in the mirror and see Keever. Instantly, Varner lowered the glass and started to spin, but he caught himself and whispered something to his cousins. Mason was over near the end of the bar, watching Johnny Vance and a townsman play poker.

"Gentlemen!" Marshal Keever said in that big, friendly voice of his. "Allow me to introduce myself." He did, while studying the faces of Varner and the cousins. "Do you plan to be in Cottonwood long?"

"Not long at all, Marshal," Varner said. "In fact, we're about ready to ride out." He displayed his buck teeth in a lopsided grin that had all the warmth of a coyote baring its fangs.

"Come a long way, have you?" Marshal Keever asked. Ordinarily it was close to a sin for anyone to pry into another's affairs. But the lawman's badge gave him that privilege.

"Long enough," Varner replied edgily.

"Where from?"

The tip of Varner's tongue appeared under his buck teeth and he gave the lawman a strange look. "You sure are a curious jasper."

"I'm paid to be," Marshal Keever said, and tapped his badge. "It's the only job there is where a man can be a busybody and not be shot for it." He paused. "So where are you from, again?"

"Nebraska," Varner said. "Me and my cousins are from near a small town called Lexington. We were raised on farms but farm life was borin' as hell, so we took to driftin'."

"Farm life is short on excitement," the lawman agreed.

Willis marveled at how easily Keever got the small man to talk about himself and share details Varner would likely as not never share with anyone otherwise. It was part of what made Keever such a good lawman — he used friendliness to do what other lawmen had to threaten to find out.

"Ain't that the truth," Varner was saying. "If I'd had to plow one more field or shuck one more ear of corn, I'd have blown my brains out."

"How have you been makin' ends meet?" Marshal Keever asked.

"Oh, however we can," Varner said. "We worked at a ranch near Sterlin' for a spell but ranchin' ain't any more excitin' than farmin'. So we drifted to Denver."

"I've been there a few times, back before I wore a badge," Keever said. "The whiskey is fine and the women are finer."

Grinning, Varner nodded. "I'd still be there now if it were up to me. I landed a job as a hog reeve but that didn't last long. I'd had enough of hogs on the farm. So then I hired on as a freighter but the hours were too long and the work about killed my back."

"You're a hard man to please when it comes to employment."

"I have my principles. I don't like takin' orders from bossy know-it-alls. I don't like sweatin' to make another man rich. And I don't like bein' paid pennies."

"I reckon that leaves everything out except winnin' a lottery and robbin' banks," Marshal Keever commented.

The man called Varner seemed to tense, then chuckled. "Lotteries are a fool's proposition. Most are rigged."

"That leaves banks."

Cocking his head, Varner looked up. "How stupid do you think I am, Marshal? The only quicker way to the gallows is rustlin'."

"Speakin' of which, some cows have gone missin' of late up to the Bar T," Keever said. "Maybe the rustlers reckon the Bar T has so many cows a few won't be missed but Abe Tyler keeps a tight tally."

"Is that a fact?" Varner asked, sounding uninterested.

Marshal Keever nodded. "He's got his hands on the lookout, and mark my words, they're a salty bunch — as loyal to the brand as can be." He leaned on the bar. "I wouldn't want to be in the rustlers' boots if the Bar T boys get hold of them. Trees are handier than gallows up in Bar T country."

"My cousins and me have too much sense to rustle."

"That reminds me," Marshal Keever said, giving the burly pair a close appraisal, "You haven't introduced them yet."

"This here is Thatch," Varner pointed at one, "and this here is Tote." He pointed at the other.

The pair just stood there, staring straight ahead into the mirror, showing no more emotion or interest than a pair of tree stumps.

"I haven't heard any last names," Marshal Keever said.

"Smith. All three of us are named Smith."

"Is that a fact?" Marshal Keever mimicked Varner, only he made it sound as if it were not a fact at all. "It couldn't be you're lyin' to me, could it?"

"Why would we do that?"

"Because it could be your last names aren't Smith at all. It could be your last name is Wilkes and the last name of your

130

two cousins there is Nargent. And it could be all three of you are wanted." Marshal Keever suddenly moved away from the bar with his hand on his revolver. "I'll thank you not to do anything hasty, boys, but to come along peaceful. I'd rather not kill you unless you force me."

Varner slowly lowered his drink. "Damned decent of you. Our wanted posters came across your desk — is that it?"

"A couple weeks ago," Marshal Keever said, "along with one on the Flour Sack Kid. The rate we're goin', Wyomin' Territory will soon have more outlaws than the Badlands."

It was a joke but no one laughed or cracked a grin. Willis wanted to yell at Keever to draw his revolver and cover them but he figured the lawman knew what he was doing. Then he caught movement out of the corner of his eye.

Mason had drawn his ivory-handled pistols. He pointed one at Johnny Vance, who froze with cards in his hands, and pointed the other at Marshal Keever's broad back. Keever had either forgotten there was a fourth rider or else he had not realized it was Mason because Mason was over by the poker table. Now Keever's back was to the man in gray, and it was Keever's turn to stiffen when Mason cocked the two pistols. Everyone in the saloon heard the twin clicks.

Timmy Easton started to rise out of his chair but Jim Palmer grabbed his arm and shook his head.

"Here's how this will be," Mason announced in a loud, clear drawl. "My pards and I are leavin'. If no one tries to stop us, everyone goes on livin'." He sidled toward the batwings, careful to move so he could cover Johnny Vance, Palmer, Easton, and the lawman all at the same time.

"I can't let you ride out," Marshal Keever said.

"You can't stop us, neither," Mason responded. "Don't be rash. You can round up a posse and come after us."

"Like hell," Varner Wilkes said. Drawing his revolver, he shot Marshal Keever in the stomach. Keever staggered, a look of astonishment on his face, and clutched at a crimson stain low on his shirt.

"No!" Mason cried.

Varner shot the lawman again, high in the chest. Keever staggered to the bar, clung to it a few seconds, then crumpled to the floor, quaking like he had the ague.

By then Thatch and Tote Nargent had unlimbered their hardware and were backing toward the door, their beady eyes glittering with bloodlust.

"Try and stop us and there will be hell to pay!" Thatch warned.

"We're curly wolves and proud of it!" Tote howled.

The only way Willis could tell them apart was that Thatch had a red bandanna and Tote wore a blue one. Tote swung toward him and he hiked his hands. He was no gun hand. In the time it would take him to draw and aim, the cousins would shoot him dead.

Mason glared at Varner Wilkes. "Damn yuh! Now we'll have the whole town down on our heads."

"Then what are you waitin' for?" Varner snapped, retreating with his revolver leveled. "Let's light a shuck while we can."

Timmy Easton was trembling worse than the marshal. "We can't let them get away!" he bawled. "We just can't!" With a wrench he tore loose of Jim Palmer and stabbed for his pistol.

Quick as thought, Mason shot him. Both of Mason's pistols blasted smoke and lead, and Timmy Easton was flung against his chair. He crashed down with the chair half on top of him and two holes spaced close together above his heart.

Jim Palmer bellowed and started to stand but the smoking pistols in Mason's hands swiveled toward him and he stayed put.

Slim was in shock. Johnny Vance was staring at Mason and only at Mason, and there was something about his eyes that was terrible to behold. Mason returned the look with a sad sort of sigh.

Willis was aghast. His brainstorm had gone all wrong. Two men shot and probably dead and he was to blame.

The Nargent brothers were at the batwings. Tote poked his head out, then yelled to Varner, "Folks are comin' on the run!"

"Change their minds for them. Thatch, you hold the horses ready. We'll be right out." Varner swung his pistol at Willis. "How about you? Got bright notions of bein' a hero?"

"Not at the moment," Willis said.

The brothers had rushed outside. Now shots boomed, women and children screamed, somewhere a man cursed, and more shots came from up and down the long street.

"Hurry it up, Mason," Varner goaded.

The man in gray was looking at Johnny Vance. Unexpectedly, Mason twirled his pistols into their holsters and turned his back on the gambler. "Another time," he said, and strolled casually to the batwings.

"Another time," Johnny Vance said after him.

Varner had his back to the wall. "We should kill every last one of these bastards. It's not smart to leave witnesses."

"No," Mason said.

"You don't tell me what to do," Varner said, but he went out without shooting anyone else.

Mason paused and glanced back at Johnny Vance and touched the brim of his gray hat. To Jim Palmer he said, "I'm sorry about the boy." Then he, too, was gone, and the batwings swung back and forth on empty air.

Out in the street a battle had broke out. Pistols and rifles were cracking and thundering from all quarters. Horses whinnied and stamped. Shouts and screams added to the bedlam.

Jim Palmer was out of his chair in a rush, drawing his revolver as he rose. "We've got to stop them!"

Willis drew his own revolver. Slim snatched a shotgun from under the bar. Only Johnny Vance did not resort to a weapon; he began playing solitaire.

About to peer out, Willis jerked back when a stray slug struck the right batwing with a loud *chuk*. Slivers flew every which way.

One stung his cheek, another his ear. He hunkered as the firing rose to a feverish frenzy.

Heedless of the flying lead, Jim Palmer was about to barrel past him when two swift shots shattered part of the left batwing, narrowly missing him. Palmer followed Willis' example. "We can't let them get away! They have to pay for Tim!"

Willis was gazing at Walt Keever. The lawman had stopped trembling and lay still, his eyes wide and vacant.

"Stop them!" someone out in the street bawled. "Shoot their horses out from under them!"

It sounded to Willis like Deputy Ivers. More shots banged, nearly drowning out rapidly fading hoofbeats.

The next moment the batwings burst inward and Deputy Ivers stormed into the saloon, a revolver in his hand. "What happened in here? Has anyone seen the mar —" Ivers spied the big body by the bar. He lurched to a halt and all the blood drained from his face. "Walt?"

"It was the little one who done it," Slim said. "Varner Wilkes, Marshal Keever called him."

"Walt?" Deputy Ivers said again. He took a few halting steps, riveted to the spreading scarlet pool.

Jim Palmer grabbed Ivers by the shoulder. "The marshal's not the only one," he said and pointed at the upended chair and Timmy Easton.

Willis limped outside. Men and women were peeking from windows and doorways, unsure if the gunplay was over. A number of glass panes had bullet holes in them. So did more than a few buildings. Down the street lay a body. Willis heard someone say it was Granger, the man who owned the feed and grain. He moved past the hitch rail and spotted another body near the buckboard. People were gathering around it and he could not see who it was but he could tell that whoever had been shot wore a dress.

"God, no," Willis breathed, and limped as fast as he could limp. Without slowing he pushed several onlookers aside, demanding, "Let me through! Let me through, damn it!"

"Mr. Lander, contain yourself."

Elfie was by the body, unhurt. Willis glanced down and discovered the dead woman was Martha Baxter, the wife of Fred Baxter, who ran the general store. The top of her head had been blown clean off by a heavy-caliber slug.

"The poor woman," someone said.

"Where's her husband?" another asked.

As if in answer, out of the store rushed Fred Baxter. A stocky man who wore spectacles and always had an apron on, he took one look and shrieked in horror. "Martha!" he wailed. Breaking into great racking sobs, he threw himself on her and clasped her gore-spattered head to his white apron.

Willis turned away. He realized he was still holding his revolver and slid it into his holster.

"Whoever did this can't swing soon enough," a man remarked. "Where's the marshal, anyhow?"

"Dead," Willis said. "He was the first one they killed."

Five or six citizens ran toward the saloon. Before they reached it, the batwings were slammed open yet again and out strode Deputy Jared Ivers. Wrath roiled on his brow like a thunderhead as he hollered, "I need a posse and I need it now! Every man with a gun and horse, meet me in front of the jail in ten minutes!"

Elfie was at Willis' elbow. "I imagine you want to go but your horse is at the Bar T. It's just as well. There's no one else to take me back and I don't want to stay with all these dead people lying around."

"I wouldn't be of much use to the posse,"

138

Willis said. He thought of Keever and Timmy Easton, and what little self-respect he had left shriveled and died.

CHAPTER 8

The way Willis later heard the story, the posse brought the disaster down on their own heads.

Fully three-fourths of the able-bodied men in Cottonwood were set to ride out when someone asked Deputy Ivers if it was smart to leave the town with so few defenders. What if the killers circled around and came back? It set off a ten-minute argument that ended with Ivers deciding to take only twenty men. Those who remained were to go about armed at all times. Guards were to be posted at both ends of the street and on various rooftops.

Then off the posse rode, shouting and whooping and filled with zeal to avenge those who had been slain. The tracks were so fresh, a ten-year-old could have followed them, and soon the posse was pounding hard to the northwest with Deputy Ivers at the forefront, urging them on.

Some of the posse members were confident it would all be over in an hour or two, and end with the four killers decorating cottonwood limbs. But the outlaws had good horses and the posse did not overtake them before the outlaws reached the mountains. Here the outlaws had done their best to shake the posse off. The avengers were forced to go much slower, and by late afternoon a few grumbled that the avenging might take longer than they figured.

Since Ivers had rushed them out of Cottonwood without packhorses and without thinking to ask the men to bring food and water, by nightfall the mood had turned sour. They camped next to a creek, which solved their thirst, but the only game they could find to shoot were two rabbits and a grouse a townsman accidentally flushed when he walked past a thicket and sneezed.

What was worse, only one man had coffee, and nearly every man wanted some. They sat around the campfire without saying much but the looks they cast in Deputy Ivers' direction said a lot.

Sunrise found them in the saddle and on the go. Renewed confidence coursed through them. The outlaws could not be that far ahead. By noon it would be over. But noon came and went and the posse had yet to catch sight of their quarry.

By three the mood had soured again. By four it was one of general discontent. What if the posse never caught up? Everyone was wasting their time. Deputy Ivers insisted the Wilkes gang were as good as dead, and he had the persuasive support of Jim Palmer to back him up.

Palmer had not said much until then. The previous night, he had sat glumly staring into the flames, overcome with remorse for Timmy Easton. So when some of the posse talked about turning back, Palmer put his hand on his revolver and informed them that he would "shoot the first son of a bitch who tried it."

That settled matters, for a while. But some of the townsmen, resentful of the treatment, dragged their mounts' hooves, with the result that Deputy Ivers had to tell them several times to quit slowing up the proceedings.

By evening the discontent had spread. They camped in a clearing barely large enough for the men and the horses to fit. There was no creek, so they went without water. The hunters among them failed to find game, so they went without food. The coffee had all been used up the night before. So they sat and glared at Ivers and Palmer, and Ivers glared right back.

Jim Palmer did not seem to notice he was one of the two least-liked people on the posse, or if he did, he did not care. All he did was stare into the flames, never moving, hardly ever blinking. He had not shaved or combed his hair, and the handsomest rider on the Bar T did not look quite as handsome.

The next morning another dispute broke out. Half the men were for heading back to Cottonwood. Their spokesman was Floyd Treach. They picked well. As the biggest man present, with more muscles than most of them ever dreamed of having, he presented an imposing figure when he walked up to Deputy Ivers and announced some of the men were leaving whether Ivers liked it or not.

No one noticed Jim Palmer. No one saw him draw his Colt. Suddenly he was beside Floyd Treach, and to everyone's incredulous disbelief, even Deputy Ivers', Palmer slammed the barrel across Floyd Treach's jaw and the mountain of muscle fell to his knees, dazed.

"Get him on his horse," Palmer said. Climbing on his own, he waved his Colt and hollered, "Let's ride!"

No one objected. They were too stunned.

Palmer had always been well thought of. He wasn't as rowdy or as rude as some of the cowhands could be when under the influence of bug juice, and he was always extraordinarily nice to the ladies. To have this easygoing man who had never lifted his voice in anger suddenly become a blacksmith beater was a considerable shock.

A lot of muttering took place, and many whispers were exchanged. By noon, when Deputy Ivers called a brief halt to rest the horses, several of the older posse members quietly took him aside and flatly told him enough was enough. They were not properly prepared for an extended stay in the high country. They should turn back before more than Floyd Treach's jaw was hurt.

Jared Ivers listened. He was pigheaded but he wasn't entirely stupid, and he announced that while he was pressing on, anyone who wanted could turn back. He gave Jim Palmer a pointed look but the cowboy did not make an issue of it.

An hour was spent debating how many should go back and how many should go on. Some of the men wanted to go back but they were afraid of being called quitters, and of looking bad in the eyes of their wives.

In the end, nine continued the chase while eleven tired, sore, hungry townsmen plodded gratefully homeward, Floyd Treach and his sore jaw among them.

The outlaws had been traveling steadily to the northwest, into a rugged, remote region. Ivers and the rest kept hoping for a glimpse of them but night fell and the posse still had not caught up, and of the nine who had stayed, two left the next morning.

Now the odds were seven to four, and Deputy Ivers had never been much of a gambling man. By midday he called another stop and said that they had done all they could but it was not enough, that they could not keep going without food and only occasional water, and that in his opinion it was best if they all returned to Cottonwood, rested a few days, and struck out again with packhorses and enough supplies to do the job right.

Jim Palmer did not say a word. When Ivers finished, he simply raised his reins and rode on. Deputy Ivers called after him but was ignored.

"Damn that cowboy, anyhow!" a townsman fumed.

"He's not the only one who's ever lost a friend," said another.

"Martha Baxter and my wife were like two peas in a pod," Harvey Stuckman declared.

Deputy Ivers sighed and informed them

he was going on. "For a day or so yet, enough to talk sense into Palmer."

Guilt cropped up. Three of the men did not let it sway them into what they deemed a foolish effort, and turned around. That left Stuckman and two others to catch up to Jim Palmer.

The deputy tried. He truly tried. He talked to Palmer for nearly two hours, seeking to persuade him to head back. He pointed out that the outlaws had the advantage. That Wilkes and company were natural-born killers who would love to bushwhack them. That Palmer could always have his revenge another day.

Once again Jim Palmer did not say a word. He rode on, his face set in rigid lines, his eyes always fixed on the next ridge, the next stand of timber, the next slope.

"This is getting ridiculous," Ted Yost said. "He's going to get us ambushed. I've stuck as long as I'm going to out of respect for Marshal Keever."

"We'll miss his funeral," remarked the last townsman.

That caused Deputy Ivers to draw rein, and Yost and the other man stopped, too. "I didn't think of that," Ivers said. "I should be there to say somethin' over the grave. He was my best friend."

"If we ride really hard maybe we can make it," Yost said.

"Maybe," said the last man.

All three of them glanced at the top of the slope they were climbing. Jim Palmer had gone over the crest.

"I say we try to talk sense into him one more time," Deputy Ivers suggested, "and if he won't go back with us, he's on his own."

"You're wearing the badge," Yost noted.

At that, Ivers frowned. "There's only so much I can do. You saw me earlier. I did all I could to convince him this is a mistake. It was like talkin' to a rock."

"I saw you," the last townsman, Nesbitt, said. "You did all anyone could do, and then some."

Yost nodded. "It's not your fault. That cowboy is half out of his mind. If he's not careful, he'll get himself killed."

At that exact instant the mountains echoed to the boom of a rifle shot. Deputy Ivers straightened, swore, and used his reins and his spurs on his horse. He was first to reach the top and the first to behold the prone figure. A slug had caught Jim Palmer in the middle of his left cheek and made a mess of the right half of his head. His handsome face would never be handsome again.

"Over there!" Yost yelled.

Two hundred yards to their left was a shelf slightly higher than the slope. A figure dressed all in gray was astride a gray horse, holding a rifle with the stock on his thigh.

Deputy Ivers bent to shuck his own rifle from its saddle scabbard but he did not pull it out. The man in gray was making no move to take aim at them. "It's the one called Mason."

"They say he's a Reb, like Johnny Vance," Yost said.

"That's a hell of a long shot he made. He must be a sharpshooter," Nesbitt breathlessly commented. "He could probably pick us off without half trying."

"We're easy targets for him here," Deputy Ivers agreed, and promptly reined around and down the other side a dozen yards.

"What about the cowboy?" Yost asked when they reined up. "We should bury him."

"Maybe that's what the outlaws are waiting for," Nesbitt said. "I didn't see the other three. They might be hiding. When we go down to the body, they'll pop up and blast away."

Both townsmen looked at Jared Ivers. "You make the decisions," Yost said. "What do we do?"

Ivers gnawed on his lower lip. He rose in the stirrups and sank back down. He put his hand on his revolver and took it off again. "They're only three of us now. We're outnumbered. It would be foolish for us to die for a man who is already dead." He squared his shoulders. "I say we head back."

"About damn time," Nesbitt said.

"I don't like the idea of leaving that cowboy lying there," Yost mentioned. "I liked him."

"Everyone liked Jim Palmer," Deputy Ivers said. "I liked him, too, but I didn't like him enough to die for him when he's past help."

"But his body," Yost persisted. "His horse."

"The outlaws will take his horse and whatever else they can use," Ivers predicted. "The body won't be there long, not with all the coyotes and buzzards and bears in this part of the country."

"That's not very Christian," Yost said.

"No, it's not," Deputy Ivers agreed, "but Jim Palmer wasn't Christ." He gigged his mount to the southwest, saying over a shoulder, "If you want to give the coyotes more to eat, you go right ahead. I'll let your wife know you died doing what was right."

Nesbitt was already following. Ted Yost stared up the slope a few seconds; then the young bank clerk wheeled his horse and started down after the others. "Wait for me!"

The three rode hard the rest of the day, or as hard as they dared given that their mounts were about played out. They continually scoured their back trail for sign of pursuit but it appeared the outlaws were not after them.

"That's a relief," Nesbitt said. "I half expected them to come after us and wipe us out."

"We're not safe yet," Deputy Ivers scowled.

That night they had neither water nor food. The next morning they were under way as soon as the pink flush of dawn marked the horizon. It was Ivers' intention to push on to the stream the posse had camped beside the first night out. "Once we reach it, we'll be all right."

By the sun it was close to eleven and they were descending a rocky slope when suddenly a harsh rattling sound caused the deputy's animal to rear and whinny. Ivers palmed his pistol and snapped a shot at the rattlesnake but the snake was too fast and slithered into some boulders.

"Whoa there, boy!" he said to his horse as it abruptly bolted. He hauled on the reins but it did no good. Another moment, and the horse squealed and catapulted into a forward roll. Ivers left the saddle and threw his arms over his head. He hit and rolled and came to a stop against a log.

"Are you all right?" Yost called down.

Deputy Ivers was fine but his horse had a broken leg. Jagged white bone stuck six inches from ruptured flesh. "Hell," he said, standing over the thrashing animal and cocking his revolver. "Hell, hell, hell."

The shot pealed off the mountain and the horse stopped thrashing.

Ted Yost and Nesbitt fidgeted in their saddles and Nesbitt asked, "Now what? There's three of us but only two horses."

"I'll ride double with Yost and you can bring my saddle." Ivers squatted by his former mount.

"No," Nesbitt said.

"No, what?"

"No, I'm not taking your saddle. My horse is tired enough. Hell, I'm about done in, and we have a long way to go. We should leave your saddle and effects here and you can come back for them."

"I'm not leavin' my saddle," the deputy said. "It cost me pretty near half a month's pay."

"You can't make us take it," Nesbitt said, and Ted Yost nodded.

Jared Ivers' thin lips twitched. He glared as best he could glare and he cursed them with a vehemence a mule skinner would envy, but in the end Nesbitt and Yost sat firm and refused to take the saddle.

"I'll remember this," Ivers spat. "The next time you need a favor of the law, don't come to me."

"Be reasonable, Jared," Nesbitt said.

But Ivers would not be reasonable, and for the rest of the day, he griped about their ill treatment of him and his saddle. Nightfall found them at the creek, where their horses drank too much and had to be pulled from the water. Deputy Ivers took his rifle and prowled in search of game but came back empty-handed.

"I'm so hungry I'd eat your dead horse," Yost mentioned, which was perhaps not the wisest comment to make as it brought a new torrent of curses from Ivers and a vow that if it was the last thing he ever did, he would repay them for the injustice of abandoning his saddle.

They did not sleep well. They tossed and turned. Their stomachs growled like ravenous bears. Each got up several times to drink. Sunrise brought them out from under their blankets stiff and sore and famished.

Deputy Ivers stood and arched his back to stretch and saw the Flour Sack Kid not ten feet away holding the matched pair of black-handled revolvers on him. "What the hell?" he blurted.

"Mornin'," the Kid said. "You sure are a sorry-lookin' bunch."

Yost and Nesbitt were too stupefied to speak.

Not Deputy Ivers. "What are you doin' here? What do you want?" he demanded.

"I heard some shots yesterday and came for a look-see," the Kid said. "Found a dead horse and the tracks of two others, and here I am." His eyes regarded them from under the flour sack. "The question is, what are *you* doin' here?"

"We're a posse out after the Wilkes gang," Deputy Ivers informed him.

"A posse? All three of you?"

"There were twenty. It's a long story."

"I'll spare you the tongue waggin'," the Kid said. "I've got somewhere I need to be tonight, so hand over your money."

Yost made a gurgling noise, then bleated, "You're robbing us?"

"It's how I make my livin', remember?" the Kid replied. "Why else do you reckon I followed you all this way? Dig in your pockets and I'll be out of your hair."

"No, by God!" Deputy Ivers fell into a crouch with his hand poised to draw. "There's three of us and only one of you!

You might get me but you can't get Yost and Nesbitt, too. Compared to the Wilkes gang, you'll be easy."

"I wouldn't say that," the Flour Sack Kid said, and shot him in the leg.

Deputy Ivers howled as he fell. Clutching his right thigh, he rolled back and forth, spewing swear words through his clenched teeth.

Walking up to him, the Kid relieved Ivers of his revolver, then collected pistols from Yost and Nesbitt. He threw the revolvers and rifles into the brush and held out a hand. "Now for the money."

Between them, Yost and Nesbitt had six dollars and forty-three cents.

"Mighty slim pickin's," the Kid said, "but every little bit helps." He stood over Jared Ivers and nudged him with a boot. "How about you, lawdog?"

"Go to hell."

Hunkering, the Kid pressed a pistol barrel to Ivers' head and patted down each of Ivers' pockets. His search yielded another dollar and twenty cents. "And folks wonder why I don't work for a livin'," he said.

"I'll see your neck stretched if it's the last thing I do," Jared Ivers vowed. His hands were slick with blood and his face was a mask of pain.

"You're welcome to try." The Kid whistled. Out of the brush came the Appaloosa. It cantered to his side and waited for him to climb on.

"That's some horse," Nesbitt said.

Deputy Ivers had not used up his store of swear words. When he was done, he snarled, "I'm lyin' here bleedin' to death and you compliment his cayuse."

"But it *is* some horse. My uncle back in Indiana was a horse breeder and I know a fine animal when I see one."

"I wish I could hang you, too," Ivers said.

Ted Yost tried to soothe him. "Look at the bright side. Things can't get any worse."

"I'm takin' your horses as well," the Flour Sack Kid announced as he swung onto the Appaloosa.

"But we need them!" Yost cried. "We need to get the deputy to a doctor as soon as possible."

The Kid reined the Appaloosa over to Ivers and looked down at him. "Wrap your belt real tight around your leg and the bleedin' will stop. If I were you, I'd lie here and take it easy while these other two go for help."

"Oh, sure," Ivers said. "Shoot me. Then pretend you give a damn."

The Flour Sack Kid looped a lead rope

over the two horses. He saw Yost and Nesbitt watching him and said, "What are you waitin' for? If you don't light a shuck, Jared there will be dead inside of twenty-four hours."

Ivers rose onto an elbow. "How is it you know my first name?"

"I know a lot of first names," the Kid said. With that, he departed in a flurry of hooves.

"You heard him!" Ivers barked at the bank clerk and the assistant at the feed and grain. "If you don't make it back in time and I die, I'll come back and haunt the both of you, so help me God."

"He's delirious," Yost said.

The two men maintained a brisk pace for a half mile or so, at which point fatigue and hunger conspired to hold them to a less-than-brisk walk. They wanted to go faster but they had dwelled in towns their entire lives and were as adept in the woods as newborn infants. Again and again they stumbled or tore their clothes or tripped over a rock or their own feet. They were clammy with sweat and their legs became leaden.

Then fickle fate came to their rescue. Three of the men who had turned back with Treach lost battles to their consciences and, after buying provisions, had set right back out again. The surprise was mutual when they came on Yost and Nesbitt at close to four o'clock that afternoon.

It was decided one man would ride like the wind back to Cottonwood for the doctor. The others hastened to the clearing by the creek, Yost and Nesbitt riding double.

"Ivers! We're back! You're saved!" Yost hollered as he jumped down. He ran to where they had left the deputy propped against a tree but Ivers wasn't there. "Where in the world . . . ?"

"I thought you said he couldn't hardly walk." This from Isaac Jorgenson, who had a small spread ten miles south of Cottonwood and happened to be in town the day of the shootings.

"He was," Nesbitt said. "I don't understand where he could have gotten to."

They commenced a search and were at it five minutes when Ted Yost strayed near the stream and happened to glance at a shallow pool. What he saw turned his blood to ice and tore a yelp from his throat. The others rushed to find out why, and Nesbitt turned and retched.

"That's a hand," Jorgenson said. "A human hand."

On the other side of the stream, they came on an arm and then a half-eaten leg. They were not trackers but the tracks of the culprit were impossible to miss.

"What a horrible way to die," Yost said.

"I can't think of any good ways," Jorgenson responded, and squatted to place his left hand over a paw print. "The blood must have drawn it in. Old-timers says a grizzly can smell blood a mile off."

"Eaten by a bear," Nesbitt said. "Ivers never counted on having that on his tombstone."

"What tombstone?" Jorgenson asked.

"All I know," Ted Yost said, taking off his hat and mopping his brow with a sleeve, "is that this was one hell of a posse."

CHAPTER 9

A pall of gloom hung over the Bar T and it did not sit well with Elfie Tyler. She complained about it to Abe, and he called all the hands who were not out on the range to the stable. Or, rather, Reuben Marsh did. To all questions about why the big augur wanted to see them, the foreman would only say they must wait and hear him out.

Willis was there. So were Charlie Weaver and Sam Tinsdale and Gus the cook and more than a dozen others. Willis did not speak to anyone. He had not said much since the other day at the saloon.

Abe and Elfie came from the big house and Abe stood in the open double doors to the stable and raised his hands for quiet. Then he cleared his throat and began right in. "We've got to shake it off, boys. Losing Jim and Timmy was awful, yes, but we can't mope about it. We have to get on with our lives."

"I'll get on with mine when they hang the vermin who done it," Gus the cook said. He was the only one who dared interrupt. It came from being the only man on the spread who was indispensable.

"I'm sure the law will bring them to justice," Abe said, "just as soon as Cottonwood gets around to appointing a new lawman." He paused. "In the meantime, we have a ranch to run."

"And a ranch to sell," Elfie interjected.

Willis had always been skeptical of her but now an active tendril of dislike crawled up through him, and even though he was not as indispensable as the cook he dared to say, "We can't let Jim's and Timmy's deaths put a stop to that."

"Exactly," Elfie beamed. "It won't do for the prospective new owner to arrive today and find the Bar T as lively as a funeral. We need to put on the best face we can."

Some of the men shifted and glanced at one another, and Abe Tyler coughed and said, "What my wife is trying to say is that, just as the Good Book says, there is a time and a place for everything, and today is not the time and the Bar T is not the place to give the lady from Texas the notion we're a bunch of quitters."

"Quitters?" Gus said.

"In the sense of whipped dogs, yes," Abe said. "Have you looked at yourselves — all of you walking around as if you're only half here? No one smiles. No one laughs. I joined you men for supper last night, if you'll recall, and I never saw a gloomier outfit in my life."

"You can't blame us," Sam Tinsdale said.

"No one is being blamed for anything," Abe declared. "All I'm asking is that we try to be more like our old selves. The Hendershot woman will arrive in a couple of hours and I'd like for her to see the Bar T at its best. Is that too much to ask?"

No one answered.

Abe smiled. "I didn't think it was. Believe you me, I know how rough this is. No one here liked Jim Palmer more than I did. And Timmy Easton, while young, was a top hand. They will both be missed."

Willis wondered if anyone would say the same of him when his time came.

"But miss them in private," Abe continued, "not when you're forking hay or riding herd or branding. Show this woman from Texas that Wyoming cowboys are every bit as hardy as the Texas variety."

"We sure are!" Leroy Fisher declared. He was the only puncher Willis ever met who hailed from Connecticut.

"That's the spirit!" Abe said. "Now let's get everything as presentable as we can. Sam, you make sure the bunkhouse is tidied up and stays tidied up the whole time Laurella Hendershot is here. Charlie, make the rounds of the home valley and advise the men on herd to be on their best behavior. Hendershot will want to inspect the cattle and I don't want her catching any of our boys shirking work. Gus, you'll have those pies we talked about ready?"

"In the oven already," Gus said. "They'll be baked brown before the hour is up."

"Excellent," Elfie said.

"That's all, then, I guess," Abe said, and started to turn but stopped. "Oh, except for Willis. We need to see you up at the house in ten minutes or so, if you don't mind."

"Not at all," Willis said, the butterflies in his stomach multiplying. The whole escort business had about ruined his sleep the past few nights. He was deathly afraid he would make some blunder that would spoil the sale.

Abe smiled and nodded and took his wife's elbow. She was wearing a new dress and new shoes and had a ribbon in her hair.

"Well," Charlie Weaver said.

"Well," Willis echoed.

"I reckon I'd best saddle up." Charlie put

162

a hand on Willis's shoulder. "Is it me or are you lookin' a mite peaked? Does havin' to chaperon the filly have you that spooked?"

"No more than stickin' my head in a rattlesnake den would."

Charlie chuckled. "Look at it this way. The first bite, and your worries are all over."

"That's supposed to cheer me up? As a friend you would make a fine disease."

"Now, now," Charlie said, "I'm on your side. Elfie and Abe should show this Texas gal around. It's their ranch, not ours. But we're on the payroll and we have to do as the boss wants, like it or not."

"We can always ride," Willis said.

"You're not about to quit over somethin' as silly as this, are you?" Charlie asked. "You didn't quit over your leg, and that's a hell of a lot worse." He caught himself. "Sorry, pard. That was plumb thoughtless."

"I'd best get up to the ranch house." Willis limped on past the corral. The last thing he needed was to be reminded of his condition. He only hoped Laurella Hendershot wasn't one of those who wore her pity on her sleeve. There was nothing worse, when a man was crippled, to be treated *as* a cripple.

Elfie and Abe were on the porch, in their rocking chairs. Little Sparrow had just brought a silver tray with a pitcher of lemonade.

"Would you care for a glass, Mr. Lander? We've had it special made for the occasion."

Part of Willis wanted to say no but it had been a coon's age and then some since he had tasted lemonade. "I'll have a glass if you can spare it."

Abe was looking pleased with himself. "How do you think the men took to my little speech?"

"They're rarin' to go," Willis said.

"Good." Abe smiled at Elfie. "We've done all we can. Now the sale is in the hands of Providence."

"True," Elfie said, "but my grandmother always said it never hurts to lend Providence a helping hand. That's why the floors are clean enough to eat off of. That's why the stable looks as clean as the house. That's why we have the lemonade and the pies and the rest of it."

"We've done all we can," Abe agreed.

"Not quite." Elfie looked at Willis. "Please don't mind my asking, Mr. Lander, but is that the best you can do with yourself?"

"Ma'am?"

"Have you availed yourself of a mirror of late? You need a shave. You need your hair trimmed. That shirt needs a washing. The

164

pants, well, the less said about them, the better." Elfie's face reminded Willis of a hawk about to swoop on prey. "We want to put on our best face for Miss Hendershot."

"There's plenty of time for me to shave and whatnot."

"That there is, but why leave anything to chance? What if Miss Hendershot shows up early?" Elfie gazed across the valley but the ribbon of a road that led out of it and eventually to Cottonwood was empty save for a few cowboys on horseback. "No, if you will indulge me, I'd rather we tend to your deficiencies here and now."

"Sure. I'll go shave," Willis said, and shifted his good leg.

"You've misunderstood. By here and now I mean right here and right now. Little Sparrow will take you out back and see to your stubble and your hair, among other things. I've already talked it over with her."

"You have?" Willis glanced at the Shoshone girl, who might as well have been carved from stone for all the emotion she showed.

"Yes. Furthermore, I won't take no for an answer. This is too important to me, Mr. Lander, as you well know. So off you go, please, and do try not to scuff the floor. We had it polished yesterday."

"Dearest," Abe said softly.

At a nod from Elfie, Little Sparrow opened the door and held it for Willis to go in. His ears burning, Willis limped past her and on down the long hall to the kitchen. He had taken Elfie literally and had his hand on the back door when Little Sparrow said in her clipped English, "Here will do."

Willis sank into the chair she indicated and folded his hands in his lap and then unfolded them again.

"There is no reason to be nervous," Little Sparrow said. "I have shaved Mr. Tyler many times, and cut his hair. Reuben's, too."

"You do?" This was incredible news to Willis, who had always assumed that was something a man did on his own except for an occasional visit to a barbershop.

"Mrs. Tyler has me do many things," Little Sparrow said, but whether she was stating a fact, bragging, or complaining, Willis couldn't say. "She says I am the next best thing to having her own maid."

"You speak the white tongue really good."

"Thank you." Little Sparrow took a shallow pan from under the counter and placed it on the table. A larger pan was on the stove, filled with steaming water, half of which she poured into the first pan. Then she went out of the kitchen and returned shortly with a razor, a pair of scissors, and a folded towel.

"Ever cut anyone's ear off by mistake?" Willis joked.

"No. But I did cut a man's upper lip off once when he talked when he should not have." Little Sparrow's dark eyes glowed with amusement.

Willis laughed and said, "So Indians do have a sense of humor. Some folks say they don't."

"Yes, we have a sense of humor," Little Sparrow said. "We also sweat when it is hot and shiver when it is cold and cough when we breathe in too much dust."

Willis grinned. "I reckon I had that comin'. But you're the only Indian I've ever talked to, and you're female, besides."

Little Sparrow had opened the razor and was testing the edge by lightly running a finger along it. "Which is worse — the Indian part or the female part?"

"Neither. Don't put words in my head." Willis squirmed in his chair. "I've always liked you. I'm just not much when it comes to small talk."

"They say you are a good man," Little Sparrow said, "but a man whose spirit was broken the day his leg was broken."

"Who says that?" Willis bristled. "My

spirit is just fine, thank you very much. Even if it weren't, what do they know? I was a cowboy. A bronc buster. One of the best. Now I'll never bust another horse as long as I live."

Little Sparrow stepped back and looked him up and down. "You wear a hat like a cowboy. You wear cowboy clothes. You wear the boots cowboys wear."

Willis's anger climbed. "You don't savvy. I can't hardly walk. What good does it do me to rope a cow if I can't climb down and get to the cow as fast as I'd need to? If a steer acted up, I couldn't get out of the way. I can't brand. I can't do any of the things a cowboy does. Not any of the things that count, anyway."

"You have much sadness inside you," Little Sparrow said.

"Just shave me." Willis refused to say another word to her until she was done. When she held up an oval mirror for him to examine his chin, he merely grunted.

"Please take off your hat."

The amount of hair she snipped appalled him. Willis had worn his hair long for so long that he felt uncomfortable with it short. When she held up the mirror again, he begrudgingly said, "Nice job." He reached for his hat.

"First your bath."

"My what?" Willis did not recollect any mention of a bath out on the front porch. "Who says?"

"Mrs. Tyler. She had Gus bring the tub from the bath shed and put it out back." Little Sparrow walked to the door and opened it. "After you."

"What gall," Willis said. But he got up and went out, and there, over under the overhang to the wood shed, was the tub, brimming with water. "She had you fill it before I got here?"

"Mrs. Tyler says that sometimes the men go into the bath shed and come out drier than when they went in."

Willis had half a mind to limp out front and tell Elfie what she could do with her tub. "I'm not takin' a bath out here in front of everybody."

Little Sparrow indicated the short fence that hemmed the wood shed on three sides to keep out the snow in the winter. "No one will see you. I will be inside." Her hand rose and in it was a towel and a bar of lye soap.

Willis glared and Little Sparrow waited, and after half a minute, Willis took the bar of soap and slung the towel over a shoulder. "This is a fine how do you do."

"It is just a bath."

"And jumpin' off a cliff is just jumpin' off a cliff." Willis went to the tub and tested it with a finger. The water was close to hot. He turned to tell the Shoshone girl that he did not blame her for the indignity but she had gone back inside. "Fine," he muttered. Walking around the tub, he sat on the ground and hurriedly undressed. He set the brace aside with extra care, then wrapped the towel around his midriff and stood to climb in.

Little Sparrow was a few yards away, holding a shirt and a pair of pants.

"What in blazes!" Willis exclaimed, hunkering down. "You promised you wouldn't peek."

"Mrs. Tyler wants you to wear these after your bath," Little Sparrow informed him. "She says they are yours to keep."

Both the shirt and pants were store-bought. Willis needed new duds, but not like this. It was humiliating. "I can make do with my own."

"Mrs. Tyler says your own clothes are not fit for being in public," Little Sparrow said. "She says an escort must look his best or he is not much of an escort."

"She sure says a lot," Willis groused. "All right. You've had her say. Now scat and let a man wash in peace."

"I can wash you if you like. I often wash Mr. and Mrs. Tyler."

"You do? Mrs. Tyler, too?" Willis didn't know what to think of that. To him, the notion that a human being would let another human being be that intimate was unthinkable. "Abe never mentioned it."

"Where should I place the clothes?" Little Sparrow asked.

"Anywhere. I don't care. Just so you let me be until I'm finished and dressed. And no peekin' out the windows, neither."

"I have four brothers. You do not have anything I have not seen before, Mr. Lander."

"Maybe not, but it's mine and I'm particular about who I show it to. Now off you go," Willis shooed her. He stayed behind the tub until the door closed, then quickly slipped over the side, holding the towel in front of him so even if she did peek out she would not see anything. He placed his good leg in first, then had to help his left leg by lifting it. Sinking down, he dropped the towel to the ground. The water felt nice. He had almost forgotten what a bath was like.

Willis couldn't get over how much trouble Elfie had gone to. The shave, the haircut, the bath, the clothes. She was determined he be as presentable as possible for Laurella

Hendershot. The more he thought about it, though, the more it stoked his anger. He resented being treated as if he were ten years old and had to be not only told what to do but led around as if he had a ring in his nose.

Still, Willis enjoyed the sensation of soaking in the water. Bending his left leg at the knee by hand, he leaned back and closed his eyes and felt the tension drain from him like water from a punctured water skin. Damn, it felt good. He thought of the line shack. Strange, but he did not miss it near as much as he did for the two or three days right after he left it. He thought of Jim Palmer and Timmy Easton and Marshal Keever and Deputy Ivers, and how a person never knew when the sands in the hourglass of their life would run out. He thought of the Flour Sack Kid and felt his body tense up again, so he stopped thinking about the Kid and emptied his head of all thoughts whatsoever.

Willis seemed to be drifting. He was warm and then he was cold, and the next thing he knew, he heard someone cough and he opened his eyes to find Little Sparrow staring at him. He figured maybe he was dreaming until she spoke.

"Mr. Lander? You have been in there forty

minutes. Mrs. Tyler sent me to fetch you. She says you were to bathe yourself, not turn into a fish."

"She said that?" Willis said, then yelped and reached for the towel. But to get it he had to rise out of the water and he was not about to do that with the maiden present. "Scoot, dang it! Tell her I'll be out in five minutes."

Little Sparrow bent and picked up the bar of lye soap from the grass. "Maybe I should tell her ten minutes. This is not wet. You have not washed yourself yet."

"I had no idea Shoshones were so blamed pushy," Willis griped, accepting the bar with as much dignity as he could muster.

The second the door closed behind her, Willis commenced rubbing the bar over his skin fit to rub himself raw. He made a special point to rub it over his feet, which on hot days, when his boots were off, were enough to gag a mule. He also rubbed it over his hair and lathered vigorously to remove any lice he might have. His skin acquired a pink hue. Soon his whole body tingled.

Smiling at how invigorated he felt, Willis gripped the edge of the tub with one hand and started to rise. He was halfway out when pain spiked his left thigh and his left leg buckled out from under him. He tried to catch himself but fell back into the water. More pain lanced up his spine. His right elbow struck the side of the tub so hard, it nearly went numb. Furious for forgetting about his knee, Willis bit off a string of fiery curses. It was stupid of him. Stupid, stupid, stupid. Gritting his teeth, he hooked his left elbow over the edge and then his throbbing right elbow and managed to slide his right leg up and out. Only when he was braced did he rise the rest of the way.

Acutely aware of his nakedness, Willis quickly toweled himself dry and sat on the ground to put on his brace. Once the straps were tight, he sighed in relief and hastily dressed in the new clothes Little Sparrow had left. He switched his belt from his old pants to the news ones, tugged into his boots, strapped on his revolver, and looked up. "What is it now?"

"Mrs. Tyler wishes you would go a little faster," Little Sparrow relayed. "The Hendershot woman can come at any time."

"I'm ready," Willis announced, and bent to pick up his old shirt and his old britches.

"Leave those for me to dispose of," Little Sparrow said.

"Dispose my foot. They have a few years of wear left," Willis set her straight. "I'll get them after this silly escort business is over."

"You do not want to show the woman from Texas around the ranch?"

"I'd rather walk on hot coals," Willis said. He adjusted his hat. "How do I look, missy?"

"Afraid."

"Who wouldn't be? It isn't natural for a man to stick his head in a bear's mouth. I'd as soon someone else did it but Mrs. Tyler elected me and her vote is all that counts around these parts."

"Mr. Tyler gave her the idea," Little Sparrow revealed. "I heard him say you were the perfect choice."

"Abe stabbed me in the back like that?" Willis was stricken. "You think you know some folks."

The Tylers were in their rocking chairs. Elfie raked Willis from hat to boots and nodded approvingly. "I do declare, Mr. Lander, that it's like night and day. You look positively respectable."

"How was I before?" Willis asked but was not treated to an answer.

"Doesn't he, Abe?" Elfie addressed her husband instead. "He'll make a fine impression on Miss Hendershot."

"That's what we're counting on," Abe said. "Now all that's left is the waiting. It could be today, like she wrote us, or it could be any day this week if she was delayed."

"She's a Texan," Elfie said. "She'll be here when she said she would."

Willis had met a Texican or two whose idea of being punctual was to show up, but he bit off the comment. "What do I do until then, ma'am?"

"Try not to get yourself or your new clothes dirty. And for goodness' sake, no drinking or traipsing off into Cottonwood. We want you handy when the time comes." Elfie gazed down the valley and her eyes narrowed. "Say, is that what I think it is?"

In the far distance a buckboard had appeared and was winding along the dirt road.

"What perfect timing!" Elfie crowed, delighted.

"Don't get your hopes up," Abe said. "It could be someone from town. Or maybe the doc was out this way and decided to see you. I've never seen a doctor so fond of a patient."

"Don't start. An ingrown toenail is nothing to take lightly. There was this woman in Saint Louis whose foot became infected and they had to cut it off, or so a friend claimed."

Willis limped to a porch post and leaned against it. His butterflies were back. More than ever. He needed a drink, needed it as much as he needed a new knee. Licking his dry lips, he rubbed his damp palms on his new pants.

The buckboard took forever to reach the ranch house. Word had spread, and hands came from the bunkhouse and the stable to watch it approach. Two people were perched on the seat. One a tall, dark man in dark clothes and a dark sombrero. The other, a woman in a calico dress and wearing, of all things, a wide-brimmed hat with a veil.

Willis had only ever seen a woman wear a veil once, and that was at a funeral. He straightened and fiddled with his bandanna and belt. Sweat broke out on his brow.

Now they could hear the clatter of the wheels. Soon the driver brought the team past the stable to the house. Swinging lithely down, he came around and held out his arms. He had a sweeping mustache and, if Willis had to guess, must have been in his forties or perhaps even his fifties. "Senorita." High on his right hip was a pearl-handled Colt. His gun belt was studded with silver conchas.

"Since when am I helpless, Armando?" the woman said, and climbed down without his help. For a woman, she had a deep voice laced with a Texas drawl.

Willis stayed where he was while the Tylers warmly greeted Laurella Hendershot. Elfie pumped the Texas woman's hand, asking if the trip had been tiring and if there had been any incidents and if Miss Hendershot needed to clean up. The woman from Texas said yes, a few, and no, but she could use something to drink.

Elfie motioned for Little Sparrow to bring a lemonade. Then Elfie said, "Allow me to introduce the man we've chosen to show you around the Bar T."

The butterflies had turned into scorpions. Willis limped down the steps and smiled his best smile and held out his hand. "How do you do, ma'am?"

CHAPTER 10

Laurella Hendershot had been on the Bar T before, so it was only natural that Willis had asked the hands at the bunkhouse what she looked like. They all said the same thing — they never got a good look at her face but she was well-dressed and from the neck down was "all female," as Charlie Weaver phrased it. No one mentioned a veil and it never occurred to Willis to ask if she wore one since so few women of his acquaintance ever had.

"How do you do?" the woman from Texas said in her low and somewhat hard voice.

Willis was surprised at her grip. She shook his hand firmly and strongly. Her hand was not pale and callus-free, like Elfie's. It was bronzed from the sun and had seen a lot of work.

"Why don't you come inside?" Elfie was offering. "You must be tired. Rest up today and begin your inventory tomorrow."

"In Texas we get things done and then we rest," Laurella Hendershot said. "But I wouldn't mind a glass of that lemonade I see on your porch."

Willis was trying to see her face through the veil and could not. The veil was peculiar in that while Hendershot could plainly see out, no one could see through it. He stepped back, unsure what he should do, and figured it best to await instructions.

"I'll have one of the hands bring your things inside," Abe said to Laurella.

"That's not necessary. Armando sees to my needs. But I thank you for your kindness." The woman from Texas turned to Armando and the pair exchanged a flurry of Spanish. The end result was that the tall man in black began toting her trunks and bags inside.

Willis would have dearly liked to help but he could not carry anything heavy on account of his shattered knee. So he stood there, feeling as useless as a wart on a toad. Armando looked at him once as he went by but did not say anything.

Little Sparrow had given Laurella Hendershot a glass of lemonade and Hendershot lifted her veil to drink it.

Hoping for a look at her features, Willis was disappointed when she shifted toward the house. He could tell nothing other than that she had a mouth.

"I can't tell you how happy I am to have you here," Elfie said. "Anything you need, anything at all, you have only to ask. Our home is your home."

"Maybe soon in more ways than one, eh?" Hendershot said, a suggestion of a grin in her lilt.

"That is my fervent prayer," Elfie said.

"You don't cotton to ranch life much, do you, Mrs. Tyler?" Laurella Hendershot asked. She had finished the glass in great gulps, as a man would, and lowered her veil.

"Please. It's Elfie, remember? And no, I freely admit I do not. I was born and raised in a city and I am a city girl at heart. The country life has its charms but they are not enough to keep me here."

"We're opposites, then. I was born and bred on my pa's ranch and ranchin' is the only life I've ever known or wanted to know." Hendershot stepped to the rail and gazed out over the Bar T. "I've been wantin' a ranch of my own for some time now. I've looked and looked but none have impressed me as much as this one. Your spread is right fine, from what I've seen of it so far."

"You'll see every square inch if you want," Abe said. "I have my books ready for you to inspect, too."

"The ranch first, the books second. I trust you keep a close tally and can account for any discrepancies I might come across?"

"I count my cattle regularly," Abe assured her.

Willis saw Abe give him a sidelong glance but could not begin to guess what it signified.

"Well then," Hendershot said, "why don't you have your man there give me a tour of the bunkhouse and whatnot?"

"I'll do that myself, if you don't mind," Elfie said merrily. "It's so rare to have another woman to talk to."

Willis went to follow them but Abe gestured, so he stayed where he was. Suddenly Armando flashed by him and caught up to the women. At a word from Laurella Hendershot, he fell into step behind them.

"What do you think of her?" Abe was at Willis' elbow.

"Too soon to say. But I have to wonder. What sort of woman wears a veil everywhere? She doesn't strike me as shy, so she must have another reason."

"She does," Abe said, then leaned toward him. "Forget that right now. What's important is that you don't mention anything about the rustlers to her."

"I don't?"

"No. If she finds out the Wilkes gang are helping themselves to our cows, it might reflect on the sale. Elfie wouldn't want that."

"So I'm to lie?" As a general rule Willis avoided lying but he was not overfussy about it.

"Not at all. I'm simply asking you not to bring the subject up. If she does, then yes, of course, be honest with her. But don't volunteer any information she doesn't ask for. Understand?"

"I savvy," Willis said.

"Don't be angry. I know I can trust you to do the right thing. It's part of the reason I chose you."

"What's the other part?"

As if to change the subject, Abe said, "Have you heard about the Flour Sack Kid hanging around?"

"Around where?" Willis asked, confused by the abrupt change of direction.

"Here. The Bar T. Karn and Posey swear they saw the Kid watching them through his spyglass from up in the trees in the north valley two days ago. And last night Ed says he thought he saw a rider with something over his head right here in the home valley."

Willis forgot all about Laurella Hendershot and the rustlers and everything else.

"Why would the Kid be sneakin' around the Bar T?" He knew the answer but he had to pretend it was a mystery.

"Who the hell knows?" Abe responded. "As if I didn't have enough on my mind with the Wilkes gang and Hendershot and the sale and everything. It's enough to make me think I did something to get the Almighty mad at me."

"Maybe Ed only thought he saw the Kid."

"Did Karn and Posey only think they saw him, too?" Abe pursed his lips in thought. "Odd that he should be nosing around. Surely he's not thinking of robbing me? I've never made a secret of the fact I keep all my money at the bank."

"Who can explain outlaws?"

"You have a point. It stands to reason that the Wilkes gang would have left the territory by now, what with everyone out to treat them to a hemp social after the shoot-out in town. But we had more cows go missing in the past few days, so they must still be around." Abe sighed. "When it rains, it pours, and then it pours some more."

"I won't mention the missing stock to Miss Hendershot."

"Thank you. With any luck she won't notice. She can't possibly expect to count every last head." But Abe did not sound certain of that.

Willis was thinking about the Kid. "Too bad Keever and Ivers got themselves killed. Where's a lawman when we need one?"

"Fred Baxter at the general store asked me if I knew someone who might want the job," Abe revealed. "There aren't any takers as yet."

"No one likes to be a walkin' target."

"True. It takes a gent with a lot of grit to wear a tin star."

"Or someone with a hankerin' to die." It had been Willis' experience that lawmen as a rule lived shorter lives than most everyone else.

"Baxter was wondering if perhaps you were interested."

"If that was a joke, it was in poor taste."

"No joke. The townsmen have a list of candidates — locals who can take over the job right away and do a halfway decent job. Your name is high on their list."

"Hell, I don't know a damn thing about the law," Willis said. The notion was absolutely preposterous.

"Baxter says learning the law is the easy part. It's enforcing it that's the challenge. But you don't need to be a gun hand, like Wild Bill Hickok. All you need is to be able to talk to people and keep calm in a crisis."

"I don't talk much." Willis had a dozen objections and that was only the second.

"You can when you want to. The problem is you haven't wanted to since your mishap."

"Don't tiptoe around it. Call it what it was. My stupidity."

"We all make mistakes," Abe said. "Personally, I admire you for trying to save the stallion. You always did love horses."

"Folks say love is blind and they're right."

"That applies to loving people, not horses," Abe said. "But what you did was commendable."

"What I tried to do."

"It's the trying that counts," Abe declared. "We never accomplish anything in this world without trying. Look at me and the Bar T. If I'd never tried, I wouldn't own one of the best ranches in the territory."

"You won't own it much longer."

"That was cruel," Abe said. "You think I'm happy about it? I'm not. Well, part of me is, the part that loves Elfie, but the part that loves the ranch wants to tell that Texas woman to go on back to Texas. The Bar T is mine, damn it!"

"Told your wife any of this?" Willis asked, overstepping himself but not caring. Abe had brought it on himself.

"Some," Abe said defensively, "but I

186

didn't put my foot down, if that's what you're hinting at. When you're married, you will understand. There's give and take involved. Sometimes the man gives and the woman takes and sometime the woman gives and the man takes."

"You're talkin' Greek," Willis said.

Abe smiled. "You faker. You're the same with people as you were with horses. You care but you won't admit you care because when you care you get hurt more than when you don't care."

"Say that again real slow. You lost me after the second care."

Abe indulged in a rare expletive. "The only one you're fooling is yourself. But that's your right and I won't criticize."

"Thank you." Willis looked for the women but they were in the stable. "How much longer, you reckon?"

"It could be ten minutes. It could be an hour. What say we wait on the porch out of the sun and treat ourselves to more lemonade?"

"No chance of whiskey?"

"I would love one myself but Elfie wouldn't approve. Escorts should not reek of liquor."

"One drink isn't a reek. It's a whiff." But Willis resigned himself to going dry for the duration of his official responsibility.

Abe rested his boots on the rail and looked down the valley. "Do you remember how it was in the old days? In the beginning when there was nothing here but grass and more grass? I took a big risk having that herd brought up. Every last cent I had was invested in those cows. A stampede would have ruined me."

"When we're young risks seem smaller than they are," Willis observed. "It's a miracle most of us live to old age."

"Do you ever wonder why things are the way they are? Why God puts us through so much hardship? Why suffering and misery are our lot in life?"

Willis glanced at his left leg. "I think about it every damn day." He refrained from adding that Abe had no idea what true suffering was like.

"If the sale goes through, you will come visit us in Saint Louis, won't you?"

"Sure." Willis would never set foot east of the Mississippi River.

"Bring some of the others. Charlie would love it. So many fine women, he'd walk around with his mouth hanging open."

"I hope you're happy there, Abe. I really do." In Willis' case, true happiness was as rare as a hen's teeth.

"I'll be with Elfie," Abe said. "When a man is with the woman he loves, he has all he'll ever need." He pointed. "There they are now."

The women had emerged from the stable and were sashaying toward the bunkhouse. Elfie, Willis noted, did most of the sashaying. Laurella Hendershot's stride had none of the enticing sway and bounce of a typical female.

Little Sparrow brought a new pitcher of lemonade. A fly buzzed about the porch but lost interest. Somewhere a cow lowed. Down by the chicken coop, the hens were pecking and scratching. The rooster strutted among them, and when he wasn't strutting, he preened.

"I'll miss this life," Abe said softly.

"It's not too late to change your mind," Willis suggested.

"It was too late the moment I said 'I do' but I didn't realize it at the time. Not that I ever regret saying it. If I had it to do all over again, I would do it the same. I love her that much, Will."

"You're a lucky man, Abe." Secretly Willis did not consider Abe lucky at all.

An hour and ten minutes was the total. Elfie bubbled over with smiles as the women and their shadow came to the porch and she graciously offered her guests more refreshment. But the veiled hat moved as if on a pivot.

"I'd rather have your man give me a tour of the home valley, as you call it. He can take me to the north valley tomorrow and the south valley the day after."

Willis had hoped to have it over in one day, not three. Pushing out of the rocking chair, he limped to the steps. "I'll have the team hitched to the buckboard. Your team must be tuckered out."

"They had ample rest earlier," Hendershot said. "Armando, you will wait here until I return."

"Por favor, Senorita Hendershot," Armando said, and launched into rapid Spanish. The woman from Texas answered in kind. Whatever she said brought a scowl to Armando's swarthy face but he bowed slightly and said in English, "Whatever you want. But I still think it unwise. Your father would agree."

"This is not Texas. There are no Comanches." The veil rose toward Abe. "Have you had any Indian troubles recently, Mr. Tyler?"

"None in ages," Abe said.

"See, Armando? I am perfectly safe. You worry too much."

Willis limped to the buckboard as quickly

as he could to help her up but she climbed on herself and folded her hands in her lap. The veil followed him as he limped around to the other side and pulled himself up. He adjusted his left leg with his hands, then bent for the reins. "How would you like to go about this, ma'am?"

"The important thing is for me to see all the cattle. Can we do it in the buckboard or should we ride?"

"We can do it in the buckboard." Willis avoided looking at the Tylers and flicked the reins. The buckboard was larger than the Bar T's but handled as well as any buckboard could. He drove slowly, racking his brain for things to say.

"You seem uncomfortable, Mr. Lander. Is something the matter?"

"No, ma'am," Willis said. It was a good thing he wasn't fussy about lying because he was doing a lot of it lately. "It's just I've never escorted anyone before."

"Rest easy. I won't be a burden, I promise." Laurella Hendershot paused. "To be honest, I am a bit surprised Mr. Tyler didn't handle this himself. It's customary where I come from."

"You're no more surprised than me," Willis admitted.

They passed the stable and the bunkhouse, where several of the punchers stared in envy. The buckboard hit a rut and the seat bounced and Laurella Hendershot grabbed at her hat as if afraid it would fly off. "Mrs. Tyler has told me a lot about you," she commented.

"There's not that much to say."

"Oh, I don't know. At one time you were the best bronc squeezer in the territory. There wasn't a horse you couldn't break."

"There was one," Willis said.

"You never hurt the horses. You never broke their spirits. You treated them with respect."

Willis said nothing.

"I admire that. How a man treats animals says a lot about the man. I've met many a bronc fighter who spoiled more horses than they tamed."

"The bad ones do. The lazy ones. The busters who don't learn the trade as it should be done. The ones who think beatin' a horse is the same as tamin' one." Talking about his passion made him want to talk more. "My pa reared me to treat every livin' thing as I treat myself. Do unto others, he always said. To animals as well as people. A horse is an animal, sure, but it has feelin's the same as we do. Treat a horse kindly and it will be kindly to you" — he frowned —

"most of the time."

"We could have used you on my pa's ranch. He always complained half his bronc twisters were worthless."

Before Willis could stop himself, he heard himself ask, "What's a Texas gal doin' all the way up here in Wyomin' Territory, anyhow? Last I heard, Texas had enough space for more ranches than Wyomin' has trees."

"Oh, I could have a ranch in Texas if I wanted," Laurella Hendershot said. "But I don't want to."

Since the conversation was going so well, Willis made bold to inquire, "Is your pa leavin' his spread to a brother? Is that how it goes, Miss Hendershot?"

"I'm an only child."

"Oh."

"I want out of Texas, Mr. Lander. I want to live somewhere new — a place where no one knows me or has ever heard of me."

"I never heard of you."

For some reason Laurella Hendershot laughed softly. "I value my privacy. Almost as much as I value my self-respect."

Now she had lost him and Willis grappled for a reply. "You can have as much self-respect as you want in Wyomin'."

Again she laughed. "You're quite the wit,

Mr. Lander. But self-respect doesn't come from outside a person. It comes from inside a person. And it's a lot like teeth in that you never miss it until it's gone."

"Teeth?" Willis was completely perplexed. Texican women could talk rings around a tree.

"Ever had a tooth pulled? You don't miss it until it's gone. My grandma had an entire mouth of false teeth and she used to cry sometimes, she missed her real teeth so much."

"I'd cry, too," Willis said. "Thank God I've still got all mine." He was beginning to like talking to her. She was easy to talk to. But then she brought his world crashing down about him.

"Mrs. Tyler told me about your leg. It's a pity."

A red haze filled Willis' vision and a lump formed in his throat. "It's a hell of a lot more than that, ma'am. Pardon my language."

"You're excused. I would be upset, too, if I lost the full use of one of my legs and my livelihood, besides."

"I get by."

"I'm sorry if I've upset you. And I admire you for that, too — for not lettin' your loss turn you into a wreck. I've seen men drown

194

themselves in bottles over far, far less."

"I'm not all that admirable, ma'am," Willis said. Evidently Elfie had not mentioned anything about the line shack.

"None of us are to ourselves except for those who can't stop lookin' into every mirror they pass. I never saw much to admire about myself — at least, from the age of ten on."

Willis drifted back in time to when he was ten, to when he had dreamed of one day being a stagecoach driver or a patent-medicine salesman. Boys that age sure were silly. "Kids don't know much," he said.

"They know when they are treated differently from everyone else. They know when they are outcasts."

"I suppose."

"Don't you ever feel like an outcast — as if your leg sets you apart from everyone else?"

"It *does* set me apart, ma'am," Willis said, struggling to control his temper. "There are things I can't do that other people can. I'm not an outcast so much as I am less than I should be."

" 'Less than I should be,' " Laurella Hendershot repeated. "That about sums up most of my life."

Willis suspected she was looking at him,

waiting for him to say something, so he responded, "You're about to buy your own ranch. Your life can't have been all that rotten."

"If you only knew," Hendershot said quietly. "And only part of the purchase money is my money. My parents are helpin' out with the rest. They're against me movin' so far from home but it's for the best for everyone — me most of all." She paused. "But to get back to why I admire you, would you like to know the most important reason?"

"Sure," Willis said.

"Stop the buckboard."

"Ma'am?"

"Stop the buckboard. I don't want you veerin' off the road and wreckin'. I've had that effect."

Completely confused, Willis did as she requested. "What difference does stoppin' make?"

"I want to show you why I admire how you have handled your leg," Laurella Hendershot said. She took a deep breath and lifted her veil.

CHAPTER 11

Willis had never been struck speechless before. He had been confused a lot, as he was until the woman from Texas lifted her veil. He had often been stumped by things that other people seemed to savvy. But he had never been as astonished as he was at that moment, so astonished his mouth fell open and a bewildering array of emotions buffeted him like the strong winds before a thunderstorm.

Laurella Hendershot sat completely still, her eyes slightly averted, apparently waiting for him to say something. Her hands were folded in her lap, her fingers clenched so tightly her knuckles were white. When he did not say anything, she said, "Well? What do you think?"

Willis didn't know what to think so he blurted, "How?"

"When I was ten I was out ridin' with my mother and a rattler spooked my mare. I was thrown off. Before I could get out of the way, the mare kicked at the rattler and hit me."

"Dear Lord," Willis breathed.

"Repulsive, aren't I?"

"No, not at all," Willis said, and fought down a shudder. "Half your face is right pretty."

And it was. The right half of Laurella Hendershot's face was smooth and unblemished, the right half of her mouth full as ripe cherries, her right cheek as round as a walnut, her eye a striking shade of blue. The left half of her face, however, was something that would give children nightmares and make adults queasy. Her left cheek had been caved in by the mare's hoof, leaving a sunken hollow laced with lines, as if the skin had partially withered and died. The left half of her mouth was grotesquely twisted, the left half of her lips flattened as thin as a flapjack. Her nose had a crook in it. Her left eye, as a result of the hollow where her cheek had been, drooped lower than her right eye.

The effect was shocking: as beautiful as could be on the right, as horrible as could be on the left. Willis blinked and tore his gaze away and frantically sought to collect his wits. "When you were ten, you say?"

198

Laurella Hendershot lowered the veil. Her chin dipped and she nodded. "My whole life was changed from that day on. I didn't know it at first. I was so young, I thought things would go on as they had before."

Willis had to clear his throat to say, "They didn't?"

"Little girls are treated special. Their parents fawn over them. Other folks treat them as princesses. I was used to that — used to smiles and praise and love. So when I started to notice the new looks, it was like being stabbed in the heart."

"The looks?"

"It was in their eyes. Deep down in their depths, they thought I was hideous." When Willis went to comment, she held up her hand. "No. Don't make excuses for them. You weren't there. You didn't experience it." Now she was the one who had to cough. "People I had known since I was old enough to toddle, people I thought loved me with a love that was boundless, looked at me as if I were their worst imaginin' come to life."

"You're bein' too harsh," Willis said. "You were little. Naturally you would think that."

"Not harsh enough. I wasn't so young I couldn't tell the difference between how they looked at me before I was thrown and how they looked at me after. To them I wasn't the same girl. Not even to my mother. Before the accident she called me Sunshine all the time. It was her nickname for me. After the accident, she never did."

"People get hurt in accidents every day," Willis said absently.

"But people do not get disfigured every day," Laurella Hendershot replied. "People do not lose the use of their legs every day."

Glancing at his knee, Willis was silent.

"You know what I went through, what it did to me." The veil turned away from him. "I wanted to curl up and die. I must have cried myself to sleep every night for a year. I broke the mirror in my room and the mirror in the parlor and told my parents if they replaced the mirrors, I would break the new mirrors as well. When people came to visit, I refused to go down to see them. I wanted nothing to do with anyone. For years I was left pretty much to myself. Oh, my mother and father made it a point to spend as much time as they could with me, but I wouldn't hardly talk to them, and when they would suggest we go do this or that, I always said no. I refused to go to school. They were mad, but I couldn't take the looks and the teasin'. Girls who had been my best friends wanted nothin' to do with me. They couldn't stand bein' near me. A few boys took to callin' me the Monster."

"Damn them," Willis said, and quickly amended, "Sorry about my language, ma'am."

"Call me Laurella. Please."

"All right. But only if you call me Will."

"Do you understand now why I admire you? Like me, you've been afflicted. But you've gotten on with your life. You haven't let it change you."

Willis thought of the line shack and was ashamed. "You're makin' me out to be more than I am."

Laurella did not seem to hear him. "I couldn't go anywhere without people pointin' and whisperin'. Word about me spread. Everyone in Texas must have heard about the pretty girl who turned ugly. It go so, I started wearin' veils, even around the house." She paused. "Perhaps now you can also understand why I want to buy a ranch in Wyomin' Territory. No one here has heard of me. The only ones who know about my face are the Tylers, and now you. I can start a whole new life for myself."

"You're fixin' to wear that veil outdoors the rest of your days?"

Laurella turned back toward him. "Of course. Indoors, mostly, too. If I don't, the same thing that happened in Texas will happen here."

"Thank you for confidin' in me." It struck Willis that she must think he was special, to share her secret, and then it struck him that she thought he was special because of his knee, because he had been permanently scarred just like she had. They shared a bond no one else did. Somehow that made him feel all warm inside.

"It wasn't easy," Luarella said. "In fact, it was about the hardest thing I've had to do and I've had to do a lot of hard things."

Willis picked up the reins, lowered them, then picked them up again. "Should we keep goin' or sit here and talk?"

"I'd rather sit a bit if you don't mind."

"Not at all." Willis stared at the blue sky sprinkled with puffy white clouds and at nearby cattle grazing contentedly. Then he said, "I was luckier than you, Laurella. I didn't get hurt until I was a lot older."

"Yes, you were luckier."

"And you're right. I know how you felt. Like you, I wanted nothin' to do with the world. But this past week has made me see that life ain't much worth livin' if we hide from it."

"That's quite poetical," Laurella said.

"I wasn't tryin' to be."

"You're scrupulously honest. I admire that, too."

Willis was glad when Laurella stopped talking because the more she talked, the more confounded he became. Yet when a couple of minutes had gone by, he grew nervous with her silence and said, "So."

"So," Laurella said.

"Should we keep goin' now?"

The veil was fixed on him for a while before Laurella said, "Yes, I suppose we better. Thank you."

Willis got the buckboard rolling, but more slowly. He was in no hurry. The sun on his skin, the wind in his face, the thud of hooves, the creak of the seat — he was noticing things he had not noticed earlier.

From under the seat, Laurella produced a handbag, and from the handbag, she produced a tally book and a pencil. "May I ask you a few questions, Will?"

"Ask whatever you want," Willis said, his skin growing warmer.

"If you had the wherewithal, would you buy the Bar T?"

"In a heartbeat," Willis said. "It's a fine ranch, ma'am. I mean, Laurella. Grass, water, timber — the Bar T has all you could want."

"Any of the cattle diseased?"

Willis glanced sharply at her. "That's near an insult. Abe takes pride in his cows. He takes pride in everything he does, everything he has. There hasn't ever been a sick cow here. I'd swear it on a stack of Bibles."

"Any Indian trouble?"

"Back in the beginnin'," Willis said. "The Blackfeet stole some horses. The Bannocks helped themselves to some cows. But none of the hands ever lost their scalps. Abe is on real good terms with the Shoshones. One winter he sent ten beeves to their chief when the tribe was goin' hungry on account of the snow and cold."

"Much in the way of predator problems?"

"Oh, a griz kills a cow every blue moon or so. There's a mountain lion with a hungry tooth for horseflesh but I aim to settle with him myself. And a while back we had a wolf that thought it had the right to help itself to our calves but Abe brought in a hunter who turned it into a wolfskin rug."

"How about rustlers?"

"Every place has them, I reckon," Willis hedged, as Elfie wanted him to do, but he did not like it. He did not like it one little bit.

"Have any ever bothered the Bar T?"

Willis stared straight ahead. He dared not look at her veil. "About ten years ago there were a couple of brand blotters who reckoned the Bar T had too many cows and decided they should have the extras. They were sneakin' south with thirty head when we caught up with 'em and held a lynchin' bee. We left 'em lookin' up through the cottonwood leaves as a warnin' to anyone else tempted to use a runnin' iron on our cattle."

"My father had to do the same five or six times before the rustlers in our neck of the woods decided it was healthier to change climates."

Laurella asked more questions, impressing Willis with her knowledge of ranching and cattle. He answered each query as honestly as he was able. But he could not stop thinking about the one he had not answered honestly.

They came to the southeast end of the home valley and Laurella asked if he would swing west and follow the tree line around to the ranch buildings.

"It will be rough. We'll be bouncin' and up and down until our —" Willis stopped. He had almost said "backsides are raw."

"I don't mind. I'm not fragile. I don't break easy."

Willis cut overland, slowing the team so the seat would not jounce as much. Laurella counted cows and marked her tally book. They were halfway along the return loop when she closed the tally book and said, "Why don't we stop a while?"

"Whatever you want."

A convenient patch of shade beckoned. Willis brought the buckboard in close to the trees, carefully got down, and came around to help Laurella. Only she had climbed down herself and stood with her hands on her hips and her back arched. He quickly looked away from her bosom.

"It's so beautiful here," Laurella said. "Those are the Tetons way off to the west, aren't they?"

"Sure are. Some days you can see them better. It's hazy today."

"Why haven't you ever married, Will?"

"Ma'am?" Willis blurted.

"You heard me. I'm curious. Are you one of those bachelors who refuses to say I do? Or is it something else?"

"I never gave it much thought," Willis said, his skin prickling as if he had a heat rash. Pulling at his collar, he limped closer to the trees. A shadow crawled across the ground toward him from the rear and a warm hand pressed his arm.

"I'm sorry. Have I embarrassed you?"

"No."

"You're a terrible liar. I shouldn't have

been so forward. It's just that we have so much in common." Laurella removed her hand and came around so she faced him. "My social graces are not what they should be."

"You are as fine as fine can be," Willis said.

"Not in every respect." Laurella raised a finger and touched her veil. "But it's awful kind of you to lie for my sake."

If lies made him kind, Willis thought, then he was the kindest person on the planet right then. "You don't give yourself enough credit."

"To the contrary," Laurella said. "I refuse to kid myself. All I need do is look in a mirror to disabuse myself of the notion of —"

"The notion of what?"

"Nothin'. Silly female chatter. Pay me no mind, Will. Sometimes my feelin's get the better of me." Laurella toyed with a button on the front of her dress. "Frankly, I surprise myself. I haven't talked so openly with a man, any man, ever."

"Well," Willis said, and shifted his weight from one foot to the other.

Laurella looked up at the clouds. Her chin was visible, the half that was perfect and the half that resembled lined leather. "The sky isn't the same here. It seems higher. Like there's more of it."

"Maybe there is," Willis said, unable to take his gaze off her chin. He did the next moment, though, when a figure stepped from behind a pine with a pair of pistols pointed at them. In pure instinct Willis grabbed Laurella and swung her behind him. "You!" he exclaimed.

Laurella's fingernails bit into his arm. "Who is he?"

"Isn't this sweet?" the Flour Sack Kid said. "A lunkhead and his lady."

"What do you want?" Laurella demadned. "If it's money you're after, I don't have any with me."

"Stifle yourself, woman." The green eyes under the flour sack were fixed on Willis. "All I'm after is the pleasure of your company."

"Lay a hand on me and I'll have every man in the territory after you," Laurella vowed. "This might not be Texas but abusin' a woman is as vile as can be."

"Good Lord," the Kid said. "You think awful highly of yourself, don't you? You must be pretty under that silly veil. Why don't you show me?"

"I'll be damned if I will."

"Such language," the Flour Sack Kid said, and thumbed back the hammers on his black-handled revolvers. "You'll show me or

I'll shoot your friend here in his good leg."

"No," Willis said.

"Stay out of this. She's the one who got snippy."

"No," Willis repeated.

Laurella started to step in front of him but Willis held her back. "I don't want him to shoot you, Will."

"He won't."

The Kid snickered. "Don't be too sure, lunkhead."

"Stop callin' me that."

"The veil," the Kid said to Laurella. "Or have the lunkhead do it for you. Either way, I'm entitled."

"You son of a bitch," Willis said.

"Don't you have that backward, lunkhead?" The Flour Sack Kid wagged a pistol at the veil. "Today would be nice."

"You don't want to see me."

"The hat, lady."

"Really, you don't."

To Willis the Kid said, "Ever notice how talkin' to a woman is like talkin' to a wall?" Then, to Laurella, he said, "Did I hear you say you're from Texas? Don't they have desperadoes down there? Or does everyone walk around with a flour sack over his head? When a man wearin' a sack and wavin' pistols threatens to shoot you, you should believe him."

"You threatened to shoot me," Willis said.

Laurella balled her fists. "I hate you," she told the Kid. "If I had a pistol of my own, I would be the one doin' the shootin'." Both her arms rose and she removed her hat with a sharp, defiant gesture. "There. Happy now?"

"Good God." The Flour Sack Kid took a step back. His pistols drooped and his green eyes widened. "You're —"

Willis hit him. He took a quick limping step and planted his right fist about where the Kid's jaw should be. His knuckles connected solidly and the Kid tottered and fell onto his back. Drawing his Colt, Willis said, "I hate you, too."

The Flour Sack Kid rose on his elbows. "No, you don't." He made no attempt to aim his pistols or even to lift them. "You only think you do."

"Shoot him," Laurella said.

As much as Willis yearned to, he didn't.

"Bloodthirsty fillies, these Texas gals," the Kid declared. "Does she want to chop off my fingers and toes for keepsakes?"

"Take his guns."

Willis shoved his Colt back into its holster and bent and extended an arm. "I hate you so much."

"You would like to," the Flour Sack Kid said. Chuckling, he sat up and slid his revolvers into their holsters, then placed a palm to the flour sack about where his jaw would be. "That was some punch. A little harder and you would have broke half my teeth."

"Did I break any at all?" Willis asked.

The flour sack wriggled from within. "Not a one."

"Damn." Willis pulled the Kid to his feet. "I forgot. You always did have an iron jaw. Must come from all your clean livin'."

The Kid chuckled louder and the sack swung toward Laurella. "Did you hear him, ma'am? He poked fun at me. There's hope yet."

"There's no hope," Willis said.

"I don't understand." Laurella looked from Willis to the sack and back again. "Why didn't you shoot him? I would have shot him."

"Bloodthirsty as hell," the Kid said. He was staring at her face. Specifically, the left half of her face.

"You're a badman, aren't you? Why else go around in that sack?"

"Why do you go around in that veil?" the Kid retorted.

"Are you sayin' that you're like me?" Laurella asked.

"No. You're a heap prettier." The Kid winked at her but she did not react. "You were right the first time. I'm an outlaw. I deserve to be shot or hung or both."

"You sure do," Willis said. "What in God's name are you doin' here? In broad daylight, no less."

"What else? Lookin' for you. I've been spyin' on the ranch for days now, waitin' for a chance to talk to you. Some of the punchers saw me a day or so ago, I think."

"No think about it." Willis sighed and glanced toward the distant buildings. "So talk before we're spotted. I won't help if they throw a noose around your neck."

"Yes, you will," the Kid said confidently, and winked a second time at Laurella. "He talks mean but he's a kitten."

"You two know each other?"

"Nothin' gets past you, does it, Texas?" the Kid said. "Oh, you can put your hat back on. I'm sorry I had you take it off. But it's a shame you hide the pretty half."

"I wish I had a gun," Laurella said.

Willis had to brace his left leg to stoop and pick up her hat. Brushing it off, he said, "This is the Flour Sack Kid. He's been robbin' folks since shortly after the war. Every marshal and sheriff in the territory is on the lookout for him. He went to Colorado for a spell but didn't have the sense to stay."

"I got homesick."

"We don't have a home anymore," Willis said. "Ma went to her reward long ago, if you'll recollect, and sis died about a year after you left us. Uncle Jessup, last I heard, was in California, workin' as a clerk."

"He never did have any dash," the Kid said.

"Is that what you call robbin' folks? Dash? Hereabouts most call it despicable, or worse." Willis sadly shook his head. "You should have given it up and gone straight years ago. Now it can only end one way."

"We all die."

"Not at the end of a rope." Willis was growing mad. "Not on the wrong side of the law. Not on the wrong side of the Good Book."

"Oh, please. Did you get religion while I was gone? You've had no more truck with the parson than I have. We both went our own path, the devil be damned."

"Just go," Willis said.

"I only wanted to see how you were," the Kid explained, "maybe spend a night around a campfire swappin' stories about how it used to be. They were happy times back then."

"They were," Willis agreed, "but they don't excuse what you've done. Go away and don't come near me ever again."

"If that's what you really want," the Flour Sack Kid said. When Willis did not respond, the Kid slowly turned and melted into the underbrush. He looked back only once, and gave a little wave.

"I hate him," Willis said.

"How many people know your brother is an outlaw?"

Willis was thinking of the many happy times before his mother died. Thinking of the first time they had hunted and the first time they had fished and his first pony. "He sounds young, doesn't he? Younger than me. So I guess it's only natural you reckon he's my brother. But he's not." Willis' chest was tight and his nose felt congested. "The Flour Sack Kid is my pa."

CHAPTER 12

Willis did not eat much at supper. Gus grumbled that his cooking was never appreciated but Willis had no appetite. Afterward, he lay on his bunk staring at the ceiling and waiting for Abe to show up at the bunkhouse or for Reuben Marsh to come in and tell him Abe wanted to see him. But Abe never came and there was no summons.

He was the last to fall asleep. He tried, truly tried, but he could not get comfortable enough. He refused to fool himself into thinking it was the bed. It was him. Deep down inside he was a boiling cauldron of twisted emotions.

Eventually, though, his exhausted body refused to be denied, and Willis slept fitfully until the crow of the cock. He was first up, first at the washbasin, first out of the bunkhouse. He opened the stable doors and brought out the team and the harness and had the buckboard ready before the sun fully rose.

Laurella had told Willis she wanted to start early for the north valley. His idea of early was first light. He did not know what her idea of early was but he deemed it best to be ready, just in case. It proved to be smart. Not ten minutes after he was done hitching the team, the front door to the big house opened and out came the Tylers and their guest from Texas and her protector, Armando.

Willis went up the path to the porch. He could not bring himself to look at her. He nodded at Abe and said, "Mornin'."

"Good morning, Will. Miss Hendershot tells us you did a marvelous job yesterday. She was extremely pleased."

"I did my best," Willis said quietly.

Elfie bestowed a warm smile. "I knew I picked the right man for the job. I expect the same performance today."

Laurella was holding a bundle. "I've brought food for our midday meal. Chicken and bread and apples and more."

"I expect I'll be hungry by then," Willis said.

"Well then, off you go," Elfie said. "Remember, my dear. If you have any questions Mr. Lander can't answer, any questions at all, bring them up with Abe and me. We're at your beck and call."

"So far I've liked what I've seen," Laurella said.

"Excellent." Elfie was as subtle as an avalanche. "A few more days and we can sign the papers and I'm off to Saint Louis."

Laurella turned to Armando. "Stay close to the house until I return. I can't say when that will be."

"I am to stay by you at all times, senorita."

"Must we go through this again?" Laurella asked. "I'm perfectly safe. Nothin' happened to me yesterday. Nothin' will happen to me today."

Willis contained himself until they were almost to the buckboard. Then he said out of the side of his mouth, "You didn't tell them."

"You thought I would?"

Until that moment Willis had never truly hated veils. "I'd hoped you wouldn't. But I wouldn't blame you if you did."

"We're friends, aren't we?" Laurella placed the bundle in the bed.

"I hadn't thought of it like that," Willis said, "but yes, I reckon we are."

"There are many ways to think of it. The important thing is which one you want. I was up most of the night and I came to peace with myself about which one I want."

Willis wanted to kick something. Here they had not started out yet and already he was confused. He helped her up, climbed on, and gave a holler and a flick of the reins. No one watched from the stable or the bunkhouse.

In the yellow glow of dawn, the cattle were astir. Some grazed. Some had their legs curled under them, chewing. A few late calves frolicked in the only play their short lives would know. The green grass glistened with dew. On the surrounding slopes the timber stood in shadowed ranks. Way to the west reared the mountains, crowned by the Tetons. The air was crisp and clear and there was no dust yet.

"Why?" Laurella asked.

Willis tried to associate her question with a reason for asking it, and couldn't. "Why what?"

"Why did your pa turn to the owlhoot trail?"

"It was after the war," Willis answered. "He had gone off to fight for the Union. He'd known a black family once, back in Indiana, and he wanted to do his part to free all blacks. My ma got a few letters from him, then nothin'. We all thought he was dead until he showed up on our doorstep."

"Go on," Laurella coaxed when Willis stopped.

"My ma was so happy for a while. Happy, but sick. Consumption, the doctor said. All he could do was give her laudanum. We had no money. No money at all. And the doctor had to be paid and the laudanum had to be bought." Willis lost his interest in the beautiful morning. "So my pa went out and stole some money."

"Oh my," Laurella said.

"He emptied out the little bit of flour we had left and took the flour sack with him," Willis related, "and when he came back, the flour sack had holes in it that had not been in it when he left, and he had twenty-two dollars. I'll never forget how much because he counted it at the table in front of us kids."

"How bad was it for your mother?"

"She just sort of shrunk away. Her skin became a sickly gray. Her face was as white as a picket fence except for her eyes. The laudanum helped with the pain for a while but then it didn't do any good and she was in pain all the time. Pain in her back and hips, mostly, until it spread. She couldn't go, you know, in the outhouse, and toward the end she got all puffy and couldn't move, couldn't lift her arms more than a tiny bit, and she would scream and scream and pass out and then wake up and scream and scream some more."

"Dear God in heaven."

"Do you really think so? I used to. Before my ma died. But after what she went through, I couldn't look up at the sky without bein' mad. How could God let someone suffer like that? I haven't been sure of nothin' since."

"Your pa — how did he take it?"

"He was crushed. I caught him cryin' a few times. Then he got mad. Madder than me. He said ma died because we were poor — that if we had more money, we might have saved her."

"There's no cure for consumption."

"I know. I think my pa knew, too. But like I said, he was mad, and crazy with grief. There he was, a soldier who had served his country, and no one offered to help us except the doctor. I guess that's why he turned bad for good."

"He kept on robbin', I take it."

"Not a lot at first. Enough to feed us and clothe us. He always wore the flour sack so no one would know who he was, and soon folks were callin' him the Flour Sack Kid. He thought it was funny, him being mistook for a kid. Came a time when he up and left us. We were old enough to make it on our own, he said. That, and he did not want us to be blamed in any way for what he was doin'. So off he went. It wasn't long after that my sister came down with consumption, too, and within a year she was dead."

"A lot of people die of it."

"People die from a lot of things. But I'll be one of the few who can say his pa was hung by the neck until dead."

"You're gettin' ahead of yourself."

Willis looked at the veil for the first time that morning. "He's overdue to be caught. No one can go around stealin' as long as he has without payin' the price. Sooner or later the odds always catch up with you."

"He's lasted this long," Laurella said. "Don't underestimate him."

"Now who is bein' kind? I'd rather not think of him at all but how can I not when I'm his own flesh and blood?"

"He must love you very much."

Willis hauled on the reins much too hard, much harder than anyone ever should, and when the buckboard stopped he turned in the seat and demanded, "How can you be so cruel?"

"He came all the way back from Colorado just to see you again," Laurella said, unfazed. "He would not do that if he did not care."

"If he cared, he would have stopped robbin' folks when my sister and I asked him to after that first time. If he cared, he would throw that flour sack in a river and start a new life."

"We get set in our ways," Laurella said.

"Why are you defendin' him? Why speak up for a man who chose the wrong road and stayed on it even though he knew it was wrong and those he cared for wanted him to take the straight and narrow? What is he to you that you like him so much?"

"He is nothin' to me and I don't like or dislike him. I like you."

"Honestly, if I lived to be a thousand I will never —" Willis' tongue froze in his mouth. He blinked at the veil, and when he could talk, he said, "You like me?"

"You."

"Like me as in like or as in something else?"

"I couldn't sleep last night for thinkin' about you."

"Oh," Willis said. "Oh."

"Sorry if that was too forward or if it shocked you. But I enjoy bein' with you. I enjoy talkin' to you. You've seen my face and you still talk to me like I'm normal, and that means more to me than you can imagine."

"Oh," Willis said again.

"You're upset, aren't you? Someone as hideous as me sayin' what I'm sayin' — it's stupid of me."

"Don't you ever talk about yourself like that again." Willis raised the reins and clucked to the team and tried to organize the jumble in his head but it was hopeless. He had never had such a jumble. When they came to the turnoff to the north valley, he took it without paying much attention to what he was doing. He was too far inside himself.

It took slightly over an hour by buckboard. Several times they passed Bar T hands who smiled or waved or both.

Laurella took out her tally book and her pencil and counted cows, the veil rising and dipping as she looked at the cows and then down at the tally book.

Willis drove for as long as he could stand it, and when he could not stand it anymore, he brought the buckboard to another stop. The veil shifted toward him. He coughed and said, "I lied to you."

"How?"

"Well, it wasn't exactly a lie but it wasn't the whole truth, either, and my insides feel as if a knife is twistin' into me."

"How?" Laurella repeated, her voice very

tiny and fragile.

"About the rustlers. There's a gang, the Wilkes gang — they've been helpin' themselves to Bar T cows. There was a gunfight in Cottonwood and they killed the marshal and a Bar T hand, and later they killed another Bar T hand who went with the posse. The deputy was killed too but a grizzly was to blame, not Varner Wilkes or those cousins of his or the Southerner."

"That's it?" Laurella said when he did not say anything else.

"That's enough. Eflie and Abe were worried if you knew it would sour the sale. They asked me not to say anything unless you asked but you never asked and I couldn't take not tellin' you." Willis had got it all out and slumped back, no longer tense. He waited for her to say something and instead heard the last thing he expected. "Are you laughin'?"

"Call it a loud smile."

"It was important to me and you're laughin'."

"Do you know what it means? What you just did?"

"No. Yes. Maybe." Willis resumed driving. "It means Abe and Elfie will be mad at me if we tell them."

"Then we won't tell them. We will have

two secrets. Secrets only we share. That makes them special."

"You're plumb wonderful," Willis blurted.

Laurella did not reply and she did not count cows, either. She sat with her arms clasped to her bosom.

Willis began whistling. For a while he forgot about his leg and the brace and everything, or almost everything.

The north valley was not as long or as straight as the home valley. The green grass of the valley floor twisted and turned like a winding garter snake for five miles from end to end. Timber was low down on the slopes. The creek that nourished the grass flowed on the north side, a stick toss from the trees.

Willis brought the rattling buckboard around another bend. To the northwest were more cowboys.

"We could stop early for our meal," Laurella suggested.

Across a strip of grass was a pool overlooked by cottonwoods. There were fish in the pool. Willis had been here before, back when he took a regular turn riding herd if there were no broncs to break. He left the road and they rolled across the flat cushion of grass into the shade of the cottonwoods. He stopped the buckboard and climbed down and limped around to help Laurella down. This time she waited for him to help her. Her body was full and warm. The veil brushed his chest as her feet touched the ground.

"Let me get the bundle," she said.

Willis limped to the edge of the pool. The water was as clear as the air. Several fish were in the middle, suspended in the current. "If I had line and a hook we could have fish, too."

Laurella moved to a tall cottonwood, sank to her knees, and opened the bundle. She set out the chicken and the bread and the apples and slices of cherry pie. "I hope this will do."

Willis looked at her and at the pool and at the food. "I have never been happier."

"Come." Laurella patted the grass next to her. "Don't be shy. I'm shy enough for both of us. This can't be happenin' and yet it is."

"Appears to be, huh?" Willis said. He sat, placed his callused hands on his knee, and admired how the surface of the pool reflected the sun like a burnished mirror. "It's real yet it's not real."

"It can't be both."

Willis thought she was grinning but he could not tell for the veil. "Take off your hat," he said softly.

"I'd rather not."

"Take off the hat. I want to look into your eyes."

"My eye, you mean. The other one isn't for looking at." Laurella's fingers fluttered to the hat but she did not take it off. "I'm scared."

"You're a Texan. I heard Texans weren't ever afraid."

"I'm afraid of myself. I'm afraid of you. I'm afraid like I have never been afraid of anythin'."

"Off," Willis said.

Laurella slowly removed the hat and slowly laid it down. She was kneeling so her right side was to him, and she shifted so none of the left half of her face could be seen. "I guess this isn't so bad."

"You're beautiful."

"Half of me, maybe. The other half would spoil your meal. It spoils mine and it's my face."

"Turn so I can see both halves."

Laurella's throat moved. "I can't. It's too soon. This is hard enough. Can't we take small steps before we take big steps?"

"Small steps then," Willis said, and helped himself to a piece of chicken. He bit down hungrily; chicken had never tasted so delicious.

Laurella took a small piece and nibbled.

"You're not hungry?"

"When I take big bites I can feel the other half. The skin is so tight, like leather after a rain, I can feel it stretch. I don't want to feel the other half right now."

"It will take gettin' used to," Willis said.

The sun was bright, the pool was bright, and the leaves of the cottonwoods were bright. They ate and watched some cows and some cows watched them.

Willis was fit to burst, he ate so much. "So this is what it's like to live? I'd forgotten."

"I'm afraid to live."

"You're afraid of your shadow today," Willis teased, grinning. "But it makes more sense to be afraid when you're at the top of the steps, not at the bottom."

"It will be a long climb," Laurella agreed. She forgot herself and looked squarely at him. "Are you sure, Will? Are you absolutely and completely sure?"

The left half did not have the effect it had the day before. Willis smiled and gazed into her good eye and answered, "I haven't been sure since that day in the corral but I'm as sure as I'm sittin' here."

Luarella looked away again. "We're movin' too fast. Either that or I'm dreamin'. I should pinch myself and wake up."

"Pinch both of us," Willis said.

"You'll change your mind. You'll wake up tomorrow and wonder what in God's name you were thinkin', and that will be fine because it's more than I ever thought could happen and a day or two of illusion is better than none."

"I'm not rightly sure I know what an illusion is but I do know one thing." Willis placed his hand on hers.

"Oh, Will," Laurella said, and the right half of her face flushed red.

"You can slap me if you want."

Laurella laughed. "I should beat you."

"That would be somethin' to see."

"This is the happiest I've been since I was ten. Maybe the happiest I've ever been. Thank you."

"I should be thankin' you. You forget. I haven't exactly been up to my neck in females."

"You better not have been." Laurella flinched as if she had been pricked by a pin, and exclaimed, "Oh my! I felt a twinge. A real twinge."

"All we've done is hold hands."

"I know, I know," Laurella said. "I'm gettin' ahead of myself. Or maybe I'm catchin' up."

"If that made sense, I'm a heifer."

"I hope not!" Laurella blushed darker. "Goodness. Will you listen to me? Women must be hussies at heart."

"You wouldn't know how to be a hussy if you wanted to," Willis said.

"I might surprise you. All women have a naughty streak. Some lock it up and never let it out. Others let it run wild. I suspect I'll be somewhere in the middle."

"I reckon the middle will be wild enough for me. I'm an infant yet."

Willis leaned back and glanced about himself in disbelief. He gazed at her and an ache he had long denied would no longer be denied. Suddenly he felt hot. Easing onto his good knee, he moved on his hands and the good knee to the pool and dipped a hand in. The water was cool and welcome.

Laurella came up beside him and knelt with her right side toward him. She, too, cupped her palm, but to drink, not to cool herself. "The Bar T has a lot more water than my pa's ranch, and a lot more prime grazin' ground. I could have twice as many cows as Abe does."

"You aim to be the Cattle Queen of the West?"

"I take the business end serious," Laurella said. "But listen to me, will you? Business at a moment like this. You would think I've never been by a pool under a cottonwood with a man before."

"Have you?"

"Oh, every day and twice on Sundays." Laurella grinned at him but was careful not to turn her face too far.

"Since I'm being so honest today, I might as well tell you I don't know how to go about this. What I should do and what I shouldn't. What I should say and what I shouldn't. It's a mite more complicated than folks let on."

"It's like learnin' to ride," Laurella said. "You make mistakes but you keep ridin' until you get it right."

Willis had a thought that made him hotter. He splashed more water on his face and neck and drank a few handfuls.

"We're gettin' ahead of ourselves, aren't we? Maybe I should put my hat back on."

"It would please me if you didn't."

"I'm not used to being without it, except at home with my ma and pa. I'm afraid there's so much I'm not used to."

"Makes two of us." Willis placed his wet hand on her wet hand. "If Elfie could see us now, she'd have kittens. This wasn't what she had in mind when she asked me to be your escort."

"She can have all the kittens she wants.

You're a marvelous escort."

"I must be comin' down with something. I'd swear I have a fever." Willis removed his hat and lowered his whole head into the pool. Goose bumps broke out all over. A fish was so close he could swear he could reach out and touch it. Unfurling, he sat up and shook his head from side to side, shedding drops. He smiled at Laurella, but she was not there. Fear brought him upright but she was only putting on her hat. "So much for pleasin' me."

"We have company comin'," Laurella said.

Three cowboys were trotting toward the pool. Willis recognized Charlie Weaver, Bob Ashlon, and a new hand he had seen around but had not met yet. "They're sure in a hurry."

Charlie Weaver motioned as he drew rein. "Will! We just found a couple of dead cows. You've got to come see."

"Was it the griz or the mountain lion?" Willis asked.

"Neither. It was the Wilkes gang."

CHAPTER 13

"This was mean," Bob Ashlon said.

The dead cows were in the timber a hundred yards in from the grass. Both their throats had been slit. One was on its side with its tongue lying like a limp washcloth over its lower jaw. The other had collapsed on its belly and its head was twisted so that its wide, glazed eyes seemed to be staring in appeal at the sky.

"They went this way," Charlie Weaver mentioned, pointing at where hooves had churned the soil.

Willis had left the buckboard at the tree line and limped in. Laurella had walked at his side, and every few yards, her arm had brushed his. Now she squatted and touched the cow with its eyes on the heavens.

"In Texas we shoot people who would do this."

The prints revealed there had been two rustlers, not four as Willis expected, and that they had led a half dozen cattle off to the north. He made up his mind so quickly, it half startled him. "Lend me your horse, pard."

Charlie Weaver was his best friend but that was asking a lot. "What for? You're not thinkin' of goin' after the buzzards without tellin' Abe first?"

"This was done about sunrise," Willis estimated. The pools of blood had a dry sheen but were not yet completely dry. "They can't have gotten far with six cows." Not when the timber thickened considerably ahead.

"Abe would be happy as can be if we caught them," Bob Ashlon said.

Willis was not doing it for Abe. "Lend me your sorrel," he repeated.

"If we've got this to do," Charlie said, "then we do it together, like in the old days." He looked at the new cowboy. "Rafe, lend him your cayuse and stay with the lady until we get back."

"Can't he stay and I go?"

"Abe put me in charge in the north valley until we're relieved," Charlie said, "so it's your horse and no guff, and I need it a minute ago."

"I wasn't givin' you guff," Rafe said, but he was not terrifically happy. Swinging down, he held out the reins to Willis. "Watch my saddlebags. Half the things I own in this world are in them."

"I won't let them come to harm." Willis gripped the saddle horn with both hands and swung up. He bent and slid his left boot into the stirrup, then glanced at Laurella Hendershot. "I won't go if you say not to."

"If we don't do it now, they may do this again after I've bought the ranch." Laurella straightened. "No one does this to my cows and lives."

Charlie Weaver pushed his hat back on his head. "Are all Texas gals like you, ma'am?"

"Most, I reckon," Laurella said from under her veil. "We won't be imposed on and we don't take sass and Lord help the man who doesn't treat us like ladies."

"I might just move there if I ever get into a marryin' mood," Charlie said. "How do Texas gals feel about Wyomin' cowboys?"

"If a cowboy can ride and rope and shoot and takes off his hat when he meets a lady, he has all the qualifications most Texas women look for."

"Your social life can wait," Willis said to his friend, and clucked to the claybank. He assumed the lead, riding at a brisk walk, the tracks easy to follow. When the trees thickened, he threaded through them with skill.

He thought he had lost it but it was coming back to him.

Charlie Weaver cleared his throat. "Mind if I ask you a question?"

"Yes."

"Did you get up on the wrong side of the bunk or is it what I think it is?"

"We won't talk about my social life, either," Willis said.

After a few suitable seconds, Charlie declared, "I would swear I was awake."

"I'm out to shoot someone and it could just as well be a blockhead with eyes like a hawk."

"It wasn't my eyes so much as my ears," Charlie said. "Either you are comin' down with a cold or you talk different to her than you do to anyone else."

"I said we won't talk about it."

"And we won't. I was just marvelin' out loud. It ain't every day the world turns upside down."

Despite himself, Willis grinned. "You're no more puzzled than me. I'm not rightly sure how it came about. It snuck up on me when I wasn't lookin'."

"Are you talkin' about your social life or is it one of those cows we're talkin' about, because I would swear your social life was taboo?"

"You're a sorry human being."

"I take after a bronc buster I know."

Bob Ashlon said from behind Charlie, "Talk a little louder, why don't you two? That way the rustlers will hear us comin' that much sooner and shoot us dead that much quicker."

"Sorry," Charlie said, "but it's not every day a miracle happens."

The rustlers had pushed the cattle as hard as they could but cows could not move fast in heavy timber. It did not help that over the first slope were several steep ridges littered with deadfall, for if there was anything that slowed cows down more than heavy timber it was deadfall.

"They weren't too bright, these rustlers," Charlie commented. "They should pick better ground."

"What has me stumped," Willis said, "is why only two?"

"We can ask them before we shoot the sons of bitches."

They were near the crest of the first ridge when they heard thrashing and rustling and the soft moo of a cow in distress. Willis jabbed his right spur into the claybank and came to the top with his hand on his revolver. But it wasn't the rustlers. It was just one cow. The critter had blundered into deadfall and some of the wind-flattened trees had given way under its weight. Now it lay amid the wreckage, the bone of one of its front legs white against the brown and the green.

The cow looked at them and lowed.

Charlie swore, then said, "The polecats just left it. They didn't put it out of its misery."

"They didn't want the shot heard," Willis figured. "It's too close to the valley."

"They could have slit its throat like they did to those others," Charlie said. "But they didn't want to stop."

Bob Ashlon shucked his rifle. "Want me to take care of it?"

"A shot can carry for a mile in these mountains," Willis said, "so we'd best do it on the way back."

The cow watched them ride north. If it was possible for a cow to look sad, this one looked sad as hell.

"I hate to see animals mistreated," Charlie remarked. "People have it comin' sometimes but animals only do what it's their nature to do."

"Deputy Ivers probably isn't too fond of animals right about now," Willis said.

"I had an aunt bit by a rattlesnake when she was little," Charlie mentioned. "She lived, but from then on, she killed every snake she came across. Garter snakes, racers, it made no never mind if they were harmless. All they had to be was a snake."

"I'm not too fond of stallions, myself."

Bob Ashlon muttered something, then said louder, "Am I the only one takin' this serious? If it's not females, it's snakes."

"Touchy hombre, ain't he?" Willis said.

"He was born in New Jersey and his family didn't move west until he was ten or eleven."

"Say no more."

"I hope you both get palsy," Bob Ashlon said.

The rustlers had continued to push the cows on over the ridge and the next ridge after that and the ridge after that . . . then down into a narrow valley with barely enough grass to feed a goat and across it and up the next mountain, heading more to the northwest than to the north.

"We're gettin' close," Charlie Weaver said.

Willis was thinking of Laurella, of their morning together. That she liked him, genuinely and honestly liked him, was the most incredible thing that had ever happened to him. She liked him and she didn't care about his knee. That was even more incredible. He had always assumed no woman would want a man who was crippled. What was a cripple good for? he had often asked himself, and answered himself, "Nothin' at all."

But that was not entirely true. He could ride. He could walk, if imperfectly. He could cook. He could chop wood. He could do a lot of things. Maybe not as well as he did them before the stallion shattered his knee. Maybe not as well as he would like. But he could *do* them and that counted for something. It counted for something for the first time in a very long time. It counted for something, but not because of him.

It made him dizzy to think of her. To think of how soft and warm her voice could be. To think of the half of her face that had not been stove in, and the warmth of her hand when her hand touched his.

He imagined how her life must have been. For her it had been far worse than for him. Especially as she was female. Girls relied more on their looks than most men. Jim Palmer had been fond of a mirror but he had been uncommonly handsome, so he had had good cause.

Willis thought of the hurt she had endured. A pretty girl turned into a monstrosity by a fluke of fate. A monstrosity in her eyes, anyway. In his eyes she was anything but. She was kindly and gentle and she liked him, but she could be strong, too. And she was smart. She had learned a lot from her folks and she was smart enough to run her own ranch.

Willis envisioned the two of them seated in the rocking chairs the Tylers normally sat in on the porch of the ranch house, smiling and holding hands and as happy as two people had ever been and ever would be. He almost reined up in surprise at his silliness. He was getting ahead of himself. Yes, she liked him, and God yes, he liked her, but it was a long way from holding hands to sitting on the porch of the ranch house as a married couple. Maybe she didn't have that in mind. Maybe — and the thought jarred him — maybe she was only interested because he was the first man ever to show an interest in her. Maybe when she had more time to think about it, she would realize he was not much of a catch and she could do better.

What if she does change her mind? Willis thought, and was suddenly more afraid than he had ever been of anything, ever. He was so afraid, he grew as chill as the creek water had been. "Please, no," he whispered. "Please let her think me worthy."

That was when he decided he would catch

the two rustlers or die trying. He must not fail. He must not go back without the stolen cattle. He must show her that although he was a cripple he wasn't worthless. He could do whatever needed doing when he had to.

"Smoke," Charlie Weaver said.

Willis looked up. Beyond the next ridge, tendrils of smoke curled skyward from a campfire.

"They stopped?" Bob Ashlon said. "How brainless is that?"

"They were up all night and they're tired and they think they got away clean," Willis said.

"Or maybe they're waitin' for the other two," Charlie said.

Willis hadn't thought of that. Four rustlers would be too many unless they were lucky and luck couldn't always be counted on to stop a bullet. "We have to hit them before the others show up."

The rustlers had made their fire right out in the open in a large bowl-shaped area between two slopes and had a coffeepot on to boil.

"It's the cousins," Willis said. "The Nargent brothers, Tote and Thatch." They were still wearing their red-and-blue bandannas. "Tote is the one on the right."

"Do we make wolf meat of them or take

them back to swing?" Bob Ashlon wanted to know.

Willis would as soon shoot the Nargents dead but Abe might want them alive to do it himself, and then there were the towns-people to think of. They had a stake in the outcome, too. "We'll try alive."

"Why take the risk?" Charlie asked. "Sneak in with our rifles and it's all over. The best part is we won't have any new holes where we shouldn't."

"Stay if you want."

"That was uncalled for, pard."

Willis dismounted, looped the reins around a limb, and slid the rifle from the saddle scabbard. It was a Spencer. He had never fired one but they were supposed to be reliable. He wondered if it was loaded. The trigger guard, as he recollected, worked the same as a Winchester lever. He experi-mented and fed a round into the chamber.

Charlie and Bob Ashlon had climbed down and were checking their Winchesters. Charlie bent and began removing his spurs.

That was a good idea, Willis thought. The slightest jingle could give them away. Lean-ing the Spencer against the tree, he took off his spurs. He was going to put them in the saddlebags but they were not his saddlebags. He settled for leaving them next to the tree and reclaimed the Spencer.

"I can circle around to cut off their escape," Bob Ashlon volunteered. He had his spurs off, too.

"Can you do it quiet?"

"If I couldn't, I wouldn't ask. I won't shoot unless I have to."

"We'll give you about fifteen minutes to get into position."

When the undergrowth had swallowed Bob, Willis crept toward the bowl, carefully placing his boots so his bad leg would not buckle, until he had an unobstructed view of the Nargents. By his inner clock there were five minutes to go when he eased onto his stomach behind a log.

Charlie sank beside him.

"Yes?" Willis whispered when his friend stared at him as if he had his head on backward. "Somethin' on your mind?"

"How fond are you of this filly?"

"I don't kiss and tell," Willis whispered.

"You've *kissed* her?" In his excitement Charlie nearly sat up. "And she let you? You still have all your teeth?"

"Most of them," Willis whispered. "Now hush. We have to be ready for when Ashlon is in place."

"You're not gettin' off that easy. We've been through too much together. I've cleaned up after you've had too much to drink and made a mess of your clothes. I practically carried you that time our horses were spooked by wolves and your knee gave out. Want me to go on?"

"No." Willis owed him a lot more than that. "All I say is that she seems to like me. But we haven't had a baby yet, if that's what you're wonderin'."

"She has money, you know. Lots of money. I heard it from Reuben and he heard it from the Tylers."

"I don't care how much she has or doesn't have," Willis said. "It's her that's important. Who and what she is."

"She's a woman." Charlie smirked. "What more do you need?"

"I need you to shut up."

"Does she have a sister?"

"Not that I know of. She has a brother but you might not be his type." Willis smiled at his cleverness.

"What does she look like under that veil? I saw she had it off when we spotted the two of you by the pool but she put it back on before we got there."

"She has eyes and a nose like everybody else."

"Is she pretty though? Plain is fine but pretty is better. But not so pretty that she'll draw other men like honey draws bears."

"I wouldn't have to worry there," Willis said.

"Damn, you're one lucky coon."

Thankfully for Willis, Charlie fell silent. They lay and watched the Nargent brothers. Tote poured coffee into tin cups and gave one to Thatch. Thatch added enough sugar to make ten pies, stirred it with a stick, and gulped.

"I want to hear what they're sayin'," Willis whispered. "You stay here." Holding the Spencer in front of him, he crawled around the end of the log and on through the high growth, avoiding twigs and dry leaves.

It was his hope the Nargents might mention where the other two were. Willis rated Varner Wilkes and Mason as much more dangerous. Varner was the brains of the gang, and Varner was deadly, but he was nowhere near as deadly as Mason. Which was strange, since of the pair, Varner struck him as more vicious. Mason was good at killing, which wasn't the same thing. But when a man was on the wrong side of the law, the distinction didn't much matter.

Willis slid his right elbow forward and then his left and then his right again. A patch of high weeds separated him from the bowl. Parting them, he saw the brothers and their horses and the weary cows.

"I hope you're right," Thatch was commenting. "I hope he doesn't get mad."

"What right does he have?" Tote responded. "We're grown men. We can do as we damned well please."

"But he said not to go near the herds while he was away. He made it plain, and you know how he gets when he's crossed."

"We're his kin. He won't lift a finger."

Thatch took another gulp from his cup of sugar with coffee added. "I wouldn't put anythin' past him, brother. He's snake mean, that cousin of ours. Hell, he shot his own pa, didn't he?"

"His pa asked for it. Took him out to the woodshed and raised welts on his back, and it wasn't the first time."

"Our pa beat us but we never shot him," Thatch said.

Tote puffed out his chest like a drunk spoiling for a fight. "Quit your frettin', damn it. You're worse than a woman. Varner will be glad we rustled more head. Now we have more to sell."

"Too bad about the one that busted its leg."

"If you'd kept a closer eye on them like I told you, it wouldn't have happened."

"You always blame me for everythin',"

Thatch complained.

"Don't start. All we should be thinkin' about is gettin' back before Varner and Mason. He's less likely to be mad."

"See? You're as worried as I am."

"Damned if I am!" Tote snarled, but there was an element of uncertainty to his tone that suggested his brother was right. He glanced at the cows, then rested his forearms on his knees. "I've got a proposition for you, brother."

"I'm listenin'." Thatch was also adding another spoonful of sugar to what was left of his coffee.

"What would you say to the two of us goin' our own way?"

Thatch nearly dropped the spoon. "Break up with Varner? Why in tarnation would we want to do that? We've had it pretty good with him."

"Have we?" Tote said. "He always takes a bigger cut, doesn't he? He always has us do most of the hard work while he sits back and takes it easy. Then there's the whole business with Mason."

"I never did savvy why Varner keeps that Reb around if he hates him so much."

"He keeps him around because Mason is better with a gun than all three of us put together. And he's scared of him, I think."

"Varner?" Thatch snorted. "He's never been afraid of anyone or anythin' in his life."

"Maybe so. But he doesn't like sass, yet he didn't do a thing the other day when Mason sassed him about shootin' that good-lookin' cowboy."

"What was it Mason said?" Thatch's broad brow furrowed. "Oh. Now I remember. He said, 'Why don't you do it yourself? Or can't you shoot a rifle as well as you flap your gums?' " Thatch laughed. "That took sand."

"But it wasn't very smart. If Mason keeps ridin' our cousin, then as sure as shootin', our cousin is goin' to shoot him. I'd rather not be around when that happens. Mason might think we had a hand in it."

"You reckon Mason will buck Varner out?"

"If Varner is dumb enough to try it facin' him, sure. But as Varner likes to say, he's never yet met a man who isn't easier to kill from the back than the front."

Willis felt a sharp jab in his side and twisted to find Charlie beside him. "I told you to stay put," he whispered.

"Good thing I didn't. Or is he supposed to wait forever for you to quit daydreamin' about your filly?" Charlie pointed across the bowl.

Bob Ashlon had made it around to the other side and was waving at them from behind a tree.

Willis gestured, and Ashlon stopped waving. "I'll go right," he whispered. "You go left. When you see me stand, you do the same."

"This better work. I'm not ready to die yet."

"Who is?" Willis whispered at Charlie's retreating back. What he had said surprised him so much that he lay there for half a minute before he started to crawl to the right.

One of the brothers had fished jerky from a saddlebag and they were both chewing hungrily.

"We'll let these cows rest an hour, no more," Tote said. "Then we drive them until they drop or we reach the meadow."

Willis crawled twenty feet. Thirty feet. He coiled his good leg under him and looked to his left but did not spot Charlie. Wedging the Spencer's stock to his shoulder, he pushed up off the ground. "Move and you're dead men!"

Both brothers moved. Tote leaped to his feet. Thatch dropped his coffee cup and clawed for his revolver but froze when Charlie rose on the rim farther down and Bob Ashlon stepped into the open and hollered, "Don't you dare!"

Tote was furious. "Damn!" He glowered at each of them. "Damn! Damn! Damn!"

"What do we do?" Thatch asked him.

"Unbuckle your gun belts and let them fall!" Willis commanded. "Keep your hands where we can see them and you'll live a while yet."

Tote was no fool. "Only until you stretch our necks! And I don't aim to end my days gurglin' on a rope!" He went for his pistol.

CHAPTER 14

Willis had Tote Nargent in the Spencer's sights. All he had to do was squeeze the trigger. But when he did, nothing happened. There was no booming report or kick of the stock. Disbelief rooted him in place as Charlie Weaver's rifle blasted and Bob Ashlon joined in from the trees across the way. But Tote did not go down, and both he and Thatch returned fire on the run. They were making for their horses, weaving madly to avoid taking a slug.

A lead hornet buzzed past Willis. He stopped staring dumbly at the Spencer and limped quickly toward a tree. Belatedly, he remembered someone telling him once that Spencers had to be cocked before they were fired. Sure enough, the hammer was down. Hastily thumbing it back, he sought to take a bead on the brothers. But they had reached their mounts. Tote was already in the saddle and firing to cover his brother, whose mount had shied.

Charlie was cursing fiercely. There was no sign of Bob Ashlon.

Anxious to prevent their escape, Willis banged off a shot. He knew he had missed even as he squeezed the trigger. Jacking the lever, he cocked the hammer and fixed the sights on Thatch, who was now half on the frightened horse, clinging to the saddle horn. He fired again, but just as he did the horse bounded forward. Again he missed.

"Let's go!" Tote Nargent bawled, and spurred his horse toward the woods.

Still clinging to his saddle, Thatch somehow got his mount to follow. Or maybe it bolted on its own.

Boiling with frustration, Willis got off one more shot just as the vegetation closed around them. He thought he saw Thatch jerk but he could not be certain. Then they were gone and the sudden silence rang in his ears like the peal of the church bell in Cottonwood.

Boots pounded the earth, and Charlie was at his side. "That sure went well! We couldn't hit the broadside of a barn if it was sittin' on us."

"We got the cows back," Willis said.

"Only because those polecats didn't think to run the critters off." Charlie's eyes narrowed. "Say, where's Ashlon?" He cupped a hand to his mouth. "Bob! Are you all right? Where did you get to?"

When they did not get an answer, Willis hobbled into the bowl. The slope was not that steep but he nearly slipped on his way down. Charlie ran on ahead and was about to the campfire when Bob Ashlon appeared on the rim, his right hand pressed to his left arm.

"You're shot!" Charlie exclaimed, making it sound like an extremely stupid thing to do.

"One of the buzzards winged me," Ashlon said, descending.

A twinge of guilt stabbed Willis. He was the one who had insisted they go after the rustlers — all to prove to a certain lady from Texas he wasn't the complete waste of manhood he tended to think he was. "How bad is it?"

It wasn't bad at all. The bullet had barely broken the skin but there was plenty of blood. The shock of being hit had brought Ashlon to his knees, where he stayed until he heard the brother galloping off.

"Now I know why I'm not a lawman."

"You and me, both," Charlie said. "I'd rather be stung by flies than bullets any day." He examined the wound. "We need to clean you up. I have a canteen on my horse. I'll be right back."

"Bring all of them," Willis said.

Charlie gave him a strange glance and hustled off.

"We were lucky," Bob Ashlon said.

Willis nodded. His grandpa used to say that the only reason idiots lived to old age was because the Almighty had a soft spot in His heart for them.

"It sure hurts," Ashlon complained. "You would think I'd been kicked by a mule."

"Sit and rest," Willis advised. Now that it was over, he had a powerful hankering to return to the north valley as fast as they could, but he had to be practical. "Charlie won't be very long."

"I never gave much thought to dyin' before," Bob Ashlon commented, "but I reckon I'd rather die lyin' in bed than lyin' in the dirt."

"We never know when and where," Willis said. A few days ago he hadn't much cared. Now he found that he did. He cared very much.

It gave him more to ponder on their way back. All of a sudden everything had changed. Changed so drastically that he wondered if maybe he wasn't setting himself up for a hard fall. It had been so dreamlike until the rustlers. His innermost longing had been answered, and it seemed too good to be true.

The cows plodded slowly along. Willis swore he could limp faster. But they were worn-out and pushing them would only make matters worse.

Charlie had been to one side to keep any from drifting but now that it was obvious they were too tired to act up, he came over alongside the claybank. "I thought your thumb was broke and you forgot to tell me."

"You saw?" Willis said, braced for a teasing.

"You looked as if you were layin' an egg," Charlie mentioned. "Good thing you're a cowherder."

"Can we keep it between ourselves?"

"For my own sake," Charlie said. "If I told the story, I'd have to tell how we fired close to twenty shots at those polecats and they still got away. We would never hear the end of it."

"We're not gun hands," Willis said.

"Thank God. As poor as we are at it, we wouldn't last a week. But we got the cows. Abe should be right pleased."

With all that had gone on, Willis had forgotten about his boss and his boss's wife.

Suddenly he was glad the cows couldn't go faster.

"I've been meanin' to ask you," Charlie said. "Does Miss Hendershot happen to have a sister? Or a cousin? I'm not fussy. So long as they aren't too ugly, because, Lord knows, I'm no prize myself."

"Pick another subject."

"Hell, if they are, I can always put a potato sack over their heads," Charlie said jokingly.

"That's not funny. Not one little bit."

Charlie was watching the cows and did not notice Willis' expression. "Marryin' a pretty girl can give a man fits. Other men are always lookin', and then there are those who have to test the waters to see if they get a nibble. I'd like as not end up in prison for shootin' some fool who couldn't read the no-fishin' sign."

"I don't care if a woman is pretty or not," Willis said.

"Seems to me you did that time in Cheyenne. That gal with the wart on her nose didn't appeal to you one bit."

"It wasn't the wart. It was her breath. She was too fond of raw onions, not that I have anythin' against onions. I just don't cotton to suckin' on a tongue that tastes like one."

"You suck on their tongues?" Charlie was flabbergasted. "Kissin' their lips is enough of a challenge. Some have terrible teeth. Remember Iowa Sue? Hers were brown."

Willis shuddered. "I'd as soon *not* remember her, thank you very much." He had been drunk. Very drunk.

"If your Texas gal doesn't have a sister, that's all right. There's always Gerty. Did I tell you how nice she hums?"

A cow picked that moment to stumble and nearly fall, and Charlie gigged his mount to check if it was hurt.

The best thing to do was rest the cows awhile. The Nargents had pushed the animals so hard, they were near exhausted. But Willis hesitated. He yearned to be with Laurella. Then another cow stumbled, and his responsibility to the Bar T could no longer be denied. "Hold them up!" he shouted, and when his companions complied, he announced his decision.

"You want me to go on with Bob and leave you here alone?" Charlie said uncertainly. "Is that wise?"

"Your job is to see to it that Miss Hendershot gets back to the ranch house. Explain to her why I had to stay, and explain to Abe so he isn't mad enough to fire me."

"I'll stick with you," Bob Ashlon offered.

"That's damned decent of you but a sawbones has to look at your arm," Willis said.

Gunshot wounds were notorious for becoming infected.

Charlie wasn't satisfied. "Bob and Rafe can take the Texas gal back. I'll keep you company."

"I want you to see to her personally."

"You're a stubborn cuss," Charlie said, but he smiled in understanding. "I'll leave her with the Tylers and bring every spare hand I can to help you get these critters back."

"Only if I don't show up by noon." Willis figured it would take him three hours once he started out. If he started at first light, he would reach the north valley by nine.

Bob Ashlon rode off but Charlie lingered to grin and remark, "That midget with the arrows sure makes us do silly things."

"Miss Hendershot is waitin'."

Presently Willis was alone except for the cows, the tall timber, and the wind. Shadows dappled him as he waved his coiled rope and hollered, "Get along there!" To the best of his recollection, there was a clearing a quarter of a mile farther.

Now that he was alone, Willis realized the risk he was taking. There was the grizzly to think of. The spot where Deputy Ivers had been ripped apart wasn't all that far as the crow flew, and grizzlies roamed a wide range. He had not seen any Indian sign but that did not mean none were around. Then he had the rustlers to consider. It could be the brothers would come back and bring Varner and Mason with them.

There was plenty to worry about but Willis surprised himself by not being worried. He had something else on his mind: thoughts of a woman who had bared her soul to him — a woman life had treated as cruelly as life had treated him; a woman who in a short span had come to mean a lot.

Thinking of her made Willis light-headed: of the half of her face that was more beautiful than any face he had ever seen; of her laughter and her touch and the smell of her hair when she sat close to him.

Laurella Hendershot was probably unaware that she had given him something precious — something no one else could; something he needed more desperately than he ever needed anything other than the use of his leg. She had given him a reason to go on living.

He was still thinking about her when he came to the clearing. He unsaddled and kindled a small fire. There might be food and coffee in Rafe's saddlebags but Willis refused to look. Whatever was in them was Rafe's.

The horse he had borrowed did not belong to Rafe. It belonged to the Bar T. Each spring all the horses were rounded up and parceled out to the returning hands and to the relative few punchers Abe kept on the payroll during the coldest of the winter months. Every man ended up with a personal string of five animals and looked after them as if they were his very own.

It had been Willis' job to tame down the wilder ones. After several months of running loose, some of the horses deemed it their God-given right to go wherever they pleased without a human on their back, and Willis had to show them they were there for a purpose. He had taken great pride in his work, in his ability to tame a horse without crushing its spirit.

The other hands had looked up to him. Cowboys generally considered bronc busters a breed apart, and wanted nothing to do with risking their own bones and sometimes their lives to show a horse who was boss.

Willis had been uncommonly good at what he did. Punchers who signed on with the Bar T did so confident the horses in their personal strings had been well broken and would perform as they should when riding herd and on roundup.

A squawk brought Willis' head up. A pair of jays flitted from tree to tree and shrieked at him as if mad he had invaded their domain. He never had liked jays much, partly because when he was a boy he saw a jay raid the nest of a songbird and kill the nestlings.

Soon the jays lost interest and flew elsewhere. Lulled by the warm sun on his face, Willis felt his eyelids grow heavy. Before long, he dozed off. He dreamed chaotic dreams of bears and mountain lions and then one of the stallion responsible for ending his days as a bronc buster. In the dream, when he went to Abe and asked to be allowed to try to break the man killer, Abe refused and had the stallion shot. He was mad, but it spared his leg, and in his dream he lived the life he had always wanted to live, breaking horses until his joints could no longer take the punishment and then working as a cowboy until he was old and gray. That was how it should have been.

A noise awakened him. Willis sat up, his hands on the Spencer. He thought the jays had returned but the woods were quiet. Too quiet, he thought. His knee protesting, he slowly stood and glanced at the sun. Judging by its position, he had been asleep for a couple hours. He was growing careless.

The cows were dozing. Rafe's string horse was nipping grass. Willis decided it had been his imagination; he was bending to sit back down when the horse raised its head and nickered.

Off in the forest to the south another horse answered.

Willis was too exposed. He limped to the trees and leaned against a fir. Hooves clomped, the brush crackled, and two riders appeared. "Charlie?" he said, then saw who was with him and limped to meet them, amazement and hope churning his insides. "Laurella? What in God's name are you doin' here?"

"I'm glad to see you, too." She drew rein, and although Willis could not see her face for the veil, he knew that under it she was smiling.

"You're supposed to be on your way back to the ranch house in the buckboard."

"The buckboard is on its way back without me." Laurella swung down and stood so near to him, he saw the veil flutter when she exhaled. "Mr. Ashlon went with it. He was kind enough to lend me the use of his horse."

"Why did you come?"

"Why do you think?" Laurella held out

the reins for him to take, then strode past to the fire. "I brought the food we had left. A man shouldn't go without his supper."

Willis glared up at his friend. "What in hell got into you? How could you let her do this?"

"I'd like to see you stop that gal when she puts her mind to somethin'!" Charlie said. "I talked until I was blue in the face but she wouldn't listen. She said it wasn't right for us to leave you out here by your lonesome and she was comin' whether I liked it or not."

"You could have forced her," Willis said. "There were three of you."

"Lay a finger on a female? A *Texas* female? Are you loco? Or maybe you didn't know she has a derringer?"

"A what?" Willis turned. Laurella had hunkered by the fire and was adding a limb she had broken.

"Somewhere in that getup of hers is a derringer. She pointed it at me when I told her she was goin' back and that was final."

"No."

"Yes."

"Damn."

"You can say that again. So since touchin' her was out of the question and bein' shot isn't high on my list of things I most like to

264

do, I agreed to bring her to you."

Willis walked over to her. "If you leave right this moment, you can reach the north valley before dark."

"When we go, we'll go together," Laurella said. "Or were you plannin' on lettin' the cows find their own way back?"

"Abe will be mad enough to spit nails. Elfie will be even madder." Willis did not care to face her wrath if he could help it.

"She won't say a word to you. It was my decision. Just as this one is." Laurella turned toward Charlie Weaver. "You can head back. Mr. Lander and I will be perfectly fine by ourselves."

Willis and Charlie both blurted, "What?"

"Wyomin' cowboys sure are hard of hearin'," Laurella said. "The Tylers are bound to be worried. As soon as Mr. Ashlon and that other cowboy reach the ranch, Abe will organize a search party and head out to find me. Mr. Weaver, you will tell him I am in no danger and there is no hurry."

"But —" Charlie said.

"But what?" Laurella prompted. "It's indecent for a lady to be alone with a man in the middle of nowhere?"

"You're puttin' words in my mouth, ma'am."

"I'm only sayin' what you were thinkin'.

Your concern for my reputation is duly noted. But it is *my* reputation, Mr. Weaver, to polish or sully as I see fit. So you will kindly head on down and put Mr. Tyler's mind at ease."

Charlie glanced at Willis.

"Miss Hendershot," Willis said formally, "my pard has a point. Folks hereabouts are bound to gossip. The parson might hear of it and then we're in for a lecture on the wickedness of the flesh." It was one of the parson's favorite sermons.

"He can lecture you if you let him but I'm no sinner and I'll be damned if I'll have him or anyone else brand me as one." Laurella's veil rose to Charlie. "Are you still here?"

"What am I to do?" Charlie asked Willis.

Laurella answered, "I've already told you. Ride down and inform Mr. and Mrs. Tyler I'm as well as well can be and they should not rush to rescue me."

"We're safer if Charlie stays," Willis said.

"Off you go, Mr. Weaver."

"Will, it's up to you," Charlie said. "Do I go or do I stay?"

The veil shifted to Willis. He smiled but he sensed she wasn't. He also sensed that he was about to make one of the most important decisions of his life. "You go," he said.

Muttering, Charlie reined his horse around. He did not look back and he did not wave.

"I don't blame him for bein' mad," Laurella said when he was out of sight. "But we have to find out, one way or the other."

Willis commenced unsaddling Ashlon's horse. He had only the vaguest notion of what she wanted to find out and did not want to appear dumb by asking. The bundle of food was tied on behind the saddlebags.

"There's not a whole lot left, I'm afraid," Laurella said as she unwrapped it. "But I'm not all that hungry."

"Me either," Willis lied yet again. He unrolled a blanket and spread it out for her to sit on, then positioned the saddles so they were side by side. But she surprised him by sitting with her back against his.

"You must think me terribly forward."

"I don't know what to think anymore," Willis confessed. He had never been much good at it anyway. The few years he had spent in school as a youngster had taxed him to his limit. He had learned to add and subtract fair enough but the multiplication tables had been impossible for him to memorize, and long division gave him headaches.

"I've spent so much of my life hurtin'

inside," Laurella said. "If there's a chance — a real chance — the hurtin' will end, I owe it to myself not to waste time. You understand, don't you?"

"Sure," Willis said, and munched on a piece of chicken.

"Life is too short. Half of mine is over. The years go by so fast, we go from the cradle to the grave in the bat of an eye. Time is precious and I refuse to squander what I have left."

Willis munched and wrestled with his feelings. The fire crackled and the horses grazed. He made bold to drape his arm about her shoulders and she shifted to make herself more comfortable and placed her hat beside them.

"Isn't this nice? Are you happy I stayed?"

"I've never been happier," Willis said. Nor more nervous. He smelled her hair and her skin. He went to stroke her neck but lowered his fingers.

"Do you mind a headstrong woman? I can change if I have to but I would rather not have to."

"You're fine as you are," Willis said, and felt her tense up. He had to remember to choose his words carefully.

"No, I'm not, but in some respects, I can be as fine as any woman anywhere. The respects I'm not, it can't be helped."

The sun was on its downward arc. The shadows about them lengthened, and from time to time, Willis added fuel to the fire. Otherwise, they did not move or speak but simply sat with her cheek on his chest and her hand in his.

Willis' nervousness faded. Toward evening the air grew chill but the flames warmed him outside and her touch warmed him inside. He was content to sit there forever. In the gray of twilight, she twisted the unspoiled half of her face up to him. Her eyes were misting over.

"I've never been so happy. Thank you, Will."

Willis kissed her on the tip of her nose. He could not say what drove him to do it, other than he had never been happier, either. Suddenly she buried her face against his chest and began weeping in great, heaving sobs. Bewildered, he patted her shoulder and her head and said softly, "There, there."

Much later, curled up in his arms, Laurella said, "I'm a hussy. Go ahead. Say it. I won't be mad."

"You're a hussy."

"If this is a trick, tell me now. If you plan to run off, tell me now. If you'll wake up tomorrow and want to kick yourself, tell me now. There will be no hard feelin's. I promise, on my honor."

Willis pecked her on the nose again.

"Oh, Will."

The fire crackled and sputtered. The cows dozed and the horses were dozing and the wild creatures of the day retired to their dens and burrows to sleep the night away, but Willis doubted he would sleep for a week. He had never felt so filled with life and vitality.

"They will never understand," Laurella said.

"It's our life," Willis said.

CHAPTER 15

Three days later Laurella announced her decision.

Elfie arranged a special supper for the occasion, to which Willis was invited at Laurella's insistence. Armando was there, too, seated on Willis' right, and it made Willis uncomfortable.

It was Armando who had been first to show up at the clearing high in the mountains. He had ridden on ahead of Abe Tyler and the rest, pushing himself and his mount tirelessly. He arrived just at the break of dawn, and he was not in a good mood. He vaulted from his horse before it came to a stop and stalked toward Willis with his hand resting on his Colt. Fire blazed in his eyes, and Willis had been set to defend himself when Laurella stepped between them.

"Armando! *Qué tienes?*"

They exchanged a flurry of Spanish. Willis only knew a little of the lingo, but he did not need to be versed in the language to guess why Armando was so mad. Finally Laurella reverted to English.

"Do you understand now?"

"Sí, senorita," Armando said. "But I do not like it."

"You judge too quickly. He is a fine hombre, as you will learn for yourself. Until then, show him the same respect you show me."

Armando's smoldering gaze was enough to char Willis to a crisp. "I will try, senorita. For your sake."

Since then her protector had barely said ten words to Willis but Willis often caught Armando studying him. Armando had insisted on accompanying them when Laurella inspected the south valley, and although Laurella had wanted to spend more time with Willis alone, she gave in.

"He is only doin' what my father told him to do," she explained, "which is to watch over me and see that I do not come to harm." She sighed. "Ever since my accident, my parents have been overprotective. I realize they do it because they love me but I am an adult now. I do not need protectin'."

"Well, you've got a heap of protectors whether you want them or not" — Willis had grinned — "because you can add me to the list."

They went everywhere together. Willis was constantly at her side; he could not get enough of her company. They became the talk of the ranch. Punchers would point at them, and smile knowingly.

Elfie was not as pleased about the relationship as her husband. Abe accepted the news without comment but Elfie went on and on about how unseemly it was for Laurella to have spent the night alone with a man up in the mountains, and what was Laurella thinking, and why did Laurella insist on always being with him, and shouldn't she be concentrating on buying the ranch and not one of the ranch hands. Elfie might have continued in that vein had Laurella not lit into her.

"Enough is enough. My personal life is none of your business. Who I spend my time with is none of your business. And for your information, I am concentrating on the ranch. Thanks to Will, I know more about the Bar T than I could ever learn on my own. And I must say I am not happy about how you and your husband tried to trick me."

Elfie had blinked and bleated, "Why, my dear, whatever do you mean?"

"Don't play innocent. I know all about the rustlers. You should have told me about them the first day I was here. But you kept it a secret. You were afraid I would change my mind about buying your ranch."

Elfie had glanced at Willis, and not in a friendly way. "My dear, you had more than enough to occupy you. Besides, my husband and I were confident we would have the problem solved long before you assumed ownership."

"A lie by omission is still a lie," Laurella had said, "and I resent being treated so shabbily. Either start to deal with me in a forthright manner or you can find a new buyer."

Willis had been secretly tickled when Elfie backpedaled, saying how sorry she was and how it would never happen again, and could Laurella please, please, oh please forgive her?

Now, as Elfie tapped her plate with a spoon and stood, Willis smiled sweetly at her just to rub it in.

"I want to thank all of you for coming tonight, and say how delighted I am to have so many friends on hand."

Willis was not the only guest. Reuben Marsh sat near Abe, wearing a new store-bought shirt and a clean bandanna. Reuben, with his slicked-back hair, sat stiff and straight.

The parson was there, too, although why Elfie invited him was a puzzlement. Reverend Merford had bushy white sideburns and a craggy face that looked down on the rest of the world as if passing judgment.

Equally puzzling was the presence of Fred Baxter, the general store owner and Cottonwood's leading citizen.

"Miss Hendershot has promised to render her decision tonight," Elfie was saying. "And since that decision is of considerable importance to everyone here, you were all specifically invited."

"Cottonwood will welcome you warmly, ma'am," Fred Baxter said, "should you decide to buy."

Reverend Merford was not nearly as agreeable. "We are a Christian community, with Christian values. It would be well for newcomers, and some of those who are not so new, to bear that in mind." He gave Willis a pointed look.

Abe rose and tapped his own plate. "Now, now, let's be civil. Miss Hendershot will tell us after we eat, so dig in, everyone. Gus has outdone himself for the occasion."

Little Sparrow did most of the serving. She hovered around Reuben Marsh a lot, or maybe Willis only thought she did. Several times during the course of the meal, Laurella's arm brushed his, and never by accident. To watch her eat was a wonderment. She would spear a morsel with her fork or scoop it up with her spoon, and with a deft flick of her wrist, the food disappeared under her veil.

Her hat had become as much a topic of talk as Willis and Laurella, themselves. Everyone had noticed that she never took it off. Everyone wondered why. Even there at the dinner table, Fred Baxter and Reverend Merford could not keep from glancing at it from time to time. Reuben Marsh was curious, too, but he had better manners.

The meal consisted of chicken soup and a salad, followed by thick slabs of beef, a heaping bowl of potatoes, succotash, corn pone, brown betty pudding, and for those who had any room left in their bellies, slices of apple or cherry pie or, in Willis' case, slices of both.

Little Sparrow cleared the dishes. The ladies were served A & P tea, the men brimming cups of piping hot coffee. Then, at long last, they got down to business.

Laurella started things by clearing her throat and saying, "I would like to thank my host and hostess for their generous hospitality, and for being so patient with me."

"Not at all, my dear," Elfie said. "It's the least we could do."

Abe leaned forward. "The suspense is killing me. Will you or will you not buy the Bar T?"

"I will," Laurella said.

The Tylers smiled at each other. Reuben shifted in his chair, and Little Sparrow immediately refilled his cup even though it was only half empty. Fred Baxter nodded. Only the parson sat cold and unmoved.

"I will buy the Bar T," Laurella went on, "provided several conditions are met beforehand."

At this, the smiles evaporated. Willis sipped his coffee to hide his smirk.

"Conditions?" Elfie said.

Laurella addressed herself to Abe. "First, let me say you have an extremely well-run ranch. I would stack it against any in Texas even if it is small by Texas standards." The smile in her tone brought a smile to Abe. "The cattle are well-fed and well-managed. The house and the stable and the bunkhouse are well-maintained. Your punchers are as loyal to the brand as any I've seen. There's plenty of grass and plenty of water and more timber than ten Texas ranches can boast of."

"In other words," Elfie interrupted, "it's everything I told you it would be."

"And then some," Laurella acknowledged. "There are no Indian problems to speak of — at the moment, anyway. Since you've never had Comanches to contend with, you can't appreciate what a blessin' that is."

"If everything is so perfect," Elfie said, "why must you insist on imposing conditions?"

"Because I'm not a fool," Laurella bluntly responded. "My pa taught me that when it comes to business, you do what has to be done and personal feelin's be hanged."

"Then let's hear them," Abe said.

"First and foremost is that the Wilkes gang must be dealt with. I won't take over with a cloud hangin' over the ranch. Either hang them or drive them out of the country, but I want them disposed of before I sign the papers."

Reverend Merford had not said much all during the meal but now he placed his forearms on the table and said sternly, "Perhaps you have heard of the Ten Commandments, my dear? One of them is 'Thou shalt not kill.' I grant you rustlers are an odious thorn in any rancher's side, but your attitude, young lady, is much too cold for my tastes."

"With all due respect," Laurella said, "if a rancher were to turn the other cheek every time a cow was stolen, pretty soon there wouldn't be any cows left. And when it comes to killin', have you forgotten the shoot-out in town? Have you forgotten your marshal and those others?"

"Of course not," Reverend Merford said indignantly. "Marshal Keever was a close friend of mine. I was devastated by his death. I thought highly of him and he thought highly of me."

Willis happened to know different. He had been in the saloon one night over a year ago when the subject of the minister came up. The marshal had been there, and had made the comment that for a man of the cloth, the reverend was remarkably short on forgiveness. As Keever had put it, "I'd like him a lot better if he wasn't always lookin' down his nose at everyone who doesn't measure up to his idea of perfection."

"If the two of you were so close, then you should want to see his murderers brought to justice," Laurella said.

"God's justice is not necessarily man's justice. An eye for an eye has not applied since Calvary."

"That will come as a shock to most Texans," Laurella said. "And it applies for me, Parson. But we were talkin' about the rustlin'. If you have a way of gettin' the Wilkes gang to stop without gunplay, I'll gladly listen."

Abe had been tapping the table during the theological debate. Now he said, "You mentioned several conditions, Miss Hendershot. What are the others?"

"I need to know, in advance, how many of your punchers will stay on and how many refuse to work for a woman."

Elfie indulged in a condescending little laugh. "Your gender is of no consequence, my dear. The men have never given me any problems."

"You're the big sugar's wife," Laurella said. "I'll *be* the big sugar. There's a difference." Her veil swiveled toward the Bar T's foreman. "How about it, Mr. Marsh? Will they stay or not?"

Reuben had been staring at Little Sparrow. "You're askin' me, ma'am?" he stalled.

"Tell her, Reuben," Abe said.

"To be honest, ma'am, most haven't made up their minds yet. Charlie Weaver will do whatever Will does. And Bob Ashlon has been singin' your praises since the other day up in the mountains. He says you have sand,

and female or not, that's enough for him."

"And you, Mr. Marsh? What do you say?"

"I tend to agree with Ashlon. It's not whether the boss is a man or a woman, it's whether they can do the job."

"I'd like very much for you to stay on as foreman," Laurella said. "No one could do it better."

Marsh's cheeks became pink. "Well, I thank you, ma'am. But since we're bein' so honest with each other, I kind of thought the foreman job was already taken." He glanced meaningfully at Willis. "So do most of the other boys."

"Oh," Laurella said. "It's unwise to assume things. You should have come right up and asked me. I'd have told you that the idea of Will bein' my foreman never entered my head. As my husband, he'll be runnin' the ranch at my side."

Willis nearly choked on the coffee he was swallowing. Complete silence fell. No one moved. No one seemed to be breathing. Then Abe stirred and said, "Did I hear correctly? There's a marriage in the offing?"

"He hasn't asked me yet but I expect him to once he finds the courage," Laurella said.

All eyes swung toward Willis. The truth was, he had thought about it several times over the past few days but had not said anything for fear of her thinking he was rushing things. "You sure don't beat around the bush."

"Isn't this a bit sudden?" Elfie asked. "I mean, marriage isn't something to be taken lightly."

An unlikely ally had an opposing view. "I think it's simply marvelous," Reverend Merford declared. "When a man and a woman are in love, what does it matter if they marry after only two weeks or wait two years?"

"But it hasn't even been two weeks," Elfie said.

"I must say," Fred Baxter spoke up, "that regardless of any wedding, it will leave poor Cottonwood in the lurch. We were counting on Mr. Lander to agree to our proposition."

"What are you talkin' about?" Willis asked.

"Oh, just that a dozen of the town's leading citizens got together the other night to discuss the marshal situation. Cottonwood needs a lawman. We considered sending flyers to some of the Kansas cowtowns advertising the position but then it occurred to us that we have the perfect candidate." Baxter's thin mustache curled upward. "You."

"Were all of you drunk when you came up with this brainstorm?"

"As sober as church mice," Baxter said. "We don't want a gun hand. Lawmen with itchy trigger fingers tend to shoot before they think. We'd rather have someone dependable. Someone who knows the community. Someone who saw the town take root and grow. Someone like you."

Willis had never heard anything so silly. "Have you forgotten about my leg? I'd be no use in a scrape. And I can't run fast enough to catch a snail."

Baxter's mustache tweaked again. "That's what deputies are for. We're quite serious about the offer, Mr. Lander. I was going to present it to you before I headed back to town. Now I guess the whole issue is moot."

Laurella shifted in her chair. "I wouldn't stand in your way if you wanted to pin the badge on."

Willis took refuge in his coffee. Too much was being thrown at him all at once.

"As for the question of whether the Bar T punchers will stay on or not," Laurella said to Reuben Marsh, "I believe I can't help them make up their minds. If you would be so kind, go down to the bunkhouse and gather everyone up. I'll be out front in ten minutes to talk to them."

"Only about half the hands are here," Reuben said. "The rest are ridin' guard on the herds."

"That's all right. The ones who come can

tell those who can't all about it." Laurella paused. "I'm sure it will be the talk of the territory."

"Ma'am?" Reuben Marsh said.

"Nothin'. Off you go."

Fred Baxter was preoccupied with his own problem. "What do I tell the town's civic leaders, Mr. Lander? Will you at least consider our offer?"

"It's plumb ridiculous," Willis said.

Laurella apparently disagreed. "He'll consider it, Mr. Baxter."

Pushing back his chair, Willis stood. "If you'll excuse us," he said to Abe, "Miss Hendershot and I need to get some air." He did not wait for her but turned and limped down the hall to the parlor and out the front door. He was by the rail when she caught up. "Why are you puttin' words in my mouth?" he demanded without turning around.

"I figured you might be holdin' back on my account," Laurella said softly.

Willis faced her. "Now who is the one doin' the assumin'? And that marryin' business. We've known each other all of five days. Is that long enough for you to be sure you want to spend the rest of your life with me?"

"You can ask that after the other night?"

Willis' ears burned and he had to try twice before he could say, "I'm not that fine a catch. You can do better."

"That's the first stupid thing you've said to me since we met," Laurella responded. "You're the one who likely as not will have regrets."

"Over what? Not bein' alone anymore? Havin' someone who cares for me — honest to God cares for me as I am? What do I have to regret?"

Laurella touched her veil. "This."

"My knee. Your face. Neither of us is perfect, not in our bodies. But it's not the bodies that count. It's what's in our heads and" — Willis had so rarely said what he was about to say that he had to force the words out — "our hearts."

Her hand found his and grasped his fingers tight. "You have just made me the happiest woman alive, Will Lander."

"Don't get too happy. There are your folks to consider. How will they take it, you marryin' a Wyomin' cowboy you've barely met? Armando doesn't much like me, and I reckon your pa will feel the same."

"Armando has nothin' against you," Laurella said. "He thinks I should take it slower, is all. Have you court me for six months or so before we talk about marrying."

"Maybe we should."

"Six more months of loneliness? Six more months of the livin' hell my life has been? No, thank you. You're loco enough to want me to be your wife, and by God, I aim to take advantage of it before you come to your senses."

They both laughed, and Laurella's hands rose to his shoulders.

"Thanks to you, I realize I've been goin' about my life all wrong. I shouldn't hide like a rabbit cowerin' in a hole. I need to start livin'."

"Then set the date. But allow enough time for your folks to come. I won't step into your loop unless they do."

"We'll make Armando happy then. Six months from this very day we'll share our vows. That stuffy parson can do the honors, although I'd just as soon it was a justice of the peace."

"No, a church weddin' with all the trimmin's," Will said, "or as many as I can afford."

"As *we* can afford," Laurella corrected him. "What is mine will be yours and what is yours will be mine."

"I'm gettin' the best of it. All I have is a saddle, a horse, and a few odds and ends. You come with a ranch."

"I'd give you the whole territory if it were mine to give."

Willis embraced her and felt her tremble. "We're addlepated, the both of us. That's what people will say."

"For the first time in my life, I don't care what other people think. I don't care what they will say. I'm yours and you're mine, and nothin' else in the whole world matters."

"Well," Willis said.

"Well, indeed."

Cowhands were drifting toward the house from the bunkhouse and the cook shack and other buildings. They stood a respectful distance from the porch, some with their hands in their pockets, others with their thumbs hooked in their belts, saying little.

"What are you up to?" Willis asked.

"We need them to stay on," Laurella said. "It's too late in the season to find enough new hands for the trail drive to the railhead."

Willis hadn't thought of that. Her business savvy beat his all hollow.

Laurella put her hands on the rail and bowed her head. "Life sure is peculiar. It never works out like we think it should. When I came up here, all I wanted was a place I could live where no one knew about me — a hideaway where I could live out the rest of my days in the solitude to which I had become accustomed."

Reuben Marsh came through the assembled hands. "This is about all of them, ma'am."

A few stragglers were hurrying from the cook shack. Laurella waited until they arrived, then squeezed Willis' hand and moved to the top step. "I want to thank all of you for coming."

The sun had not yet set. Bloodred, it cast the porch and the cowboys and the lady from Texas in a crimson glow.

Armando came out of the house and moved close to Laurella. Behind him filed the Tylers, Reverend Merford, and Fred Baxter.

"I'll make this short," Laurella said. "As all of you are aware, I aim to buy the Bar T. I would like all of you to stay on, and I'm aware some of you haven't made up your minds yet. So I'll help you decide." She raised her voice. "My pa taught me that a rancher should always be honest with his hands. That he, or she, should extend the same trust to those who ride for the brand as those who ride for the brand extend to the man or woman they ride for. So I am about to show you exactly who you will be

288

workin' for. If you still want to quit, go right ahead. I won't hold it against you."

"Don't," Willis said.

Some of the cowboys were looking at one another and shrugging shoulders and shaking heads.

"Ma'am," Sam Tinsdale said, "what can you show us that we don't already know?"

"This."

Laurella took off her hat.

CHAPTER 16

The bunkhouse was the quietest Willis ever remembered it being. He lay in his bunk waiting for someone to say something but no one did — not even Charlie Weaver or Sam Tinsdale, either of whom could talk until the cows came home. He was willing to bet his last dollar that it would be one of them who broke the silence, but he was wrong.

"That there is some woman," Bob Ashlon said.

As if a dam had burst, unleashing a torrent of water, Ashlon's comment unleashed a torrent of talk. Not one cowboy made reference to Laurella's disfigurement. The talk was about her as a person: how she knew ranching inside out; how she could ride better than any female any of them had ever seen; how there wasn't a thing about cows she hadn't learned.

Then Charlie Weaver said, "Can you

290

imagine how hard it must have been, growin' up like that?"

"That there is some woman," Bob Ashlon repeated.

"I reckon I wouldn't mind ridin' for the brand with her in charge," Sam Tinsdale said.

"Me either," Rafe Carter said. "And I wouldn't stand for anyone speakin' ill of her neither."

A change had taken place. They no longer regarded her as an outsider. The fact she was female had become irrelevant. She was a cowman, whether she wore skirts or not, and she had grit. Those were the two qualities that counted most as far as the punchers were concerned — those and her honesty.

"It took courage to do what she did," Gus said, "more courage than I have — that's for sure."

"So you'll cook for her?" Charlie asked.

"And be damned proud to do so," Gus replied.

His pride was contagious. Willis detected it in all of them, in their expressions, in how they spoke of her. They seemed to have forgotten he was there but he was wrong again, for no sooner did the thought cross his mind than Charlie Weaver swiveled in his chair and looked at him.

"What I want to know," Charlie loudly declared, showing more teeth than a patent-medicine salesman, "is what a fine gal like our new boss sees in that bronc peeler yonder."

Laughter and chuckles greeted the jest but Willis was not all that amused. "She has good taste in men, is all."

"Wait until she finds out you don't bathe but three times a year," Charlie said.

Sam Tinsdale had to get his two bits in. "That will change once he says I do. I've never seen it fail. He'll be takin' a bath every day and twice on Sundays."

"Says the gent who has never been hitched," Willis said.

"I don't need to be kicked by a mule to know it hurts," Sam said, "the same as I don't need to be married to know that once a woman has a man droolin' over her, she can tell him to jump and he'll ask how high."

The door opened and in strode Reuben Marsh. He had been at the house huddled with the Tylers when Willis left. His hat was pushed back on his head and the top four or five buttons of his shirt were undone. He was whistling softly to himself but he stopped as he came down the aisle to Willis'

292

bunk. "So how do you want us to handle it?"

"Handle what?"

"You heard Miss Hendershot. One of her conditions is that the rustlers be dealt with before she'll sit down with the lawyer and sign the papers. Abe wants us to tend to it right away."

"Why are you askin' me?" Willis wondered.

"I might as well start now," Marsh said.

Willis sat up and scratched his head. "You're not makin' any kind of sense."

"Aren't I? Then let me spell it out for you. Miss Hendershot is goin' to buy the Bar T. She also has her heart set on marryin' you, and she told us at supper that you will be runnin' things as much as she does. So I might as well start takin' my orders from you now as wait until you slip a ring on her finger."

The notion of being the new boss stunned Willis. "Abe hasn't signed the Bar T over yet. He's the one you should talk to."

"Who do you think told me to come see you?" Reuben asked. "He says since you've run up against the Wilkes gang twice already, you're the expert."

"I have no idea where they are or what they will do next." But even as he said it,

Willis realized that was not entirely true.

"What's that look?" Reuben asked. He was not foreman for nothing.

"Somethin' one of the Nargent brothers said," Willis recalled, "about takin' the cows they stole to a meadow."

Charlie came out of his chair. "I remember, pard. But there are a lot of meadows up in those mountains."

"The Nargents were headin' northwest," Willis said. "That narrows it down some." He swung his good leg over the side of the bunk, then shifted his bad leg. "It has to have water, and be somewhere no one is likely to stumble across. That narrows the number more."

"I've hunted up that way a lot," Sam Tinsdale remarked. "Just last year, in fact, I went after a bull elk there."

Willis had been over much of the same area back when he hunted, and sometimes went for long rides for the joy of riding. "My guess is the meadow would also be high up so they can see anyone who comes after them."

Sam Tinsdale snapped his fingers. "I recollect a meadow up near Buzzard's Roost that fits the bill."

Buzzard's Roost was a barren peak so named because it was vaguely shaped like a bird with a big beak. Willis proposed, "Then maybe we should go have us a look-see."

"How many?" Reuben asked.

"Ten should be enough. Make sure each man has a rifle and plenty of ammunition and brings jerky and a canteen." Willis marveled at how easy it was to make decisions when he put his mind to it. "You'll be in charge."

"I figured you would be," Reuben said.

Ordinarily, Willis shunned going horseback because it reminded him of his condition. But he hadn't minded riding with Laurella. He hadn't minded that at all. "I don't know."

"I never saw it fail," Sam Tinsdale said. "It's a sad fact that when a man takes a wife, he suddenly becomes delicate."

"I'm not wed yet," Willis said gruffly, "and I'm as delicate as an anvil. So you can eat your words. We head out at first light. Reuben, you pick who goes and who stays."

"Right after I get back from fillin' Abe in." The door closed on the foreman.

Willis propped his pillow behind him. Being top dog would take some getting used to. "One more thing. Anyone who wants to quit the outfit should say so by mornin'. There's no sense in draggin' it out."

"I'll stay if you'll have me." Charlie grinned.

Willis provoked cackles when he said, "I'll have to think about it. The Bar T ain't a cocklebur outfit. Hillbilly cowboys can't keep up with us real hands."

"Why, you —" To a peal of general mirth, Charlie launched into a string of curses that would have done an army sergeant justice.

Laughing as heartily as everyone else, Willis slapped his leg and leaned back. He could not remember the last time he felt so happy, so content, so at peace with the world, and he owed it all to the lady from Texas. On an impulse he slid off the bunk and limped to the door. "I'll be up to the ranch house."

Sam Tinsdale put a hand to his chin and fluttered his eyelids. "Why, whatever could you want up there?"

"I'd shoot you but you're not worth the lead." The night air was cool. Willis pulled his hat brim low and limped up the path to the porch.

In the shadows a rocking chair creaked. "I was hopin' you would come back." Laurella took his hand. She was wearing her hat with the veil. "Let's go for a stroll."

Arm in arm, they walked to the stable and on past it until they were alone under the stars with the cows and the grass and the wind. Laurella turned to him and Willis raised her veil and kissed her.

"I could get used to that."

"You surprised me today. You never do what I expect."

Laurella rested her cheek on his chest. "How did they take it? Will there be a puncher left on the Bar T come mornin'?"

"Elfie would be jealous if she found out how popular you are. Why, they would elect you president if you were to run."

"I didn't scare any off?"

"They think you're the greatest thing since Hector was a pup." Willis kissed her hair. "I happen to feel the same myself."

"I'm afraid I'll wake up any moment now and it will all have been a dream," Laurella said. "You're too good to be true."

"I'm as ordinary as eggs. You're the special one. Just ask the punchers you swept off their feet."

Her arms rose around his neck and they were still for a very long time, until she sighed and said in that small voice she sometimes used, "Oh, Will, I'm so scared — so very, very scared."

"Of what?" Willis dreamily asked, and ran a hand through her hair.

"That you'll come to your senses. That I'll

be crushed. That I'll have to live the rest of my days as a spinster."

"I want you more than I want my knee as it used to be. If that ain't proof, I don't know what is."

"Tomorrow let's go on a picnic. I'll pack a basket and we can take the buckboard to that pool where we had a wonderful time the other day."

"Tomorrow?" Willis said. "I'm afraid I have other plans, and you only have yourself to blame."

Laurella raised her head. "How is that, dearest?"

A warm tingle spread through Willis' chest. No one had ever called him that before. He covered her good cheek with kisses and only tore himself from her with an effort.

"My head is spinnin'. Tell me about to-morrow."

Willis explained about the rustlers and the meadow. He assumed she would be pleased but felt her fingernails bite into his arm.

"Must you go yourself? Can't you have Mr. Marsh or someone else lead them? The Wilkes gang are killers, and I'd rather not be a widow before I'm even married if I can help it."

"I'm not a turtle. I can't hide in my shell

while other men do what I'm supposed to do." Willis reached for her hair but she pulled back.

"I'm serious."

"So am I. A ramrod who doesn't pull his weight is worthless. The men won't respect him."

Laurella clutched his hand. "Are you're doin' it to impress them — or to impress me?"

"Maybe it's to impress me," Willis said. "It's been so long since I could look at myself in the mirror with any kind of respect, I've forgotten what it's like."

"And if I insist you don't go?"

"You can insist. You can yell. You can scream. You can throw things. But I have to do it."

Laurella hugged him tight and did not let go. "Our first tiff. Please let there be more. If you don't come back, I won't want to live."

"Now you're spoutin' nonsense," Willis declared. "If it's meant to be, it's meant to be. Like they always say, if man is supposed to drown, he'll drown in the desert."

"Please, Will."

For a long while they were still except for their breathing. Willis thought his left leg would cramp but it didn't. It was working better than he ever dreamed it could.

"So many stars," Laurella said softly. "I've never seen the sky so lovely. A month ago I wouldn't have noticed."

"A month ago we were fools." Willis kissed her right ear and she trembled against him.

"Where I come from, callin' a girl names is not how to court her."

"What will you do while I'm gone?"

"Wear a hole in the porch. I'll have Elfie take me into town so I can send word to my parents. Be prepared in case they show up unannounced. My pa will want to take your measure and my ma will want to take my temperature."

Willis wrapped an arm around her shoulders and they began walking. "If I'm to be shot, it couldn't be for a worthier cause."

"My pa is partial to hemp. I can talk him out of it, though, if you ask real nice."

Grinning, Willis leaned down to kiss her neck but paused when hooves drummed to the southeast. "Someone is in a hurry to reach the ranch. Maybe we should go back."

"Not just yet. Please. Whatever it is can wait."

They existed in a little world all their own. Willis closed his eyes and inhaled her scent and prayed the bliss would never end. Then the rider reached the stable and shouts broke out and several figures came hurriedly out of the house and others rushed from the bunkhouse.

"Quite the commotion," Laurella commented, "but it has nothin' at all to do with us."

"We have to," Willis said.

"Is this how it will be? You always bossin' me around?" But Laurella was smiling, if wistfully, and she did not object when he bent their steps toward the buildings. She did pull her veil down.

Silhouettes moved in the light from a lantern. Men were moving in and out of the stable and bringing horses from the corral.

"It's an exodus."

"Or a war."

Abe was there, and Elfie and Reuben Marsh. Horses were being saddled as swiftly as the hands could saddle them. Rifles were being loaded. Revolvers were drawn from holsters and the cylinders checked.

"Maybe it really is a war," Willis said. He spied Fred Baxter beside a lathered horse, breathlessly relating a story to the Tylers.

"— out of nowhere, I tell you! One second we were riding along and the parson was saying how in heaven everyone has wings and can fly like a bird, and the next he was in front of us with his pistols out, ordering us to throw up our hands."

"How terrible," Elfie said.

"I threw my hands up," Baxter said, "but the parson just sat there. I whispered to him to do as we were told but he shook his head and said he did not give in to sinners and miscreants. I thought that would make the skunk mad but all he did was laugh."

"Who laughed?" Willis asked. Laurella had let go of him and was walking at his side.

"Miss Hendershot! Will! There you are!" Abe exclaimed. "For a minute I was worried you had fallen victim to him, too."

"Victim to whom?" Laurella inquired.

Fred Baxter answered. "The Flour Sack Kid. Reverend Merford and I were on our way back to Cottonwood when the Kid jumped us. He demanded our money. I gave him mine but Reverend Merford told the Kid he could rot in perdition before he would give him a cent."

Willis' dreamy feeling evaporated and was replaced by a gnawing pang of anxiety. "The Flour Sack Kid?"

"As big as life!" the store owner exclaimed. "You should have heard him. Mocking the reverend. Saying Merford was always looking down his nose at everyone when he wasn't any better than them. Calling the reverend a poor excuse for a man of the cloth."

"Oh, Lord," Elfie said.

"Reverend Merford got madder and madder. Then the Kid said that he could keep his money, that he probably got it from an old widow or took it off a body at a funeral. The parson started yelling at him, calling him names I can't repeat in mixed company."

Someone asked, "How did the Kid take that?"

"He just laughed. He thought it was funny. He started to ride off but Reverend Merford grabbed him and shouted for me to ride for help. Since we were closer to the Bar T than we were to town, I turned around and headed back. But I hadn't gone ten feet when I heard the shot."

"The Flour Sack Kid shot the parson?" Elfie was horrified.

"Maybe one of his pistols went off when they were struggling," Baxter said. "I really can't say. I heard the shot and saw Reverend Merford fall from his saddle, and then I rode like the wind to get here."

Abe turned to the punchers. "You heard him, men. Our minister is lying out there somewhere with a bullet in him, and the Flour Sack Kid is to blame. If we catch him, we'll do the same to him as we'll do to the rustlers."

The ground under Willis' feet swirled and the stars spun. A firm hand on his wrist brought him back to himself.

"You best go with them," Laurella said.

Abe overheard. "Of course he's going with us. He has a bigger stake in rooting out lawlessness and seeing that justice is served now that he has a vested interest in the territory" — he smiled — "or will soon enough."

Willis limped to the stable to saddle the zebra dun. He wanted to stall, to take so much time that his father would be long gone before they got there, but the others were impatiently waiting. As he rode into the open, Abe bawled a command and the avengers galloped down the valley.

Willis found himself in the middle of the bunch. To a man, they were as grim as hangmen. And who could blame them? A parson was the spiritual pillar of a community, the man most looked up to after the doctor. Parsons never carried guns, never lifted their hands against other human beings. Shooting one was almost as despicable as shooting a woman.

No one would argue Merford had his faults, but he *was* a reverend, and that made him special in the eyes of those he ministered to. When the townspeople heard about it, they would be as mad as riled hornets. The whole territory would be after the Kid's hide. Accident or not, it was the worst thing the Kid could have done.

They came on the horse first. It had drifted toward the ranch and was grazing at the side of the road. Abe had one of the hands bring it.

A few hundred feet farther, and a lanky form lay sprawled at the edge of the road.

"There he is!" Fred Baxter cried.

Reuben Marsh was out of his saddle first. "Reverend Merford?" he said, carefully cradling the minister's head on his leg. "Can you hear me?"

Willis held his breath, fearing calamity, but the parson groaned and opened his eyes. "Who . . ."

Abe was by their side. "It's Tyler, Reverend. Lie still." He unbuttoned Merford's jacket and bent low. When he raised his right palm, it was stained dark. "He's bleeding bad. We'd better not move him. Charlie, you and Sam ride to town and fetch the sawbones." Abe motioned at the rest of them. "What are you waiting for? The Kid can't have gotten far. Spread out and search. In pairs, not alone! Fire two shots in the air if you find him." Abe rattled off names and directions to take.

Willis was paired with Bob Ashlon and told to swing east. Willis let Ashlon take the lead. Inside him, a war raged. Part of him wanted the Kid caught and hanged. The other part, the part raised by a caring father until his mother died, wanted the Kid to get away.

"We'll never find him in the dark," Ashlon said over a shoulder.

"We have to try," Willis said. The Kid had a head start but fourteen other men were scouring the countryside, increasing the odds he would be caught.

"They'll double the reward bounty," Ashlon predicted. "If he's smart, he'll head for Alaska."

Willis had a hunch that no matter how high the bounty climbed, his father would not leave. The man was as pigheaded as the year was long.

Woodland loomed ahead. Ashlon drew rein and Willis came to a stop next to him.

"Do we risk our horses breakin' a leg?"

Before Willis could answer, two shots shattered the stillness. "The signal!" he said, and reined to the west, dreading the blast of more shots and the end to someone who once meant the world to him. But there were only a few shouts and the drum of heavy hooves. Other riders materialized and soon he was among a knot of punchers trying to pinpoint where the shots came from.

"Was that you?"

"No, it wasn't me."

"Then who fired?"

"Did you fire?"

"Am I holdin' my pistol?"

"Well, somebody sure as hell fired!"

"There!"

Rafe Carter and George Trimble hove out of the gloom and reined up. "I saw him!" Rafe shouted. "I saw the Flour Sack Kid as big as life and as plain as I'm seeing all of you!"

"Where?" someone asked.

"This way! Follow me!" Rafe cried, and used his spurs. The others raced after him, whooping and hollering as if they were having the time of their lives.

Willis hung back. He did not want to be there if they caught him. They would shoot on sight, and he could do without seeing the man who had helped bring him into the world shot to ribbons. "Please, Pa," he said. "Please."

Then there was another shout, and a shot, and more shouts, and more shots, and Willis had the impression of horsemen riding every which way in wild confusion brought to an end by one more shot and the loudest shout yet.

"I got him! I shot the Flour Sack Kid!"

CHAPTER 17

Nine or ten Bar T riders were clustered around a horse Willis recognized: the Appaloosa. Rafe Carter had hold of the animal's reins and was crowing, "I shot him! I'm sure of it!"

"Then where's the body, boy?" Gus demanded.

"He went that way," Rafe said, pointing at a dark wall of vegetation some fifty to sixty feet away.

Relief flooded through Willis. Maybe the young cowboy had missed, and in the woods, his father had a good chance of eluding them.

Hooves thundered, heralding Abe's arrival. On being told the news, he rose in the stirrups. "What are you waiting for? After him! Spread out! But stay in sight of the man to your right and your left. Don't take any chances! Don't try to take him alive. Shoot the Kid down on sight!"

"The Kid's not a rustler," Willis heard himself saying. "He deserves a trial, the same as anybody else would."

"He shot the parson," someone said.

"The parson ain't Moses," Willis responded. "If the Kid had shot Baxter, we wouldn't be so all-fired eager to string him up."

"What's gotten into you?" Casey McLeash asked. "Since when do you give a damn about outlaws, whether they're hot-brand artists or not?"

"With the marshal and the deputy dead, we're the law now," George Trimble pointed out.

"Then we should act like the law," Willis said, "and the law doesn't hang folks without a trial."

"You're gettin' soft now that you have a cow bunny," Trimble replied.

Willis almost reined over to punch him but Abe Tyler spared him from making a fool of himself.

"No. Will is right. I've always said that Wyoming isn't Montana. We can't have vigilantes take over. Yet here we are, behaving like vigilantes ourselves. My only excuse is that I think shooting a man of the cloth is as low as a badman can go." Abe smiled at Willis. "Thank you for keeping your head.

The rest of you, if we can, we'll take the Kid to town to stand trial."

"Hell," Gus said in disgust, "why don't we just paint big white bull's-eyes on our backs?"

"I didn't say not to shoot if he resists," Abe said. "If he lifts a finger against you, fill him with lead. We're justified in defending ourselves, law or no law."

"The law!" Bob Ashlon scoffed. "It's real good at protectin' those who break it but not worth a damn at protectin' those who don't."

"Save the legal niceties for later," Abe said. "As we speak, the Flour Sack Kid is getting away. After him!"

Willis trailed them into the trees. He reined wide to the left to be at the north end of the line as it advanced. More than likely his father was somewhere near the center and he did not want to be one of the punchers who caught him. He did not even try to search. He was absorbed in thoughts of life and fate and how one woman could change everything for the better.

The cowhands were shouting back and forth.

"Any sign of him yet?"

"He's not over here!"

"Nothin' this way!"

"Look up in the trees! He could be hidin' up a tree!"

"Watch for logs, too! He could be hidin' behind one!"

His head down, Willis thought of another woman who had loved him once — a woman who had doted over him as only a mother could. Lord, there were times when he missed her! He often wondered how different his life would have been had she not died.

Suddenly a hand grasped hold of his left leg and a muffled voice whispered, "Son! It's me! Don't let on that I'm here!"

Willis jerked straight in the saddle. The flour sack was pale in the night; the Kid was holding his other hand to his shoulder. "Go away," Willis whispered. "I don't want anythin' to do with you."

"I'm bleedin'."

"Serves you right for goin' around shootin' parsons," Willis whispered almost savagely. "You have no more brains than a turnip."

"It wasn't my fault," the Kid protested. "The jackass grabbed me and tried to take my pistols from me and one went off."

"It's never your fault, is it?"

"Damn it, son, I'm hurt. Are you goin' to put on airs or help me?"

Willis glanced to his right. The nearest rider, Bob Ashlon, was barely visible. "Take off that stupid sack and wad it under your shirt."

"What for?" his father balked. "I've had it for years. It's part of me, like your hat is part of you."

"Where did you get a silly notion like that? My hat is no more a part of me than my belt buckle." Willis caught himself. Now was not the time for another of their arguments. He must control his temper. "That damn sack stands out like a sheet on a clothesline. Do somethin' with it or I'll leave you and your precious sack to bleed to death."

"A fine way to talk to your pa," the Kid said, but he took off the sack, folded it, unbuttoned his shirt, and slid the sack underneath. "There. Happy now?"

"I'll be happy the day you're out of my hair for good," Willis whispered. He had been slowly drifting to the left and was now out of Ashlon's sight. "Quick," he said, lowering his arm, "grab hold and swing up. I'll get you out of here before my whole life is ruined."

"Thank you, son."

"Don't call me that. I'd rather not be reminded."

"A little inconvenience and you become

all prickly. I'm the one who's been shot, not you."

The saddle creaked. The Kid's hand gripped Willis' shoulder. Willis reined west but held the zebra dun to a walk.

"Thank the good Lord I spotted you before any of those others spotted me," the Kid whispered.

"I wouldn't be bringin' the Lord into this so soon after shootin' one of His shepherds."

"You haven't changed much, Will," the Kid grumbled.

"Neither have you, Matthew."

They went a short way, and the Kid said, "I thought maybe you had forgotten my name."

"I tried to forget you but you won't let me," Willis said. "I reckon some ties are deeper than we count on."

"I'm sorry for all the aggravation I've caused you."

"Don't you dare be nice to me," Willis snapped. "I'm entitled to want to split your skull with a brandin' iron."

"It's been that rough, has it?" Matthew whispered.

Willis was shaking, he was so mad. "I'm not foolin'. I'll push you off and you can fend for your own damn self."

"It's no less than I deserve, I guess. I took

314

the wrong road in life, and I'm not makin' excuses."

Willis half turned and jabbed a finger into his father's chest. "Quit being so all-fired reasonable! It's a little late to be apologizin'."

"I know that, son. Believe me, I know —"

"What does it take to get through to you?" Willis was practically beside himself. "I don't care, Pa. I just don't care anymore. So save your excuses for when you're lookin' in the mirror."

"If you don't care, why are you so upset?"

Willis refused to answer. For over a mile, he wound to the northwest and then headed due west, relying on the Big Dipper and the North Star to guide him.

"Where are you takin' me, son?"

"Stop callin' me that," Willis said testily. "We're goin' to the Bar T — to a gully near the ranch house. It's choked with brush you can hide in until I arrange for you to leave the country."

"Who says I'm leavin'?"

"I do," Willis declared. "The parson was the last straw. Pick a place, any place, so long as it's not within five hundred miles of the Bar T. I'll get you a horse and supplies, and I never want to set eyes on you again."

"It's that bad between us?" the Kid asked.

"When hasn't it been?"

"That's not fair. That's not fair at all. I did my best by you when you were younger. Then your ma died and I lost my head."

"And it's been lost ever since."

His father chuckled. "That was a good one."

"It wasn't meant to be. I'm serious, Pa. I want you gone. I have a chance at a new life and I don't want you to spoil it."

"Is it that filly you were with — the strange one who wears the hat and veil all over the place?"

"She's agreed to marry me," Willis revealed. "We're going to run the Bar T together, have kids of our own. I pray to God I'm a better pa to them than you ever were to me."

"Did I miss somethin'? What's that business about runnin' the Bar T?"

"I thought you knew. She's here to buy it, all the way from Texas. Once I marry her, I'll be half owner."

"So the ranch will be yours?" The Kid whistled. "That's good news, son. Mighty good news. Now I don't need to go anywhere. Your marriage is the answer to our prayers."

Reining up, Willis twisted around. He had not gotten a good look at his father earlier but now he did, and was shocked. Once a deep brown, his father's hair was nearly white, with broad gray streaks. Once smooth and rugged, his father's face was seamed with wrinkles, his father's jaw framed by a couple weeks' worth of whitish-gray stubble. "The only prayer I have is to be rid of you."

"Don't you see?" Matthew said. "Thanks to you, I can start a new life, too. I can give up my wicked ways. Isn't that what you want more than anythin'?"

"How is it thanks to me?" Willis asked suspiciously as he slapped his legs against the zebra dun.

"You'll be runnin' the Bar T. I'll throw away my flour sack, and you can hire me on as a new hand. We'll make up some name for me so no one will suspect who I really am." His father clapped him on the shoulder. "I'll work hard — you'll see. You won't have any regrets."

"No," Willis said.

"You won't hire me? Why not? No one knows what I look like under the flour sack. It's perfectly safe."

"I'll know the truth," Willis said, "and my wife will know because I won't keep it a secret from her. I can't. I care for her too much."

His father was growing angry. "I won't be

a burden. I promise. I'll do the same work as the rest of the hands, and I'll do it well. I won't give you cause to regret takin' me on."

"You're not listenin'. I've already made up my mind. You're leavin' the territory and you're not comin' back."

"I don't believe my ears. You'd deny your pa a normal life?"

"You denied me one," Willis said. "Don't make more of our relationship than there is — if we can even call it that." He let out a long sigh. "We're doin' it my way or we're not doin' it at all. Climb down and we'll part company for once and for all."

"You don't leave a man breathin' room."

"What makes you think you deserve any?"

That shut him up for a while. Willis came to a clearing and spied lights at the far end of the home valley. It would be a while yet before they reached the gully.

"What is this filly of yours like, if you don't mind my askin'?" Matthew inquired.

"I do mind." To Willis, Laurella was the one truly clean and wonderful thing in his life, and he would not discuss her with a man who had tainted the Lander family with the stamp of lawlessness.

"I would be a wonderful grandpa."

Willis had endured all he could. He drew rein and swung down, careful to put most of his weight on his good leg, then reached up and gripped the front of his father's shirt and hauled him off the zebra dun. *"No more!"* he raged, and shoved. His father fell onto his back, still clutching his wound. *"I will not put up with you anymore — do you hear me?"*

Straddling his father, Willis grabbed him by the throat and slapped him full across the face, not once but five, six, seven, eight times, slapped him hard, so hard that his father's lower lip split and blood trickled from the corner of his father's mouth. Willis raised his hand to slap him again and abruptly realized his father was not fighting back, was not making any attempt whatsoever to defend himself.

"Are you done, son?"

Willis shoved his father to the ground. Whirling, he stalked a dozen steps, his arms tight against his ribs, unable to keep his eyes from misting and furious at himself for being so weak. "I hate you."

"Sure you do."

"Stop it! You gave up your right to be my pa when you left us. And I will not inflict you on my own children."

"If you feel this strongly —"

Willis' revolver was in his hand. He thumbed back the hammer. His father was an indistinct shape in the darkness, but at that range, Willis couldn't miss him. "You deserve this."

"I've always loved you," Matthew said.

Invisible daggers sliced into Willis' insides. His finger curled around the trigger. The metal was cool to the touch. All it would take was a slight squeeze.

"I know I've done you wrong, son. There isn't a day goes by that I don't curse myself. But I couldn't stop. They took your ma from me and I can never forgive them for as long as I live."

"No one took her. It was just how things worked out."

"You're a grown man. You should know better. Did the parson take up a collection for your ma? Did any of those fine, upstandin' ladies from town come by to comfort her? Did *anyone* do *anything* for us?"

"The doctor tried his best."

"He took an oath. All doctors do. They have to help whether they want to or not. But no one else would soil themselves by reachin' out to poor white trash like us, and me a veteran. They left your ma to rot. Not one flower at her funeral. Not one person showed to mourn her."

"Have you forgotten what you did? How you got drunk and stood out in the middle of the street and cursed the town and said that if anyone showed up at the funeral, you would shoot them dead? Now you lie there and blame *them?*"

"Someone should have come. Someone should have helped."

Willis slowly slid his revolver into his holster, then helped his father to stand. Only then did he realize how much taller he was, and how much broader in the shoulders, and how frail and old his father looked without the flour sack.

It was pushing midnight by Willis' watch when they came to the gully. He turned to tell his father to climb down and discovered the Kid was asleep. Gently shaking him, he said quietly, "We're there."

"Oh. Sorry." Matthew stiffly slid down, and grimaced.

"Let me have a gander at that shoulder." Willis peeled the blood-soaked shirt partway off. The bullet had gone in under the clavicle and left a nasty exit wound. "You'll need stitchin'."

"I can get by."

"We do this my way or we don't do it. Savvy?" When his father nodded, Willis indicated the brush. "In you go. I'll be back an hour before sunrise with what food I can scrape up, a canteen, and a needle and thread."

Matthew smiled and started to turn. "What if you're caught? What will they do to you?"

"It's a little late to be thinkin' about me." Willis swung onto the hurricane deck. "In a couple of days I'll have a horse and the supplies you'll need, and you can be on your way."

"Whatever you want," Matthew said meekly.

Willis paralleled the gully. It came out forty yards from the rear of the ranch house. He reined west and then south to approach from a different direction. Lamps were on in the house, a rarity at that hour, and at the bunkhouse. He stripped the zebra dun, shouldered his saddlebags, and limped to the bunkhouse door. He had hoped everyone was asleep but voices came from within.

"Will!" Charlie Weaver exclaimed. He and several others were playing poker with toothpicks for chips since Abe did not let them play for money. "Where in hell did you get to? The boys thought maybe the Kid got you."

"My leg cramped up." Willis employed a lie they would accept since it had happened before. "I had to climb down and rest it a while. Afraid I dozed off."

"With us scourin' those woods and callin' your name?" Bob Ashlon asked.

"I was on my way back when I stopped." Willis grinned. "I guess you didn't holler loud enough." To keep them from asking more questions, he said, "What's the latest on the parson?"

"The doc has him up to the house," Charlie said. "It was too far to town, so they're operatin' on the kitchen table."

"They?"

"Abe and Elfie and your sweetheart are helpin'. She was powerful worried about you. It was all Abe could to do to keep her from ridin' out after you." Charlie added a few toothpicks to the pot. "If you haven't been up to the house yet, you might want to set her mind at rest."

"Did you ever find the Flour Sack Kid?" Willis remembered to ask.

"Not a trace of him," Rafe Carter said. "But I swear I hit him. I'll bet he's lyin' out in the timber somewhere, bleedin' to death."

"Let's hope," Sam Tinsdale said.

Willis' leg really did begin to cramp as he went up the path to the front porch. It had been a long, tiring day. His leg muscles had been neglected so long that it would be a while before he was his old self, or as close to his old self as his bad leg would let him be.

At his knock, Little Sparrow opened the door. "Mr. Lander," she said formally, "everyone has been worried."

"So I hear." Willis doffed his hat and limped past her. In a chair in the parlor sat Reuben Marsh, hat in hand. Reuben nodded. "Would you let Miss Hendershot know I'm here?"

"Certainly, sir." Little Flower bobbed her exquisite chin, smiled at Reuben, and hurried down the hall.

"Some night," the foreman said.

"Ain't it?" Willis said.

"Between the Flour Sack Kid and the Wilkes gang, we've had more excitement than we know what to do with." Reuben was gazing down the hall like a puppy that had lost its master.

"Some peace and quiet would be nice." Willis put his hat on and took it off again. He smoothed his bandanna, hitched at his belt.

"I'm happy for you, Will," Reuben Marsh said. "About Miss Hendershot, I mean. You're lucky havin' a gal you can marry without complications."

"There's not much to it. The man says I do and the woman says I do and the parson says now you are man and wife."

"Not that kind of complication," Reuben said. "Not the ceremony."

"What other kind is there?"

"Families. In-laws to be. Sometimes the man and the woman aren't the same race. You wouldn't think that would matter when two people are in love, but to some folks, it matters enough to make all those involved miserable."

Was that experience speaking? Willis wondered as Laurella flowed toward him with her arms wide open.

"Will! Oh, Will! Where have you been?"

The feel of her, her warmth, the scent of her hair, the scent of her perfume — Willis drank her in as a man who had been out in a desert for forty days and forty nights would drink from a spring. Her veil brushed his cheek, and he felt her heart hammer in her chest. Or was it his?

"I can use some air," Laurella said. "It was stuffy in the kitchen with the pot of hot water on to boil, and the smell of the blood."

"Will Reverend Merford live?"

"Accordin' to the doctor. The pastor is to rest here a few days before they take him to town." Laurella clasped his fingers and pulled him out onto the porch. The light spilling from the windows was not to her liking. She pulled him farther, to a corner shrouded in shadow.

"I missed you. Isn't it silly? You were only gone five hours and I missed you as if you had been gone five months." Laurella nuzzled his ear and whispered, "Where is your pa?"

"How did you figure it out?" Willis marveled.

"He disappeared. You disappeared. You're back, but you haven't brought him up yet, which tells me you're not worried how he is because you know."

"I'm marryin' the most brilliant gal in Texas."

"I can add two plus two without my shoes off," Laurella said. "Was he really shot? How bad is he? Will he live?"

"Unfortunately," Willis said, and explained about the gully.

"So that's how it is. But how will you look after him when you're gone?"

"Gone?" Willis said, and remembered. "Damn."

CHAPTER 18

The long ride to Buzzard's Roost was a nightmare. The days were sunny and clear, the nights crisp and brisk. Game was abundant and there were a half dozen streams along the way. The ten of them, traveling steadily higher through vast stretches of pines and firs and cottonwoods and then aspens, never wanted for food or water.

It was a nightmare because Willis could not stop thinking about Laurella and his father. She had offered to take food to him while Willis was gone. Someone had to look after him, Laurella said, and there was no one else to do it. Willis would not hear of it; he refused to go after the rustlers until he had seen his father out of the territory. But Laurella pointed out that if he delayed the trip to Buzzard's Roost it might arouse suspicion. It had been his idea, after all.

Willis still refused to give in. Then Laurella reminded him that the rustlers must be dealt with before she bought the Bar T. The sooner the Wilkes gang was eliminated, the sooner their future together started in earnest.

So the next morning, early, as Willis had arranged, ten grim cowhands headed for the high country with Willis in the lead. He was the grimmest of all.

Willis worried nearly every minute. He worried his father would get Laurella into trouble. Maybe she would be caught taking food to him. Or maybe his father would give her a hard time. The one thing he did not fear was that his father would harm her. Matthew had never raised a hand against a woman in his life.

Willis fretted, and fretted some more, and he was fretting the morning they came to a timbered switchback a mile below Buzzard's Roost. Since he was in the lead, he saw the tracks before anyone else: dozens of cow tracks left by cattle that had no business being there unless they were the cows stolen from the Bar T.

"You were right, then," Charlie Weaver said. "They are hidin' out up here."

"We should be near that meadow soon," Sam Tinsdale said.

"And they're bound to have lookouts," Rafe mentioned.

Willis pulled his Winchester from his saddle scabbard and levered a round into the chamber. "Get set, boys." He was eager to get it over with so he could return to the ranch and Laurella. As much as he worried about her, he missed her more. He had never known it was possible to miss someone so much.

"Shouldn't one of us ride on ahead and scout around?" Sam Tinsdale asked.

"I'm fixin' to do just that," Willis said. At the top of the switchback, he guided them into some brush. "Wait here. No fires. No noise. I'll be back as soon as I've made sure they're there."

"I'll go with you," Charlie offered.

"One rider makes less noise than two," Willis said, and gigged the zebra dun toward Buzzard's Roost. The meadow was a quarter mile from the peak. Dense forest masked his approach. Twice he stopped when he saw movement but each time it was an animal, the first time a mule deer, the second time a bull elk.

Then Willis smelled smoke from a campfire, and the aroma of coffee. It made him think of the food Laurella was taking to his father every day, and his worry blossomed anew. Shaking his head, he dispelled it. He must concentrate. He must stay alert. Varner Wilkes and Mason and the Nargent brothers were killers and would shoot without warning.

Willis rode slowly, stopping often to probe the shadows, and to listen. The trees did not thin out; they ended abruptly at the meadow's edge. He heard the cows before he saw them: twenty-three, all with the Bar T brand.

The Wilkes gang was not camped in the meadow. They were beyond it, in the timber on the other side, their presence given away by the tendrils from their campfire.

Since Willis couldn't very well cross in the open, he skirted the meadow and came up on them through the undergrowth. On horseback he would be easier to spot, so he dismounted, tied the reins to a low limb, and advanced on foot, barely conscious of his limp.

The smell of smoke grew stronger. Presently Willis glimpsed flames. Tote and Thatch Nargent were beside the fire. Four saddled mounts were nearby, kept saddled, no doubt so the gang could make a quick escape if they had to. Varner Wilkes was doing something with a pair of saddlebags.

Willis bent at the waist. He toyed with the notion of taking them alone, of making them drop their hardware and holding them at gunpoint until his friends joined him. Leaning against a fir, he fingered the Winchester's trigger and wondered where Mason had gotten to. The Southerner had to be around somewhere, or why were there four horses and not just three? Willis looked right and he looked left and did not see him. He took another slow step, and a second, and something touched the nape of his neck.

"Hand the rifle back nice and slow," the Southerner directed. "Stock first, if yuh don't mind."

To resist was suicide. In the time it would take Willis to turn and shoot, Mason could put three shots into him. Willis handed the rifle back and had to stand helpless as his revolver was plucked from its holster.

"Thank yuh, suh. Now walk. With your hands in the air."

A pistol barrel nudged Willis in the spine. Raising his arms, he limped into the clearing. Immediately, the Nargent brothers leaped to their feet and clawed for their revolvers.

Varner Wilkes grinned. Shutting the saddlebag, he sauntered over. "What do we have here, Reb?"

"He was sneakin' up on yuh."

"Is that so?" Varner tilted his head and said to Willis. "I remember you. You're that cripple from the Bar T."

Willis thought of Laurella and how much he adored her.

Mason came around in front of him and tossed the Winchester to Tote Nargent, who set it on the ground. "He was the only one I saw."

"But I doubt he came alone." Varner stared up into Willis' eyes. "How many are with you, cripple? And where are they?"

"Don't call me that," Willis said. He did not see the punch that caught him below the belt but he sure felt his groin explode with pain. Clutching himself, he grunted, sputtered, and nearly fell.

"Don't tell me what to do, cripple," Varner Wilkes said. "Answer my questions or I'll cripple you worse." His smile was positively vicious. "Now let's try again. What are you doin' here?"

"Huntin'," Willis said.

"You expect me to believe that?"

Willis remembered the bull elk. "This is prime elk country. I come up here every year after one."

"Most folks hunt in the fall," the runt observed.

"Usually I do, too," Willis glibly informed him, "but I needed some time to myself so I came up now."

"Let's kill him," Tote Nargent said.

"I'll do it," Thatch volunteered, and raised his revolver. "Smack between the eyes."

Without looking at them, Varner said coldly, "That's funny. I don't recollect sayin' we should buck him out. And I wouldn't want to be you if you killed him before I'm ready."

Thatch quickly said, "We'd never do a thing like that, cousin."

"I hope not, or I'd be shy two kin." Varner glanced at Mason. "Backtrack him. Make sure he's alone like he claims."

The Southerner didn't move. "Yuh didn't say please."

"Damn it, this is no time for your shenanigans," Varner growled. "Can't you for once do somethin' without givin' me a hard time?" When the man in gray did not move, Varner swore and snapped, "*Please.* Happy now?"

"Very," Mason said. "I admire a man with manners." He grinned and melted into the timber.

"Contrary son of a bitch," Varner Wilkes muttered, and pointed toward the fire. "Have a seat while we wait, cripple. Tote, give the gent some coffee. Never let it be said we're not hospitable."

"Coffee? I don't understand you sometimes, cousin," Tote said, but he bent to do as he had been told.

"That's because you have half a brain and I have a whole one." Varner poured a cup for himself and stood blowing on it and taking little sips.

Willis wondered how long it would be before Charlie and the others realized something was wrong and came after him. The pain below his belt had subsided enough for him to say, "I'm surprised you haven't left the territory yet. You havin' a brain and all."

"Another twenty head or so and we'll be on our way," Varner said. "I've got a buyer lined up."

"Who?" Willis asked. Buying stolen cattle was itself a crime, and those who did so did so at their peril.

"Marshal Keever," Varner said, and laughed.

Thatch had been studying Willis closely. "Say, this is one of the hombres who jumped Tote and me the other day." He touched his shoulder. "I'm still sore from where they nicked me."

"Is that so?" Varner smirked at Willis. "You get around for a cripple. When the Reb gets back, I'll let my cousins do what they want with you. It should be amusin'."

"Do you gun down helpless old ladies, too?"

Varner took the insult without a hint of anger. "Mister, I'll gun down anyone, anywhere, anytime. Men, women, kids — I've killed them all, even old ladies. The last was a hag with a withered arm. We stopped at her farm and she invited us in for tea and said her husband was away and wouldn't be back for a few days."

"I remember her!" Tote chortled. "She's the one you nailed to the floor and skinned alive."

"She sure could scream," Thatch said. "It hurt my ears, how she carried on."

Willis had heard of men like this: men who killed and thought nothing of the killing; men who snuffed out lives as casually as other men snuffed out candles. He had never met any until now, and until now he had thought that maybe men who did such terrible things were made up. Now he believed.

Suddenly Willis realized that Varner was speaking to him.

"— ears plugged with wax? I asked you a question and you damn well better answer me."

"Sorry."

"Maybe his ears are crippled, too," Tote

Nargent said, and he and his brother cackled.

Varner cast an annoyed glance their way, then said, "I asked if the good people of Cottonwood have got around to pinnin' a star on a new lawman?"

"Not yet," Willis said. "They want me to be the new marshal but I haven't given them an answer."

"You?" Varner Wilkes slapped his side and laughed as loud as his cousins. "You'd be plumb worthless! You can't hardly walk. And you sure don't strike me as bein' a gun hand."

"I'm not," Willis admitted. "All I've ever shot are snakes and such."

"And elk," Varner said. "Don't forget the elk." He scratched his head and sipped more coffee. "I don't rightly know what to make of you, mister. You should be tremblin' in your boots along about now."

"We all die," Willis said. Inwardly, though, he was scared as scared could be, but not of dying. He had thought about killing himself too many times to ever be scared of that. No, he was mortally afraid of being denied the years he had hoped to spend with Laurella. At long last he had a chance at genuine happiness and he would never get to experience it.

"What's keepin' Mason?" Varner asked, gazing into the trees.

Willis was glad he had left the zebra dun so far from the clearing. It would be a while before the Southerner found it. "You should leave while you can. Your days in Wyomin' are numbered."

"Says you," Varner replied. "Wyomin' is no different than anywhere else. Sheep everywhere you look, and I don't mean the four-legged kind."

"Is that all people are to you?"

"No, some are wolves. I'm a wolf. My cousins are wolves. Mason is a wolf but a wolf with a conscience, which is no wolf at all." Varner squatted with his elbows on his knees. "You're one of the sheep — you and all the other yacks who ride their asses to the bone for forty dollars a month."

"You have it all worked out," Willis said.

"The world is a lot simpler place than most think," Varner responded. "It's take or be taken. I'm one of the takers."

Thatch was gnawing on his lower lip and shifting his weight from one foot to the other. "Why are we doin' all this jawin'? Can't we shoot him and be done with it?"

"Not until we find out if he's alone," Varner said. "He might come in handy as a hostage."

"Like the time we robbed that bank in El-liston," Tote said, "and you used the bank clerk as a hostage when they surrounded the bank. We waltzed out of that town as pretty as you please."

"And you shot the clerk anyway later," Thatch said, and giggled.

Varner smiled at the memory. "Now you see why we haven't killed this cowpoke yet. Never burn your bridges until you've crossed them."

"He's a bridge?" Thatch asked in be-fuddlement. "How can that be?"

Varner sighed. "Never you mind. The important thing is to do as I tell you and we'll get out of this in one piece. I haven't let you down yet, have I?"

"Not once," Tote said. "You've outfoxed everyone who's tried to put windows in our skulls."

"We'd have been caught and hung long ago if not for you, cousin," Thatch con-curred. "You're the smartest hombre I know."

A tiny voice deep in Willis warned him not to say anything but he did anyway. "How smart is it to rob and kill?"

"It beats smellin' cow piss for a livin'," said Varner. "We do what we want, when we want, and we're beholden to no one."

"Except the ghosts of all those whose toes you've curled up," Willis said.

Varner's eyes narrowed. "That galls you, doesn't it? The killin'?"

"I wouldn't do it but I'm not like you."

"And do you know why you can never be like me? Because you're soft inside. A man has to be hard as iron to do what I did to that old woman." Varner paused. "I've never had nightmares, not one. That should tell you somethin'."

Willis said, "It tells me you're as dead inside as the people you kill."

"That's where you're wrong. I never feel more alive than I do when I squeeze the trigger or stick a knife into someone. I've always been that way. From the time I stomped a frog to death when I was seven or eight." Varner set down his tin cup. "Where in the hell is Mason? He should have been back by now."

Willis was thinking the same thing. The zebra dun wasn't *that* far, and Mason would ride it back rather than walk.

"Want me to go see?" Thatch asked.

Tote had risen on the toes of his boots and was peering intently into the timber. "Say, I think I see someone movin' around in there. A whole bunch of someones."

"A whole bunch?" Varner shot erect, his

hand swooping to his revolver.

Willis looked, and Tote was right — six or seven shadowy silhouettes were converging on the clearing. He had never been so glad to hear Charlie Weaver's voice as he was the next moment.

"Drop your guns, you polecats, or we'll fill you with lead!"

Tote and Thatch Nargent glanced at their cousin. For a span of heartbeats, Varner Wilkes was frozen in surprise, but to his credit, he was swift to recover and grab Willis by the shirt and spin him around. Jamming the muzzle of his revolver against Willis' temple, Varner backed toward the horses while hollering, "Do you see this cripple? Try to stop us, and I swear to God he's the first to die!"

The silhouettes stopped their advance. Tote and Thatch laughed and backpedaled, confident their cousin held the top card.

"Let Will go!" Sam Tinsdale shouted. "We'll let you ride out if you don't harm him!"

Varner's features twisted in a sneer of contempt. "You expect me to believe that? He's comin' with us! Any sign of any of you doggin' our trail and you'll never see him again — alive, that is."

Willis thought of the bank clerk. "Don't

believe him!" he yelled. "He'll kill me anyway!" He dug in his bootheels. Without warning, a tremendous blow to the side of his head nearly buckled his legs. The world blurred, and Willis felt a warm sticky sensation above his ear.

"Not another peep out of you!" Varner snarled. He moved faster, hauling Willis after him. "I can kill you here as well as anywhere."

Willis could not let them get him on a horse. Once the rustlers were in the clear, they would leave him lying in a pool of blood. He tried to turn but his body would not do what he wanted it to do. His ears were ringing and he was half queasy to his stomach. Varner gave a maddened tug and his left leg gave way. Too late, he braced his right leg but it would not support his weight. Down he sprawled.

Oaths blistered the air. Varner seized Willis by the back of the neck and sought to yank him to his feet. "Get up, damn you!"

"My leg —" Willis blurted, but Varner didn't care that his left knee was useless. All Varner cared about was using him as a shield.

"Get up!" the killer roared. Livid with fury, he let go of Willis' neck and grabbed Willis' belt instead. "I won't tell you again!"

That was when a rifle cracked and Tote Nargent staggered but did not go down. Tote and Thatch cut loose, firing as rapidly as they could thumb back the hammers of their pistols. The firing from the timber rose to a crescendo, compelling Varner Wilkes to join in.

A hailstorm of hot lead sizzled the air above Willis. He flattened, saw his Winchester, and scrambled toward it. A slug kicked up a dirt geyser inches from his cheek. Another missed his right hand by a whisker.

Tote had reached the horses and Thatch was boosting him onto the saddle. Varner Wilkes had unlimbered a rifle from a scabbard and was covering them, his rifle banging in measured cadence as he aimed and fired.

Another moment, and Willis had the Winchester in his hands. Rolling onto his back, he saw Varner Wilkes climbing on a roan. He fired but he rushed his shot. Varner jabbed his spurs into the roan and bent low over the saddle horn. Willis fired again but again Varner appeared to be unscathed.

Tote was reining his mount around. His face pale, he extended his pistol at Willis. "You're dead, you stinkin' cow nurse!"

Willis was a shade faster. His Winchester boomed and Tote Nargent reeled, a hole low in his side. Tote would have fallen had Thatch, now on horseback, not pulled up alongside, snatched the reins to his brother's mount, and bolted into the vegetation.

Willis looked for Varner but Varner had disappeared. Heaving on his good knee, he sighted down the barrel but there was no one to shoot. He rose unsteadily as Bar T hands poured from the woods, Charlie Weaver foremost among them.

"Pard, you all right?"

"No thanks to you," Willis said. "What took you so long?"

"You told us to stay put, remember?" Charlie began reloading his revolver while bawling, "The horses! Bring the horses!"

"Thank God you didn't. What about the fourth one — the Southerner, Mason?"

"We saw a man in gray near your horse but he vanished into thin air before we could get to him."

Rafe Carter and Sam Tinsdale came out of the trees supporting Casey McLeash, who hung as limp as a wet rag.

"McLeash has had it," Tinsdale said. "Les Stewart is dead, too, shot in the head by Varner Wilkes."

"Stewart's brains splattered all over me," Rafe Carter said. His shirt and hat were speckled with bits of hair and gore.

Out of the woods came Bob Ashlon, leading the horses.

Willis limped toward the zebra dun, calling out, "Leave the dead! We'll come back for them!" His plan had gone awry but it was not over. The skirmish had gone to the rustlers; the outcome was yet to be decided.

"Shouldn't one of us go for more men?" Rafe Carter asked. "There're only eight of us now."

"Eight is enough," Willis said. "We'll stick to their trail, and either end it or drive them clear out of the territory for good and for all."

Rafe was a seasoned nitpicker. "What about the other one? Mason, isn't that his handle? He could be anywhere."

"He's the one who shot Jim Palmer," Sam Tinsdale said. "He shot Timmy Easton, too."

Willis did not need reminding. "On your horses!" He did not wait for them. Spurring the zebra dun into the trees, he rode as he had ridden in the old days. Varner Wilkes and the Nargent brothers were out there somewhere, and Willis was going to ride them down and do to them what should have been done a long time ago. He could hardly wait.

CHAPTER 19

The cowboys charged out of the clearing whooping and hollering and bubbling with a volcanic thirst for vengeance. Rafe Carter, in his exuberance, fired a shot into the air. Willis was as eager to slay the rustlers as everyone else. More so, for he had something to prove, and he would die proving it if need be.

The thought jarred him. It was one thing to be the iron hand of justice, another to want to slay other human beings to show that he was not only worthy to be the new boss of the Bar T but to show the woman who wanted to take him for her husband that he was a worthy husband. But it did not jar him enough to change his mind.

At the forefront of the avenging pack, Willis plowed through the underbrush, avoiding trees and logs and boulders and ducking under low limbs, and always with his eyes fixed in the distance for sign of their quarry.

That sign came on them unexpectedly. Two hundred yards from the clearing the zebra dun suddenly whinnied and shied, and Willis immediately drew rein. He had spotted the same thing the zebra dun had spotted; a body sprawled in their path.

The whooping and hollering had died. Somber and silent, the cowboys ringed the fallen form.

"Well, we got one," Sam Tinsdale said. "Which one is it?"

"Tote Nargent," Willis said.

"Why is his tongue stickin' out like that?" Bob Ashlon wondered.

"He soiled himself," Charlie Weaver noticed.

"I heard they do that," Frank Donner said. "When they die, I mean. It all lets go."

Willis felt nothing. No thrill. No sense of justice or triumph. He felt nothing at all, which was strange. "One down, three to go." Flicking his reins, he brought the zebra dun to a gallop.

The sign was clear as clear could be: churned sod, broken branches, crushed bushes. So far the rustlers were making no attempt to shake them off but that was bound to change.

Willis had gone a mile before he realized that he had not thought about his bad leg once since the Southerner put a gun to his back. All he had thought about was how he did not want to die and what he could do to stay alive. Now here he was, riding hell-for-leather, and he was doing it without thinking about how much better he could ride in the old days. He was not feeling sorry for himself. That in itself was something.

The tracks came to the base of a steep slope. Willis started up it. Suddenly the trees thinned and he was confronted by a barren mountainside sprinkled with boulders. Boulders ideal for bushwhackers, or rustlers who wanted to whittle the odds.

Raising an arm, Willis brought the cowboys to a halt. He did not like the looks of that slope, and he said as much when Charlie asked why they had stopped.

"We'll climb on foot," Sam Tinsdale proposed. "It'll be harder for those polecats to hit us."

Willis was unwilling to risk more lives. "Charlie and me will circle around the mountain. If we find their tracks, we'll fire a couple of shots in the air. If not, Charlie will stay to cover the back door and I'll come back and we'll flush the coyotes out."

"Maybe there should be two of us watchin' that back door," Sam said.

A good idea, Willis reflected. "You can come with us. Bob, you keep the rest here. We've lost too many good men already."

Willis had Charlie and Sam go left and he went right. He did not mind going alone. That, too, was strange, since he figured he would be more scared than he was. He rode with his pistol in his hand, his thumb on the hammer. The woods were unnaturally quiet: not one bird or squirrel anywhere. He was going at a walk so he would not make a lot of noise but the dull clomp of the zebra dun's hooves was still much too loud to suit him.

His comment about losing good men echoed in Willis' mind. Timmy Easton. Jim Palmer. Now McLeash and Stewart. They had not deserved to die. They had never bothered anyone, never imposed on others, never done anything to merit their grisly ends. They had been simple cowboys making a living the best they knew how, only to be cut down in their prime by vermin who placed no more value on human life than they placed on flies.

Willis had never savvied how people could be so coldhearted. Killers were a breed apart from normal folks — a breed normal folks could do without.

Suddenly Willis gave an angry toss of his head. Here he was, thinking, when he should be concentrating. It would get him added to the list of the dead if he wasn't more careful.

He went a short way more and saw more tracks. But those had not been made by horse hooves. A large elk had passed by earlier. Willis recollected the last time he had been elk hunting, back before the accident, and how he would very much like to go hunting again soon. He had a lot of living to make up for.

The zebra dun's ears pricked. Instantly drawing rein, Willis scanned the mountain. He was past the boulder-strewn slope in heavy timber that covered the slope to well near the top. He started to rise in the stirrups but thought better of the notion.

His nerves jangling, Willis gigged the zebra dun on. There was a lot more to manhunting than he ever reckoned. He knew then, with absolute certainty, that he would never accept the offer to be Cottonwood's new marshal. It wasn't in him. It wasn't suited to his nature. He was happy being a cowboy and had always been happy being a cowboy, and the only thing that would make him happier was marrying Laurella and being the boss of a bunch of cowboys.

An old-timer once told him that cowboying got into the blood and stayed there, and that old-timer had been right. The cowboy life was glorious. Sure, the hours were long and the work was hard, but it was the kind of work that put muscle on a man and kept him lean and healthy, unlike being a clerk or a banker where a man sat around all day growing fat and soft.

Willis liked, too, that while a cowboy was always answerable to the foreman and the big sugar, it wasn't as if they were always looking over his shoulder telling him what to do and how to do it. Cowboys were expected to know how to do things, and do them well.

He had never put it into words before, but what he liked most about the cowboy life was the independence: the independence to make a living yet be beholden to no one; the independence to be who he was, and the rest of the world be hanged.

Willis grinned. Here he was, thinking about independence, and if Laurella Hendershot had her way, his independent days were about over. From what he had seen of marriage, a married man wasn't fancy-free like a bachelor. But giving up a little freedom for the privilege of having someone love and cherish you and always be there for you was more than a fair trade. Independence was fine but a man shouldn't be a fanatic about it.

Willis abruptly grit his teeth and gave another toss of his head. He was doing it again! As sure as shooting, he would get himself killed. He emptied his head of stray thoughts and focused on the trees.

Up ahead something moved. Willis brought up his revolver but he did not shoot. It was Charlie and Sam, waiting.

"Took you long enough," Tinsdale said. "I could have grown a beard."

"No sign of them?" Willis asked, and when Charlie shook his head, he said, "That must mean they're back in those boulders. They made a mistake. We have them boxed in."

"Don't put the cart before the horse," Charlie cautioned. "Varner Wilkes is too crafty to let himself be trapped."

"He's been lucky but his luck has run out. You two find a spot to lay low and watch this side of the mountain. I'm countin' on you not to let those buzzards slip past."

"We'll do what we can," Charlie said, "but we're neither of us Daniel Boone. I'm only fair with a rifle and no shakes at all with a revolver."

Sam Tinsdale grinned. "I can hit a barn if

it's standin' still."

"Just don't get hit yourselves," Willis said, and reined around. "Give me a quarter of an hour and the festivities will commence."

"Will?" Charlie said. "You did the right thing decidin' to come after these varmints. They'd only cause us more trouble later."

"Thanks." Willis trotted back the way he had come and soon rejoined the others, who had taken cover.

Bob Ashlon unfurled from behind a stump as he rode up. "We were gettin' set to come look for you."

"A common affliction today." Willis dismounted and shucked his Winchester. The others gathered around. He detailed his plan. He and Frank Donner would go up the middle of the slope, Bob Ashlon and Green would take the left side, Rafe Carter and Maynard the right side.

"Shouldn't someone stay with the horses?" Bob Ashlon asked. "I'd hate to be stranded afoot up here."

Willis did not see the need but the worried looks he was given prompted him to say, "Frank, you watch the animals. I'll go it alone."

"Is that smart?"

"Hell, the day I start livin' smart is the day the world comes to an end." Willis motioned and the flankers moved into position. When they were set, he pumped his arm and the five of them slowly ascended, moving from boulder to boulder and knob to knob, never showing themselves if they could help it.

Willis wasn't fooling himself. Varner Wilkes knew they were coming and would be ready. The question now was, could they kill Varner and Thatch Nargent before Varner and Thatch killed any of them?

It was slow going. Willis' left leg began to cramp on him and he had to stop and flex it. He would be damned if he would let his leg stop him now. Or from living his life as he should have been living it all these years. When he thought of the time he had wasted, when he thought of the precious years and months he had squandered in self-pity, he wanted to beat his head against one of the boulders.

Willis halted and looked down at himself. Would he never learn? As a lawman he wouldn't last two months. He glanced both ways, saw the others waiting for him, and scrambled past a small boulder to a larger one. Rising on his right knee, he removed his hat and peered over the top.

The rustlers were well hid.

"Where are you?" Willis whispered. Placing his hat back on, he crawled around the boulder and across a short space to an erosion-worn depression barely deep enough and wide enough for him to crawl into. He crawled up it until he came to a cluster of boulders. Rolling up and out, he moved to a gap between two of the largest.

Still nothing up there. Scowling, Willis crept to another cluster. No shots echoed. No angry shouts were directed at him. Yet he had to be close. Another forty or fifty yards and there was no cover left.

Perplexed, Willis sat with his back to a boulder and gazed down the mountain. It hit him that he had not seen any hoofprints on the way up. Not one track since near where the boulders began. Cupping a hand to his mouth, he called, "Bob! Rafe! Have any of you seen any tracks?"

After whispered consultations with their partners, Bob shook his head and Rafe shouted, "Not a one, Will!"

Willis had a bad feeling. Cautiously rising, he tensed for the blast of a rifle or a pistol, but there was none. He limped a few yards higher, and swore. Shouldering the Winchester, he began roving in wide loops. The others caught on and did the same, and it did not take them long to discover the galling truth.

"They're not here!" Rafe Carter exclaimed.

"How the hell did they slip away under our very noses?" Maynard wanted to know. "We had them cornered."

"We thought we did," Bob Ashlon amended.

"We're like kids at this," Green said, "bumblin' around without accomplishin' a damn thing other than gettin' ourselves killed."

Willis did not like the look Green gave him. "Are you blamin' me for McLeash and Stewart?"

Ira Green had been with the Bar T three years. He hailed from New Mexico and little was known about him other than he was a top hand with a rope and hardly ever talked. "If the boots fit," he said.

"That's not fair," Bob Ashlon came to Willis' defense. "We had to come after them. Or would you have the rustlers help themselves to all our cows?"

"They're not *ours*," Green said. "They're the Bar T's."

Willis could not let that go unchallenged. "When you ride for a brand, the brand comes first. I don't want any puncher workin' for me who doesn't think the same."

"You're not the big sugar yet," Green observed.

Willis let the insult pass. But the day after he married Laurella, there would be an opening for a new hand at the Bar T.

"Be petty, why don't you?" Bob Ashlon said to Green. "There's more than the cows at stake. We've lost friends. Our own have been killed, and it's up to us to make damn sure their killers don't live to brag about it."

"That's the only reason I came along," Ira Green said. "My pards mean more to me than cows."

Willis decided that maybe he had been a bit hasty in his judgment. "Our pards matter to all of us. An outfit where no one cares is an outfit that doesn't last long."

"So what now?" Maynard asked. "I'm for takin' McLeash and Stewart back to the ranch for buryin'."

"We'll do that soon enough," Willis promised. "Fan out. Look for tracks. Find where Wilkes and Nargent went to."

It had been slickly done. The two rustlers had only gone twenty feet up the slope and reined due west, riding as close to a row of boulders as they could so their tracks were not obvious.

Willis was furious with himself. He should have caught on sooner. He had let the

356

rustlers hoodwink him. By now they were miles away. Overtaking them in such rugged country would be next to impossible with the lead they had. "Let's collect Charlie and Sam."

It was a glum bunch of cowboys who spent the next several days winding down from the high country to the north valley. The punchers minding the north herd added the stolen cows, then told them the word from town was that the parson was on the mend and that Fred Baxter had been out to the Bar T a couple of times to talk to Abe Tyler, but no one knew what about. Willis could guess. He wanted to ask about Laurella but refrained.

The sun set before they reached the home valley. Strung out in single file, their horses as tired as they were, they came within sight of the buildings. Willis adjusted his bandanna and brushed dust from his shirt and pants.

"Well, lookee there, boys," Charlie Weaver said. "Will is takin' a bath in the saddle."

"Drop dead, you jealous goat."

"My, oh, my. Such language."

The laughter brought a smile to Willis' lips. God, he loved this life. "If it's language you want, remind me when I get to the bunkhouse later."

Charlie was quick to pounce. "Later? Where will you be in the meantime?" He snapped his fingers. "Oh. That's right. Your cow bunny will want to tighten her loop after givin' you so much slack."

"Your day will come," Willis predicted. "There's not been a man yet who is loop proof."

"When my day does, I'll likely be so booze blind, I'll be married a week before I know I'm hitched."

"Just think how drunk the dove will have to be," Willis said, and was rewarded with guffaws and glee from every puncher.

"That one is yours," Charlie conceded, "but I'll have the last laugh on your weddin' day. I'll still be single."

"I'll think of you on my weddin' night — you and your pillow."

"Dang!" Charlie said. "That's two in a row. And you haven't touched a bottle all day."

They placed the bodies in the stable on a bed of straw and covered them with blankets. Their arrival had not gone unnoticed. The Tylers had hastened from the ranch house and Reuben Marsh came from the bunkhouse to hear what had happened.

Willis was concluding his report when the one he had been yearning to see stepped through the open double doors, her ever-present shadow behind her. She was wearing her hat but he did not need to see her eyes to tell what was in them. In a few lithe bounds, she was in his arms. He held her close, intoxicated. A lump formed in his throat, and he had to cough several times before he could croak, "Did you miss me?"

"Not one bit," Laurella said, then through the veil whispered, "I missed you more than I have ever missed anyone or anything. I thought I would die, my heart hurt so."

Willis sure had been feeling light-headed a lot lately. "No man has ever been happier than I am right this moment," he whispered in her ear.

Abe Tyler was standing beside the body still draped over a horse. "You brought one of the rustlers back?"

"I figured the law might need proof," Willis said. "We can take him on to town in the mornin'."

Abe gave a few tentative sniffs and wrinkled his nose. "He's rank as it is. Find a spot close by and plant him. Mark it so we can find it again if we have to."

Reuben Marsh was standing over McLeash and Stewart. "I've buried more good men in the past few weeks than I have in the past twenty years."

"These will be the last for a spell," Charlie said. "By now the rustlers are long gone. To California, maybe. Or Arizona Territory."

"We don't know that," Sam Tinsdale said.

Abe put an arm around Elfie. "The important thing is that you ran them off and recovered our missing cattle. Now we can get on with the business of sellin' the Bar T." He looked pointedly at Laurella. "Say, tomorrow morning? We'll go into town, consult with my lawyer, and by week's end, he can have everything in order."

"Sounds fine to me," Laurella said, and squeezed Willis' arm.

The excitement had died down. Punchers drifted toward the bunkhouse or the cook shack. The Tylers walked out with Reuben.

"Armando, wait for me at the house," Laurella instructed her protector. "I'm takin' a walk with my beau."

"Sí, senorita." Armando took a few steps, then stopped. "I have been as much use to you as a fifth wheel on that buckboard."

"Who watched over me all the way here? But if it will make you feel any better, as soon as my pa arrives your ordeal will be over."

"How soon will that be?" Willis was curious.

"I wrote them but they haven't answered

me yet," Laurella said, and grinned. "It could take them a week to recover from the shock."

Soon they were alone with the bodies. Laurella pulled Willis into a dark corner, raised her veil, and kissed him on the cheek.

"Why, you hussy," Willis said, and kissed her on the mouth. She tasted as sweet as he remembered.

Laurella trembled against him. "I was so worried. I kept thinkin' that it would be you they brought back belly down, that I didn't really deserve to be happy."

"That's foolish talk," Willis said.

"Habits are hard to break," Laurella said, "and I've been in the habit of thinkin' I'm a freak since I was knee-high to a calf. It will take a while to get used to the notion that maybe I'm a normal woman."

"No maybe about it," Willis said huskily. "You're as normal as normal can be." He was slightly bewildered when she threw her arms around his neck and sobbed softly into his shoulder. "What's wrong?"

Laurella did not answer. She stopped sobbing but sniffled and wrung the collar of his shirt as if it were a washcloth.

"I'm sorry if I upset you. I don't have much experience with your kind — with women, I mean. Half the time I don't know what to say or if I do know what to say I'm not sure how to say it."

"You do fine," Laurella said softly. "It's me. I get emotional. I try not to but I can't help it." She nuzzled his neck. "I'll get better as time goes by. Wait and see."

"Do you hear me complainin'?" Willis responded. "Don't change on my account. I like you just how you are."

"You might think different a year from now."

"I won't think different ever. Don't put words in my head, especially in advance." Willis smiled to reassure her.

"Do you know that you have your father's smile?" Laurella asked.

The reminder was like a bucket of cold water in the face. "Pa!" Willis exclaimed. "I forgot all about him. How is he, anyhow? Did he give you any trouble while I was gone? If he did, he'll regret it."

Laurella drew back. "Oh. That's right. I haven't told you yet. I was too thrilled to see you."

"Told me what?"

"I don't know if I should say."

"You can't start to say somethin' and then not say it," Willis said. Although, now that he thought about it, women did it all the time.

"It can wait."

"Let me be the judge of that," Willis said.

Laurella glanced at the double doors and then leaned close. "Promise you won't be mad at me."

"How can I promise a thing like that when I don't know what it is?"

"You have to promise," Laurella insisted.

The more Willis got to know her, the more female she acted. "I give you my range word."

"Good." Laurella beamed. "Your father and I have become good friends. He asked if he could come to our weddin', said it would mean the world to him. I hope you don't mind, but I said he could."

CHAPTER 20

Willis lay on his back in his bunk staring at the bunkhouse rafters and marveling, for the hundredth time, that Laurella had done what she did. Asking her to tend to his father had been a mistake. The whole time up in the mountains, he had been worried sick his father was treating her poorly, and the whole time the two of them had been getting along like two peas in a pod.

His father would come to their wedding over his dead body, Willis vowed. That old man had caused him too much misery for much too long for him to forgive and let live. If he had his druthers, he would never set eyes on Matthew ever again.

The more Willis thought about it, the madder he became. His father had a lot of gall, asking to be at the wedding, when until now he had shown no interest in Willis' personal life or, for that matter, wanted anything to do with him. For God's sake!

Willis mentally shrieked at the rafters. His father had run out on his sister and him when they were barely old enough to fend for themselves. He did not give a good damn what the old man wanted, and he would make that clear as clear could be.

By the clock that Reuben Marsh kept on a shelf above his bunk, it was nearly three a.m. Snores rose in a grinding chorus. All the punchers except Willis were asleep. Or so he hoped. Easing his blanket off, he slowly sat up. He had removed his spurs before he turned in and he did not put them back on. Slowly rising, he moved toward the front. As he came abreast of Charlie Weaver's bunk, Charlie muttered and rolled over.

Willis froze. After he was sure Charlie had not woken up, he limped to the door. The wooden latch, worn smooth by use, worked noiselessly. Then he was outside in the brisk night air, a stiff wind at his back, hurrying past the stable and the main house to the gully.

A figure separated itself from the darkness. Laurella wore a dark dress and her hat.

They hugged, Willis pulling her close against him. "How can you see out that thing?" he whispered, although he did not need to. They were far enough from the buildings that no one would hear. But he dared not risk being caught, as much for Laurella's sake as his. Folks would not like it that they had harbored the Flour Sack Kid.

"I can see fine," Laurella whispered, then turned her good cheek to him and raised her veil. "Can you?"

Willis took the hint and kissed her on the cheek. Taking hold of her chin, he turned her face full to him and kissed her full on the mouth. She stiffened, as she always did, and when the kiss ended, she raised a hand to the ruined half of her face and touched it as if astounded anyone would ever want to put their lips on hers. Almost reluctantly, she lowered the veil.

"Take me to him," Willis said.

She had been to the gully so many times that she easily found her way. "There," she said after a while, and pointed.

Thick brush choked the bottom. Willis peered intently but did not see any trace of his father. "Are you sure?"

"Matthew, are you there?" Laurella softly called out.

Part of the brush moved, and out of the opening came the man Willis could not bear to look at without his insides churning and his hands balling into fists.

"Laury!" Matthew came up the side of the gully and gave her a quick hug. "I was beginnin' to think you weren't comin' tonight."

Willis grew even madder.

"Hello, son," Matthew said. "It's nice to see you again, too."

"Is it?" Willis coldly rejoined.

"Your gal is a peach, let me tell you. I never wanted for food or water the whole time you were gone." Matthew smiled at Laurella. "She reminds me a lot of your mother, God rest her soul."

"Have you mended enough to travel?"

Matthew seemed to give a start and tore his gaze from Willis' intended. "What? Oh. The wound isn't completely healed yet, but yes, I'm fit enough to light a shuck whenever I see fit."

"Whenever *I* see fit," Willis said.

Matthew's face was hidden in shadow. "Is that how it is, then, son?"

"That's how it is," Willis bluntly informed him. "And I told you before to stop callin' me that. Don't pretend we're somethin' we're not."

"Will!" Laurella said.

"I'm sorry," Willis said, but he was not sorry at all. "There's too much bad blood between us for me to treat him as most sons treat their fathers. He robs. He steals. He's an outlaw. He shot the parson —"

"That was his own fault," Matthew said. "If the fool had let me leave in peace, it never would have happened."

"Of course you blame him." Willis' fists were as hard as iron. "You always blame everyone else. You've conveniently forgot you tried to rob him and Fred Baxter."

"Well, there's that, too," Matthew said, "but I was polite about it."

"You're despicable. Why didn't you stay in Colorado? Better yet, why haven't you gotten yourself killed? Why keep tormentin' me?"

Laurella put a hand on his arm. "Will Lander, I won't have you talk to your father like this in my presence. Whatever he's done, he's still your father and he's always loved you very much."

"He has a damned peculiar way of showin' it," Willis rasped, his throat threatening to constrict on him.

"It's not too late," Matthew said. "I can start over."

"Just like that?" Willis uttered a brittle laugh. "I'm supposed to act as if all that's happened never did? I'm supposed to welcome you back into my life with open arms?

Is that how you have it all worked out in that lunatic mind of yours?"

"I'm perfectly normal," Matthew said.

"Oh really? When was the last time you rode into a town and saw everyone walkin' around with flour sacks over their heads? Normal folks don't do that. Normal folks don't rob other folks at gunpoint." Willis' voice was rising but he couldn't help himself. "Normal folks don't have wanted posters on them." He took a step, his fists rising. "Normal folks don't turn their backs on their son and daughter!"

"Will!" Laurella moved between them, facing him. "Don't! You'll never be able to live with yourself."

"It can't be any worse than livin' with what I've already had to put up with," Willis said.

Silence fell, broken only when Matthew finally said, "I take it I'm not invited to your weddin'."

"You're not completely stupid," Willis said.

"What would you have me do then? Leave as soon as I can? Fetch a horse and I'll be out of your hair."

"Oh, sure. I give you a mount, and by nightfall you've robbed someone and are back to your old ways." Willis shook his head. "Not this time. This time we do it right. This time I take you to Cottonwood and put you on the stage to California and we never see each other again."

Laurella bowed her head.

"If that's how you want it, son, then that is how we'll do it," Matthew said. "But I feel guilty about havin' you pay for the ticket."

"I could just shoot you," Willis said.

"I reckon I had that comin'."

"You have a lot more besides." Willis had to think a bit before he remembered what day of the week it was. "The next stage to California arrives in town the day after tomorrow. About noon, as I recollect. It heads out again at two. We'll leave the Bar T an hour before sunup, which will allow us plenty of time to get you there."

Laurella said, "I'm goin', too, and don't even think of stoppin' me."

I'd rather you didn't, Willis almost responded. But her tone convinced him to keep quiet. To his father he said, "Lie low until then. Try to sneak off, and I'll track you down and take you into town over my saddle. Savvy?"

"Whatever you want, son."

Willis had to leave before he took a swing. Wheeling, he said, "Let's go." He did not look at Laurella until they were near the mouth of the gully, and when he did, she stopped and plucked at his sleeve.

"That was mean, Will. How could you — to your own pa, the man who helped bring you into this world and who raised you until your mother died?"

"You weren't there," Willis said. "He's not the saint you paint him to be."

"I'm not sayin' he was. But he's your father, and he deserves better than to be treated as if he's the worst scum who ever lived."

"You're confusin' my pa with yours. Mine was not there when his son and daughter needed him the most. Mine wasted his life ridin' the owlhoot trail." Willis was quaking with anger. "Mine couldn't be bothered to show up at my sister's funeral."

"So you plan to hold all that against him for the rest of his life?"

"I've held it against him this long," Willis said. "Another five or ten years won't matter."

"I don't quite know what to say. I've never met anyone so bitter. I like your pa, Will. Yes, he's been an outlaw, and yes, he deserted you, but he wants to change and he's here now and that ought to count for somethin'."

"Have you asked yourself why he's here? Why he came all the way from Colorado after all this time? I'll tell you why. His misspent life is catchin' up with him. He's not as spry as he used to be. Old outlaws are soon dead outlaws unless they can dig a hole and pull the dirt in over them. That's what I am to him: his hole — his way of hidin' where the law will never find him and escapin' the fate he deserves."

"I'm sorry, but that's just not so. I've talked to him. I've heard the love for you in his voice, seen it in his eyes. He has missed you, missed you terribly, and he wants to spend what time he has left makin' amends."

"He's too late," Willis said. "The fences that needed mendin' have long since fallen down and there's nothin' left to mend."

"You don't feel any sentiment for him — not any sentiment at all?"

"What do you want me to do? Lie? I don't feel a thing for him, no." But as Willis said it, his voice broke. "I'd as soon he was dead and out of my life for good." He turned and would have stormed off but the ache in his chest would not let him. He held out his hand for her to take and she took it.

"I'm here for you. Remember that. I will always be here for you from now until the day we die."

Willis forgot about his father. He took her into her arms and raised her veil and lavished kisses on her until he was breathing fast and hard. Then she went back inside the house and he headed into the bunkhouse, afraid his pounding heart would wake the other hands.

Once again on his back in the bunk, Willis imagined the life he would live with Laurella, and felt joy such as he had never known. Thoughts of his father tried to intrude but he would not let them. He was done with his father. Oh, they were father and son, but only in blood, not in the real sense. His father had given up that right when he left his sister and him.

Laurella was kind enough not to bring up Matthew the next morning. Willis took her for a stroll in the bright sunlight and was invited to the house for coffee and cakes.

Elfie Tyler was bubbling with delight now that the sale of the Bar T was near to being finalized and she could at long last return to her beloved Saint Louis. Abe was not as gleeful, and several times Willis noticed him stare longingly out a window.

Laurella mentioned that she would like to go into Cottonwood early the next day, and Willis immediately offered to drive her. Neither said exactly *how* early they were leaving, which might spark questions.

The rest of the day was an agony of suspense and a bed of pleasure: suspense, in that Willis could not wait to be shed of his father; pleasure, in that he and Laurella went for a ride and spent the afternoon off in the timber. Armando wanted to go along but she would not let him.

That night was another night of unrelieved restlessness. Willis turned in early in order to get plenty of sleep but he could not fall asleep no matter how long he lay quiet and still. He tossed, he turned, and he fidgeted until past midnight.

With a low gasp, Willis sat up and gazed worriedly about him. He had been asleep, but he knew not how long. He glanced at Reuben's clock, the hands visible in the glow from a lamp that was always left burning low so that when punchers got up in the middle of the night to use the outhouse, they did not stumble over someone else and wake them.

It was only three. Willis had another hour before he was to hitch the team to Laurella's buckboard. He lay back down and halfheartedly sought to get more sleep. It would not come. He thought about Laurella, miracles, second chances, and the oddity called life.

A few minutes before four, he was up and limping to the door. Only a few of the cowhands were snoring, and when his right knee popped, it sounded to Willis like a gunshot. But no one stirred, and soon he was nearing the stable and rubbing his palms together to warm them against the brisk air. Unless he was mistaken, they were in for an early fall.

One of the stable doors was partway open, and from within came furtive sounds. Slowing in surprise, Willis dreaded that someone else was up early and their plans would be thwarted. He peered inside and saw Laurella.

She wasn't alone. Armando was hitching the team.

"What's this?" Willis asked.

"He insisted on comin' along, and I can hardly refuse him. My father made him give his word never to let me out of his sight."

Armando said something in Spanish, and after Laurella responded he looked at Willis and said in English, "I did give my word, senor — a promise I have broken more than once so that you and she could be alone. But I will not break it today. The town is far, and I do not trust this Flour Sack Kid, even if he is your padre."

"I don't trust him either," Willis said. To

Laurella, he asked, "How long has he known about my father?"

"I tell Armando everything. He was always nearby when I took food and water to him."

Willis wondered if Armando was always nearby when he and she were together and simply did not tell her. Surely not, he thought, and saw Armando smile.

"You need not worry, senor. Your secrets are safe with me."

"That's nice," Willis said. But it was not nice at all, and he would talk to Laurella about it after they got back from town.

"We should go get Matthew," she proposed.

The ranch house was dark yet Willis had the unsettling feeling unseen eyes were on them as they crossed to the gully. Before he could start up it, a dark figure rose up from concealment.

"I'm all set," his father announced with a smile. "I didn't want to keep you waitin', son."

As Willis retraced his steps to the stable, he caught a glimpse of someone at a ground-floor window. He could not be positive but he had the impression it was Little Sparrow. She stayed over now and then, in a guest room. He crooked his neck to see if any lamps came on but none did.

Both the stable doors were open. Armando was at the rear of the buckboard, holding up the edge of the canvas that covered the bed. "Under you go," he said it mockingly.

The Kid complied without comment. Armando walked around to the front and held out his arm to boost Laurella up. Then he climbed on beside her.

Willis climbed up on the other side and lifted the reins. The seat was not really wide enough for three people, and Laurella sat so she was closer to him than Armando, with the result she was pressed against his side, a development he had not foreseen but liked.

For a while they had the stars overhead and the northwest wind at their backs. Then pink emblazoned the horizon, the pink changed to yellow, the yellow to orange and then yellow again, and the sun rose in all its splendor.

"What a lovely sunrise," Laurella declared.

"Not nearly as lovely as you," Willis said, forgetting Armando was there. After that blunder he did not say anything for a long while.

They were over halfway to town when from under the canvas the Kid asked, "Mind if we stop for a couple of minutes? I'm not as young as I used to be and all this bouncin' around is takin' a toll."

Willis was tempted to tell his father to hold it in, but the glance Laurella gave him changed his mind. "Just hurry up," he grumbled.

The hours crawled by. Laurella talked about growing up in Texas, and a trip she had made to Arkansas once. Willis did not say much. He had something else on his mind.

A dusty haze shrouded Cottonwood. A few stick figures moved about but otherwise the town looked as lively as a cemetery.

Twisting in the seat, Willis said, "Stay under that canvas until I say it's safe to climb out."

"Whatever you want, son. But remember. No one knows me without my flour sack on."

"Maybe so, but I don't want to be seen with you if I can help it," Willis said. "I'll buy the tickets and slip them to you, and then we part company."

Fred Baxter, a broom in hand, waved at them from the boardwalk in front of the general store. A pig darted across the street and Willis had a hankering for ham.

The stagecoach was out in front of the stage station but neither the driver nor the shotgun nor any passengers nor the station manager or his wife were to be seen. Willis went on by and brought the buckboard to a stop beside the feed and grain. Smacking the canvas, he said, "Stay put. I'll be right back." He swung his good leg over, then his bad leg, and gingerly lowered himself.

"I'm taggin' along," Laurella said. "I need to stretch my legs."

Armando was already down, and followed.

The door to the stage office was closed and the shades had been pulled. Willis opened it and let Laurella and her protector enter ahead of him. He limped inside, and nearly collided with Armando, who had unaccountably stopped. Stepping past him, it took a few seconds for what Willis was seeing to sink in.

Connelly, the stage manager, was on the floor, as still as a statue and as pale as paper except for a bright scarlet smear on his head and the scarlet ring spreading outward from his body.

Over against the far wall, lined up with their hands in the air, were Jenks, the driver, and Trask, the shotgun, his crushed nose seeping blood, along with three people who must have been passengers, one a woman in a blue bonnet and blue dress with tears streaking her cheeks. But it was the three men in the middle of the room that caused

Willis to gasp and take a step.

"Well, what have we here?" Varner Wilkes said, a leveled revolver at his waist. "It's the cripple! And he's brought a lady friend and a Mex."

Thatch Nargent wagged the rifle he was holding. "Let's get out of here, cousin. We have the travelin' money we need."

"In a minute," Varner said. "I aim to have me some fun first."

Mason was by the window. His fancy revolvers with the ivory grips filled his slender hands. "We have no time for your nonsense, Wilkes."

"Don't prod me," Varner said, turning toward Laurella. "What's with the veil, lady? Are you shy?" He reached out and Laurella jerked back.

"Don't!"

Armando stepped to the left, blocking Willis' view. "You will not touch my mistress, senor."

"Is that a fact?"

"*Sí.*"

"Damned uppity Mex," Varner said, and shot him.

Willis heard the *thwack* of the slug. Armando grunted. Then Armando's pistol was out and he and Varner and Tote Nargent and Mason fired all at once.

Willis leaped, wrapping his arms around Laurella, and bore her to the floor. Letting go, he rolled onto his back and stabbed for his revolver.

Tote Nargent was on his knees. Varner had a hand to his side but was grinning as if the blasts of gunfire were music to his senses. Mason was unscathed.

But Armando had been hit three or four times and his legs were giving way. He banged a last shot at Varner as he went down.

Tote and Mason both fired and Armando stopped moving, his eyes rolling up in his head.

By then Willis had his revolver out and he fired at Tote. He snapped a shot at Varner and felt a searing pain in his side. Mason, had fired twice into him, and Mason never missed.

Suddenly everything seemed to slow down. Everyone moved as if they were made of molasses.

Willis saw Laurella scramble toward Armando's fallen pistol. Mason swung toward her but did not shoot. Varner swung toward her, too, and he was leering in sadistic glee.

"No!" Willis bawled. He tried to roll between them to take the shot himself even as he fired but he knew he could not save her.

That was when the front door crashed inward and in hurtled the Flour Sack Kid. He had a black-handled revolver in each hand and he fired both revolvers at Varner and Tote even as Mason put two into him, and then he fired as Mason fired and fired into the floor as his knees gave way and his flour sack hit the floorboards with a thud.

"Pa!" Willis cried.

Mason dashed to the door but he was not moving as fluidly as he usually did. He leaned on the jamb as he went out.

Pushing on his good knee, Willis made it to the door himself. He, too, had to cling to the jamb. He extended his arm but he did not shoot.

Just past the hitch rail stood Mason. Beyond him, in the center of the street, was Johnny Vance, and pinned on the gambler's vest was a badge, the same tin star once worn by Marshal Keever.

"Drop them!" Vance commanded.

"I can't," Mason said.

Their eyes met. There was a blur of motion, and one shot, and the man in gray tottered against the hitch rail. His body slumped until his elbows caught on the rail. He smiled at Johnny Vance and said, "I'm glad it was yuh." Then he was gone.

A warm hand turned Willis and another

touched his face and suddenly the stage station was filling with people and everyone was talking and he was being carefully lowered to the floor.

Laurella's veil brushed his face. "He only grazed you. You'll live! Do you hear me, Will? You'll live."

Willis was glad, mostly. He was suddenly very tired. Fighting the urge to close his eyes, he rose on his elbows.

"What are you doin'?" Laurella asked.

Willis did not feel strong enough to stand but he was strong enough to crawl. He slid to the Flour Sack Kid and raised the head in the flour sack and gently placed it in his lap. People were watching. He placed his hand on the flour sack and in the quiet that descended, he said, "This was my pa. He cared for me more than I thought he did. He cared an awful lot."

ABOUT THE AUTHOR

Ralph Compton stood six-foot-eight without his boots. He worked as a musician, a radio announcer, a songwriter, and a newspaper columnist. His first novel, *The Goodnight Trail,* was a finalist for the Western Writers of America's Medicine Pipe Bearer Award for best debut novel. He was also the author of the *Sundown Riders* series and the *Border Empire* series.

The employees of Thorndike Press hope you have enjoyed this Large Print book. All our Thorndike and Wheeler Large Print titles are designed for easy reading, and all our books are made to last. Other Thorndike Press Large Print books are available at your library, through selected bookstores, or directly from us.

For information about titles, please call:

(800) 223-1244

or visit our Web site at:

www.gale.com/thorndike
www.gale.com/wheeler

To share your comments, please write:

Publisher
Thorndike Press
295 Kennedy Memorial Drive
Waterville, ME 04901